V

THE NEXT HAPPIEST PLACE ON EARTH

Dear Mother March –
I so hope you enjoy
this book. Thank you
for visiting the next
happiest place on Earth.
Love Greg

Greg Triggs

authorHOUSE®

AuthorHouse™
1663 Liberty Drive
Bloomington, IN 47403
www.authorhouse.com
Phone: 1 (800) 839-8640

Published by AuthorHouse 03/11/2016

ISBN: 978-1-5049-8132-3 (sc)
ISBN: 978-1-5049-8133-0 (hc)
ISBN: 978-1-5049-8131-6 (e)

Library of Congress Control Number: 2016903105

Print information available on the last page.

For the first Frances, My Mom.

Dorothy Frances Fiore Radke Triggs

She believed everyone deserves a 2nd chance.

PROLOGUE

There are three empty airline bottles of vodka in front of me. I have named them Happy, Dopey, and Sleepy. I'm already anticipating my next Absolut Dwarf when the pilot announces that we have begun the preliminary preparation for our landing. The flight attendant takes the bottles away and looks at me as though I might have a problem.

She's right, of course. I do have a problem but it's not liquor. It's my life. I'm amazed that I don't drink more. The last few years have been rough. So many disappointments: the accident, therapy, Paul's affair, the divorce, a stalled career, maxed out credit cards and now *this*.

I cross myself like every good Catholic girl was trained to do in moments of true terror. I can't believe I left a rent-stabilized apartment on West 51st Street in the middle of Manhattan, to take a job as an Art Director at a theme park. 8th Avenue was too touristy for me. How am I going to survive Orlando, Florida?

I can see the future and it's no fairytale ending. I'm going to be a very sad girl at the happiest place on Earth.

This is the fresh start I have been hoping for, praying for. I should just clear my mind and visualize everything working out. Let the stress go. Breathe easy. Relax.

You can barely hear the landing gear over the crying babies. I feel a knot in the pit of my stomach. There are a lot of children on this flight.

I have traded the rats of Hell's Kitchen for the rug rats of Central Florida. There are going to be kids everywhere. I need another dwarf. I'm getting Grumpy.

A comforting meow comes from underneath my seat. I grab the faux Louis Vuitton feline tote, twenty bucks on 6th Avenue, thank you very much, and say hello to Katzenberg, my wonderful, fat, spoiled, friend. He grimaces. I just got a bad breath alert from something that licks its own privates. I pop a Tic Tac, put the carrier over my shoulder, smooth out my skirt and make my way up the aisle on unsteady, corporately appropriate two-inch heels with a covered toe.

I can see through the hatch at the end of the aisle. It's really bright out there. I suppose it always is here in the land of oranges. I miss the overcast and perpetually gloomy Empire State. I might have to start smoking again.

The minute Katz and I exit the plane a wall of humidity hits us. I instantly grow three inches taller thanks to the frizzy mess atop my head. Two hundred bucks of chemical straightening down the drain and I've been a Floridian for all of five seconds.

The airport is spotless and institutionally pretty. There are no stains on the carpeting.

It's not like LaGuardia or JFK at all. The ceilings are high and the terminal is flooded with sunlight.

I must remember to buy darker sunglasses.

I stop by the ladies room to splash water on my face.

I'm momentarily startled. Who is that staring back at me from the mirror? My mascara must have run while I was crying. Seeing Manhattan shrink through my little coach window had been overwhelming. It was all I could do to resist the urge to scream, "Turn the plane around!' Leaving New York was like breaking up with someone I still loved.

I looked out the window until the clouds got too thick to see anything. Goodbye Manhattan. Hello permanent humidity.

Stupid, cheap mascara … they said it was waterproof. If I still lived in New York I'd return it and ask for a refund. But, I remind myself I am no longer a New Yorker. I am an Orlandite … Orlandophile … Orlandonian. Whatever.

Two women start cooing over Katzenberg but it's in Spanish and I can't make all of it out. I think I hear the words *muy obseso* several times. Thank goodness neither of us understands them.

A tram, not unlike a subway, but outside and very, very clean takes us to Baggage Claim. A prerecorded voice welcomes us to Orlando in several languages.

Look at all the tourists, so happy to be here. Good for them. They're only here for a week. I'm in for the long haul. It says so right on my contract.

I'm working full time in the land of vacation.

My bags arrive immediately and without nick or bruise. I scan the crowd and spy a very wholesome looking young man. He must be my driver. He is, after all, holding up a sign that says, "Frances Fiore."

For a while in the 90s it was Phrances Phiore. For a while I was Mrs. Paul Bettinger but that didn't last.

Shake it off girl. This sad sack routine is beyond old. Stand up straight, blow your nose and pull up your pantyhose.

Frances Fiore, age thirty-eight, divorced theme park Art Director, and caretaker of Katzenberg, welcome to Orlando, Florida.

Your new life starts now.

CHAPTER
ONE

The driver, someone named "Bobby" according to his nametag, shakes my hand. He then hands me my very own ID pin and welcomes me with a bright, toothy smile. I've never seen hair so blonde. There are no roots. It's real. That's not fair.

His hands are big and muscular. His shoulders are broad and his waist is clearly of the gym. You could cut paper on that jaw.

And yet there is no sexual energy whatsoever. None. This guy, this child, is such milky perfection that he makes the Osmond's look like a gang of crack whores. "I hope you enjoyed your flight," he says with complete sincerity and just the slightest hint of a southern accent. It's adorable, but that's all. No pangs to play Mrs. Robinson overtake me.

He picks up my bags with next to no effort and leads the way to the car. We are on a tourist conveyer belt. I can feel my calves losing their tone. New York is a city of pedestrians. New Yorkers walk.

Don't judge. Be open-minded.

This is efficient and it's a nice chance to catch up on my reading. Oh look. They're having a

Marinara Festival at the 20 local Olive Gardens. How lovely!

There's advertising everywhere.

Oh my God. There's an ad for a place called Gatorland.

Dunkin' Donuts.

SeaWorld.

Universal.

Hotel. Hotel. Hotel.

Soon we are in the parking garage and facing the car. Oh my. The car.

I've never seen such a thing. It's like a stretch limo and a 70s conversion van had an ugly baby. Flying through a well-executed mural of a cloudy blue sky are America's best-loved animated characters. They're all holding hands, or rather paws and hooves. At the apex of the grouping, actually the hood of the limo is Binger Bunny. His head is three-dimensional. The windshield is his mouth. His ears make up the antenna for the radio.

Katz hisses. Bobby laughs and mentions that dogs regularly chase the vehicle. "The company must like you," he says. "Only VIPs get this kind of treatment." Which leaves me wondering what they do to the people they don't like. Bobby puts my bags into the trunk, closes it and grimaces as he looks into the now purple and pink sky.

"Uh-oh, we better get a hurry on."

"Why?"

"The sun's starting to set," Bobby explains. "The fireworks are going to be going off in just a little bit. That always ties up traffic."

"Fireworks? Is today a holiday?"

"Well ma'am," ouch, he thinks I'm a ma'am, "I wish I could tell you that it was in honor of your arrival but it's not. We have fireworks every night. Sometimes we even have 'em twice. All the parks do."

"Every night?"

"The locals are used to it, but the tourists stop right in the middle of the highway to watch the show. Heck, it's the only free thing most of them get!" He chuckles at his own joke, which I'm guessing he has told many times.

I can't help but notice how excited people are to see what Bobby calls the "Bunny Buggy." Children point and smile as we pass them in our rolling billboard. People get out their phones and take pictures. Thankfully the windows are tinted. I watch the scenery. Hotel. Hotel. T-shirt shop. Hotel. Chain Restaurant. Hotel.

Where is the skyline? Where are the homeless people and broken dreams? Oh New York, I miss you so.

The view is incredibly redundant, so I begin to review the information packet I was sent last week. Basically, it fleshes out the story everybody grew up hearing. The brochure, printed on very nice, heavy, glossy paper with lots of pictures, reads:

"Legends usually have humble origins and so our story begins. The Bingers were once just real people with a dream and the gift to make magic. Miss Mary Thompson and Mr. Art Binger were two young idealistic art students who fell in love on the Left Bank of Paris in the 1920s. Disliking the expatriate lifestyle and yearning for the red, white and blue shores of their American homeland, they married young, bought a small farm in California and quickly had three children to feed. This was during the Great Depression after the Stock Market crashed in 1929. Money was tight. Art and Mary couldn't even afford a simple radio. Entertainment was hard to come by. Imagination and love were the only things they had in plentiful supply. Mr. and Mrs. Binger would make up stories for their enthralled children about their cute pet bunny who shared the family's last name; and so was born Binger Bunny. How the children would delight as he got into wild mishaps and constantly bested the other animals in the family menagerie. There was Lola La Parisian, their cat, Rufus, her he-cat American beau, Whip the Wonder Dog, Bud the plow horse and two chicks named Chester and Kaboodle both of whom lovingly provided the family with eggs until passing away from natural causes after a long and healthy life."

The brochure fails to mention their mother hen named Clucker, which to the delight of stoned college students made her "Mother Clucker." You don't see her anymore. Evidently in a cross-marketing promotion, the Binger Dynasty sold her to KFC and she ended up on a plate.

"Eventually the stories were put down on paper and illustrated ..."

I love these source drawings. They're very American in a wonderful, sepia pastel tone. They're beautiful but don't really reflect the eventual style of their work. Like all things, it evolved.

"The illustrated children stories were published, quickly climbed up the best-seller list and led to a series of animated cartoons. The success of those films became the foundation of a movie studio which still exists today."

"As Art and Mary grew older, they became intrigued with some newfangled invention called television. *The Wonderful World of Art*, which premiered in the late 50s and ran for more than thirty years, was the Sunday evening foundation of American television. Mr. Binger, the gentle patriarch, became everyone's Grandpa. Weekly he would open the Binger Vaults while visiting America's homes and introduce short cartoons, animated classics or live action movies to an enthralled audience."

This was, of course, way before cable, DVRs, Hulu, Netflix and Apple TV. My sister Teresa, my brother Tommy and I were in front of our color Magnavox with the carved Mediterranean cabinet for every episode. The show was on at seven o'clock, usually just before sunset. We would watch the show together as a family while eating dinner on the wood veneer TV trays my parents got for a wedding present from Uncle Nick and his wife Aunt Josie. If the episode featured a travelogue, my mother and father would talk about how they were going to see those places in person one day.

Mom and Dad.

I thought about them so much while I was getting ready for this move. It's still hard to believe they're gone. I get weepy thinking about it, so I try not to. I thought I was past the tears. Maybe it's the vodka or perhaps this Florida humidity is actually pooling in the corner of my eyes. I fasten my seatbelt.

"Bobby, please turn on the air conditioning."

"Yes ma'am"

"It's Frances. Ma'am makes me sound like your mother," I try to say with a smile.

"Okay, then," his southern manners take a second to adjust as he pauses before adding, "Frances."

"Thank you." Temperature under control, my attention returns to the Binger brochure.

"Eventually the family farm became a theme park just outside of Los Angeles called Binger Village. This galled Mr. Walt Disney with whom the family had always had a friendly feud. He, of course, went to Anaheim and opened Disneyland; the thought being that a land is bigger than a village. It was a huge success and spawned Walt Disney World in Orlando, generally thought of as the penultimate theme park resort of its era. Of course, Binger Bunny never gives up and neither does the company named after him."

I'll take over now.

By the late 1970s, Art and Mary Binger had passed away. The business had grown, and was being run by their heirs and all the yuppity MBAs Binger Bucks could buy. Gone were the gently competitive days of Mom and Pop Studios. It was now a war and Central Florida was the battlefield. Capitalizing on miles and miles of orange groves they had bought in the 50s for a steal, the family corporation decided to outdo Disney World and open *Planet* Binger, just down the road from the Magic Kingdom.

Take that Mickey Mouse!

Everyone knows bunnies are bigger than rodents and planets are bigger than Kingdoms. Both companies have done very well and continue with their efforts to outpace and outspend each other.

In the process they have turned sleepy little Orlando, Florida into the ultimate company town. What was once a quiet place where the wealthy passed the winters in little hamlets named Winter Park, Winter Garden and Winter Haven is now the fifth largest city in the state.

I learned all this on the Internet. I'm not the kind of woman who just pulls statistics out of the air, although 100% of my former husbands might disagree.

According to my iPhone, Planet Binger and Disney World are the largest employers in the city with a workforce of more than 120,000 combined. The lure of opportunity attracts true believers in the magic of fairies and cash whores such as me from all over the world.

The car begins to slow down. Evidently, we're at the gates of my new universe right now. It's hard to imagine that someday soon this will be my version of everyday living. The road in front of the gate is a semicircle. It's called, wait a minute, there's a sign, *Orbit Drive*. Each car drives into something that looks like a space launch pod, which raises cars about ten feet into the air and through a docking station, which is actually a glorified parking booth with an attendant dressed as an alien. Our space buddy is a lavender color, medium tone, with a metallic finish. Good choices. Well executed. The parking ticket comes out of his (her?) antennae.

"Welcome Earthling. You have been transported to Planet Binger!"

The sign says it costs $20.00 to park. That can't be true, can it? Twenty bucks? That's outrageous.

"Hey Bobby" says the alien in a thick Midwestern accent.

"Siri, is that you?"

"Shush now Bobby. Guests might hear you!" warns the alien whose name is evidently Siri.

"Hey Girl, this here is Frances, she's new to the company." I roll down the window, smile and give a friendly little wave. "Frances, this is Siri, she's an intern this semester."

Where is the career path in parking attendant? I'm sure she was thrilled to get this assignment. I suppress a little scream when suddenly one of the creature's six appendages is coming through the car window and grabs my hand for a surprisingly firm shake.

"Please to meet you ma'am."

Get used to it Frances. You are now, and forevermore, a ma'am. Everyone here is going to be younger than you are. Just accept it as a fact of your new life.

"See you later at the Ale House girl," says Bobby before gunning the engine and making way for the next guest.

I am whisked through the gate and up to a larger than life hotel on top of a hill. Ironically, it is a recreation of New York, the city from which I have just come. Binger Boroughs is a sanitized version of my hometown and it brings up a question I have always had:

Why do people settle for fake versions? Go to the real thing. Get on a plane and head to New York.

That's what I'm tempted to do.

Bobby escorts me to the front desk. Evidently he has been cloned. There are twelve clean-cut, sexless replicas of him waiting to check me in. "Oooh, Frances, they're putting you up in Manhattan. They really like you. Most new hires get stuck in the Bronx," says Bobby.

"Middle management gets Staten Island," adds one of the clones.

The minute I see my room I get tired and give into what has been a very long day. Katzenberg has other plans. I let him out of his carrier and he immediately begins exploring the room, which is to be our home until we can find something more permanent. He spends a very entertaining minute or two trying to get underneath the bed, which his girth makes all but impossible.

I order a salad and a diet soda from room service. The woman is very friendly and promises it will be delivered quickly.

Clearly this is not the real New York.

I turn on the television and the room is flooded with images of all the options awaiting people on Planet Binger; followed by clips from a cable network called BTV and what looks like a lot of teenagers working in the music industry or fashion; followed by clips of classic animated films such as *Princess Hun*, which tells the story of the girl behind Attila.

It's overwhelming and feels a little bit like watching work so I settle on a music channel and am soon relaxing to some light jazz as I start to unpack.

"Hello new co-workers," I imagine myself saying. "I'm Frances. I listen to light jazz."

I'd prefer some old school rap right now, but I'm guessing that's not an option and turning on Pandora seems like too much effort.

The room has a very high, and comfortable king size bed. Katz has been trying to jump up on it for a while now and can't quite manage underneath or on. I prop up one of my suitcases to help him.

It's nice that they allow animals in the rooms. They even set up a littler box. A company of animals, for animals, that could be the Planet Binger slogan. Our slogan. Ours. Oh God. Ours.

The wallpaper is a little on the cute side but nothing I can't live with temporarily. The bathroom is like a mini spa. Creamy marble with lines of gold running through it, a deep tub with inviting Jacuzzi jets, a heat lamp (really, in Florida?), two sinks and a gift basket of soaps and lotions.

Oh look. There's a card. Linen paper. Nice.

"Welcome aboard. We're all glad to have you on the team. Sincerely, Matthew O'Connell". If I remember correctly, he's in charge of my project, which means he's my manager, I guess. How very corporate. I haven't had a manager since I worked at the Pizza Hut on Long Island.

The lotions are really nice and feel great after my flight. Mmmmmmm. They smell of lilac and lavender. How thoughtful. Bobby was right, they must really be glad that I'm here. None of the people I worked for in New York cared about my skin being properly moisturized and scented.

The phone rings. How is that possible? I haven't even told anyone where I am yet. It can only mean one thing.

"Hello Teresa."

"How did you know it was me?"

Who else?

My sister's full, married name is Teresa Maria Ann Fiore Teitelbaum. She converted when she married. Her husband Larry is a *mensch*. They have the kind of marriage I wanted, total devotion and trust.

She converted and is now, for the most part, Jewish. Although we were raised Catholic, our parents encouraged us to explore many faiths. In eighth grade, I announced I was agnostic. Later that semester I was Buddhist. To me religion is many different paths leading to one destination. Which one you choose doesn't matter all that much. God bless if you believe in God; otherwise, peace be with you.

It does however matter to my sister. She's very passionate about her Judaism; however, her version allows her to celebrate Hanukkah and Christmas. It doubles the gifts. She even expected presents on her first Yom Kippur. Yet she believes. That and family are her foundations.

"How in the world did you find me?"

"I called the main switchboard. They gave me your office number too; I already programmed into my phone, and then patched me through to your hotel room. I'll always be able to find you. How great is that?"

When my sister commits to something or someone, she does it one hundred percent. Husband, children, siblings, religion, cooking, paying the bills, dried flower arranging class, soccer mom-ing, acrylic nails, bikini waxing, *Candy Crush*: total and utter commitment. It's a mixed mitzvah.

11

"Why didn't you just call me on my cell?"

"We should both be wasting minutes?" OMG, who worries about minutes anymore? "You're single, with moving expenses. Save your money. How was the flight?"

"Fine."

"How is Katzenberg adjusting?"

My sister, who is just as generous as she is demanding, gave me Katz right after Paul and I split up. She was at temple, praying for me as the story goes, and found him underneath the steps of the synagogue. He came to me already named. "A mitzvah," she claimed. "Is it wrong to honor the rabbi?"

"He's fine Teresa. Right now he is licking the wallpaper. How are the kids?"

"Rachel is doing very well, thanks for asking. She just got a solo in choir. She's very excited. Christian, however, is disappointing the Cantor in Hebrew School."

Of course he is. You named your Jewish son Christian. Granted, it was after our father, but still. It's going to make his birthright trip to Israel very challenging.

"He'd rather study baseball statistics than scripture."

"He's a boy Teresa."

"He's a slacker who has lost his iPad until I get an acceptable report from the temple," she says more loudly. I am guessing he is within earshot.

"Wait, doesn't he use that for studying?"

She ignores me, and charges on. "This isn't a game. His Bar Mitzvah is right around the corner."

"Lay down the law Teresa." It's not like she needs encouragement. This woman was born bossy. Teresa is the oldest and just about to turn forty, then there's me at thirty-eight and our brother Tommy who is thirty-seven.

"Listen baby doll, I've got to go. I am almost to my Hadassah meeting and the traffic is *farkatke*. I just wanted to make sure my little sister arrived safely."

"I did and now you know."

"You're taking big steps. Just remember the road goes both ways. You can always come home."

"I think I'll give it at least a day before I give up."

I can actually hear her rolling her eyes. "Now I know where Christian gets it from. You two were cut from the same bolt of cloth. I'm not saying you can't do it Frances. I'm saying I miss you."

"The last seven hours have been very difficult."

"Don't be smart."

"You drove me to the airport Teresa."

"So make fun of your sister's love. It's how you cope."

"Thank you Dr. Teitelbaum. Someday when you get your therapist degree you'll be able to take on other patients." There is a pause. She's waiting. "I love you too. Goodbye."

"Goodbye," says a third voice.

"Tommy?"

"Oh! Did I forget to mention … I conferenced him in. We're having a three way."

Tommy starts coughing to stifle a giggle.

"Hi Frances," says Little Brother.

"Hi."

"Glad you got there safely."

"Thanks Tommy. How are y…"

"G'bye," and he disconnects. Not a man of many words my brother.

"Bye Frances." She throws her phone into her purse and it doesn't disconnect. The last thing I hear is, "Oh my God. Betty Stein! Wait up! I've got that money from the Trees for Israel drive for you."

There is a knock at the door so I hang up without hearing the transaction. "Room Service." I check my watch. Wow. That was less than fifteen minutes. Incredible. The salad is presented very nicely from a young man who also presents himself very nicely.

He is, however, of the Bobby mold. How can people be so beautiful and yet completely lacking in sex appeal?

This balsamic vinaigrette cannot be low fat. It tastes too good. The vegetables are shaped like the little animated characters. That's cute and frightening at the same time. How do you get a kid to eat their Binger shaped carrots? It's like eating a loved one. Multi-task! I continue unpacking as I eat.

Moving out of 51st Street was like exorcising ghosts. I got rid of the Paul triggers. Photos, souvenirs from weekend trips, gifts that cost under $50 (one has to balance sentiment and fiscal responsibilities) and things that he promised to pick up after we split up but never did. It's all out of my life and waiting to be picked up by someone from my Cousin Richie's Shelter in the Bronx. I love the idea of some homeless guy keeping warm in that jacket that my ex-husband spent way too much on at Barney's Warehouse Sale.

Maybe I should have called Paul before I left town. Typical decision, thinking I hurt him by denying myself something I wanted. I should have called.

These drawers are nice and deep. I like the shelving paper. It's cute. I wonder where they got it?

No. I did the right thing.

Clothes. This is about clothing. Keep your mind on the task. Open the closet. Hang up your clothes.

There's a mirror on the inside of the closet door. I see myself before I realize who I'm looking at. There's no time to prepare and for one split second I see the real me.

Opening the door makes my hair blow in a breeze that ends too quickly. It falls back to my shoulders and caresses my face. I smile. I'm holding up pretty well.

I love that the brown of my hair matches my eyes. I like that my eyes are big and expressive and that I don't have to wear glasses all the time, although the frames do help hide the lines starting to form in the corners of my eyes. I'm back into my size eights, down from a post-divorce size twelve. My breasts were fuller then, but being able to tuck in a blouse makes losing that perk is okay. I'm fine with who I'm looking at. Just fine.

So what if I'm alone?

Katz meows to remind me that I'm not. He's eaten his dinner and finally made it up onto the bed. His left paw is patting, okay, snagging the bedspread. His message is clear. "Stop thinking and get some sleep. Tomorrow is a big day."

CHAPTER
TWO

The phone's piercing ring shatters a lovely dream, the details of which automatically evaporate into daylight. Find the receiver without opening your eyes Frances. Maybe the phone has a snooze button.

"G-g-g-g-g-ood mooooooornin', this is J-J-Jo Jo," the stuttering cow, a Binger Studios character I have always found to be in bad taste. Her name is Jo, that's what all the other animals call her but she refers to herself as Jo Jo because she stutters.

"All the othhhher anim-m-mals in the barn-n-n-yard are a-way-way-way, up and at 'em. G-g-g-et up!"

Another voice, male, very authoritative takes over. "Press nine to have this message resent in nine minutes."

N-n-n-no thank you. Once is quite enough.

Katzenberg follows me to the window as I open the curtains. The room is flooded with that damn Florida sunshine. Where is a good old-fashioned airshaft when you need it? They do such an effective job of blocking out the morning.

The pool is already brimming with happy, giggling people. "It's 6:30 in the freaking morning people!" I say, knowing the window protects me from the insane tourists. These people must really want to get their money's worth.

I barely finish feeding Katz when room service shows up with the breakfast I ordered last night. Rebecca, according to her nametag, hands me the fluffiest omelet I have ever seen. The sourdough toast is perfection. Totally worth the carbs; but I've got to be careful.

"Don't get used to this," I say aware of the speaking to myself trend into which I'm falling. As soon as I get an apartment it's back to my morning cold cereal or leftover Chinese.

A shower follows breakfast. A quick check of my iPhone reminds me I've only got an hour to get ready for work.

If my room were animated Binger style, it would become a flurry of beauty products, powder puffs, blow dryers, curling irons, hair spray, and perfume. After forty minutes of prep and ten minutes of revision I have to admit it has come together as well as it's going to.

I smile and start to unfold my Grandma Emma's lace handkerchief. There they are. I brush my hair aside to put on the finishing touch: my mother's earrings.

I always wear them on the first day of anything new. My father gave them to her on their wedding day. They're clip-on and follow the contour of my ears up from the lobes. The stones are in a gold setting. "Mostly rhinestones," I can still hear my father saying. "One is a real diamond. Someday I'll tell you which one."

Don't get sad Frances. Do not get sad.

I love this suit too, clearance at Bloomingdales. Great deal. Hides the flaws and accentuates the positive.

Am I showing too much cleavage? One more button buttoned, grab the briefcase, pet the cat, make sure the mini coffee maker is turned off, pet the cat again, come back, check his water, grab the key card and head out the door. I come back in, get my phone, and leave.

I don't have a car yet which bothers me not at all. I have never owned one and the thought of having to buy a car freaks me out. This morning I take the Planet Binger Transportation System to work. A train, tricked out to look like a retro rocket ship picks me up at Grand Central Spaceport in front of my hotel. They play the theme to *2001: A Space Odyssey* over the speaker system. I hear it five times before getting off at my destination.

I check my watch. Ten minutes early. That's good. I'm right underneath the arch of The Binger Orion Studios, where they told me to report. It was the third of the five total parks that make up Planet Binger. This one is themed to the movies.

Thank God for the Planet Binger app.

This is my first look around in daylight. It's well rendered craziness. The execution is good. The content, however, is a little disconcerting. This place bills itself as an, "homage to the golden era of movie making." In reality, it's more like a trade show. There are posters and marketing material for all their new films and television shows. The classics get a nod, but in a totally revisionist way. Someone has taken famous films and replaced one of the actors with a Binger Studio animated character: There's *Gone With the Wind*, with Lola La Parisian standing in for Scarlet O'Hara, then *Casablanca* with Whip the Wonder Dog rather than Humphrey Bogart, and *My Fair Lady*. Instead of Audrey Hepburn, Rex Harrison is coaching that stuttering cow that woke me up this morning.

"Excuse me, are you Frances?" says someone who looks as though she has wandered in from *The Stepford Wives*. I nod. "Good morning. I'm Kellie Holden, Human Resources Specialist."

"Nice to meet you."

"Thank you. I hope you had a pleasant flight and found the accommodations accommodating." Amazing. She can laugh at her own wordplay and speak at the same time. Her voice is like a perpetual giggle.

"Everything was lovely. Thank you." Her face screws up and she take a deep breath. Afterwards she hesitates but manages to keep smiling.

"Um, oh golly, this is always awkward."

"What?"

"Was there a problem with your nametag? Bobby was supposed to give it to you."

"He did."

"Where is it?"

"Oh, I'm sorry. Am I supposed to wear that?"

She frowns in the most patronizing way imaginable. "Everyday. We wear our nametags everyday. See? I'm wearing mine." Sure as hell, there it is. Underneath her name is the glamorous Rosie Rabbit, Binger Bunny's girlfriend.

"May I ask why?"

"It's a rule."

"Really?"

"For productivity. We're a first name company, but that can lead to some problems." She points to her nametag. "Voila! Solution. No introductions, no embarrassing memory gaffes. Nametags provide total accountability. The next time you see me, you'll know my name is Kellie."

"Yes, Kellie Holden, Human Resources Specialist. I won't be forgetting that anytime soon."

"Thank you. That's so sweet. Just do yourself and me a favor and please remember to wear your nametag from now on. I hate being bad cop. Hate it. Hate it. Hate it."

"Okay, I will. I will. I will. I'm sorry. I didn't know I was supposed to wear it."

"It's on page three of our Cast Member Expectations Manual, third paragraph, left hand column. It was sent to you ten days ago. Registered. You signed for it." She pulls out her iPad. "I can show you the documentation."

"That's okay. No need. I guess that little paragraph just escaped my attention while I was getting ready to move across the eastern seaboard."

"It's really not a problem. You creative types are known for missing deadlines, but somehow you always seem to have a nametag excuse at the ready. I brought an extra one, just in case."

She opens her pink purse that almost matches her pink floral dress and her pink lipstick. Those are some strong choices for a redhead. Admittedly the brown roots distract from the overall effect.

The Human Resource Specialist hands me a nametag. Underneath my name is Sowgorney the pig, another Binger Studios character. She is perpetually messy and constantly trying to lose ten pounds. Kellie Holden may have a bunny on her nametag, but this bitch is a snake.

"Won't this poke little holes in my jacket?"

"More excuses! Not to worry Frannie …"

"Frances. I prefer Frances."

"Okay, Francessss. See? There is a magnet with a metal backing. Very strong, holds the pin nicely."

"That's clever."

"Thank you! It was one of my first innovations in the department." She points to the golden bunny cameo on her nametag. "I got a Binger Pin for it!"

Damn it all to hell, I paid her a compliment.

"By the way, I'm the dress code patrol in our Division. Time to play bad cop again." She pauses to scrunch up her face. "Those earrings are a little too big."

She can't be talking to me. I reach for my ears. "These earrings? They're fabulous."

"I'm sure you think they are, but they are larger than company policy allows."

"It said the size of a nickel in the handbook," I say, without trying to give her the pleasure of sounding defensive. Wow. First day on the job and I can already quote company policy. Good job Frances.

"Yes, and I can tell you that those are outside of the nickel limit. I'm sure. I took a class in it."

They teach a *class* in earring scale? "Okay," deep breath, "I won't wear them again."

"Thanks."

"And just to be sure I'll get two nickels set and only wear those, alright?" I smile and give a fake giggle so she thinks I'm joking.

"Just be careful. You might want to use pennies or dimes. If the setting goes outside of the perimeter of the coin, it will still be too big. One of the gals in the office tried to do that and I had to write her up. Cost her a promotion." She cocks her head to one side, "So sad."

The earring Nazi leads me through the crowd like a linebacker. Ms. Holden is a very brisk walker. Her Fitbit probably needs an extra digit. There's barely time to look around let alone remember the path. We cut through families, run past weigh-your-own frozen yogurt machines, and lines - lots of lines, many lines full of sweating tourists. We dodge frustrated parents pushing strollers as though they were driving on the West Side Highway at rush hour.

The colors, whizzing by, are primary. There is a lot of energy, lots of music playing in the background. I like that. The landscaping is very lush. There are tropical flowers everywhere. I see some signs in the Fleischer style as we head toward a gate. It says, "Cast Members Only."

We cross through and everything stops.

There is no color. Everything is gray and beige. The buildings are, for the most part, prefab and metal. No music. There are no flowers. I feel like Dorothy back in Kansas after seeing Oz. The disappointment must register in my face.

"Is something wrong?" asks the Wicked Witch of the Theme Park.

"Wrong? No. Not really."

"Oh, that's right! All your interviews took place in the New York offices, didn't they? This is your first time backstage!"

I nod.

"We save the glitz and the glamour for our guests. It's a little more utilitarian behind the scenes. We can't have magic everywhere!" Or paint either for that matter. Evidently pigment wasn't in the budget. The money was probably diverted into a nametag slush fund.

"Here we are! Home sweet home."

I look up and see a very weathered brown metal sign beige letters announce, "Creative Administration." The building has no windows and is made out of a corrugated metal. It's like a glorified three story trailer. I don't think I'll be coming here in the case of a tornado.

We walk through frosted glass doors. "Hi girls!" chirps the HR monster. The receptionists don't look up. Kellie falters a bit. She's trying not to show that it bothers her; I love these women already. Holden the Horrible picks up a little tab next to her name and slides it into the IN category on some kind of staffing flow chart, with little rectangles that are filled in with dry erase markers. "Gratciana, you were supposed to add Frances' name to the attendance board."

"Hello, nice meeting you. I'm Frances Fiore." I get a glance and a smile before she turns to face the music.

"I'm sorry Kellie. My son is sick. I had to find someone to stay with him. I got in a few minutes late."

"Update your hours on the portal please."

Gratciana's face tightens. Her, "He's fine. Thank you," is totally lost on Kellie. Evidently the Human Resource Department needs to learn a little something about humanity. We walk down a fluorescent hallway with worn gray indoor-outdoor carpeting. She opens the door marked, "Conference Room."

"Hi team," chirps Kellie, now in full cheerleader mode. "This is Frances Bettinger."

I stop cold. "Frances *Fiore*. My last name is Fiore."

"Oh, that's right," she says with doe eyes. "You went back to your maiden name." Two of the three women in the room smile and check to make sure their wedding rings are still there. The third woman looks up with sympathetic eyes. She must have recently split up with someone, a husband. The skin is still lighter on her ring finger. Kellie quickly apologizes. "I'm sorry. My bad."

This woman is good. I almost believe her. "Let's see if I can get the rest of the names right!"

"These two ladies from Finance are twin sisters, married," she says with emphasis, "to twin brothers in our Security Department. Frances Fiore meet Pauline and Petra Vogt." They both smile so it takes me a second to notice that they're dressed alike with identical hairstyles.

"Next to them is my assistant Joy." The woman with the wedding ring tan lines looks up. Clearly

Joy's name is ironic. Girlfriend needs some Cymbalta stat. Kellie's face tightens. "Could you check on the cookies for the meeting?" Joy hurries out of the room. "It's a little tradition we have here. Cookies on everyone's first day!" Under her breath just loud enough for all of us to hear she adds, "I guess I should have just done it myself."

She motions to my left. "This is Desi Perez."

We shake hands. "Very nice to meet you Frances," says the handsome man. He has a great haircut and beautiful latte skin. I take him to be in his early thirties, no wedding ring and Prada trousers from two seasons ago. I'm guessing gay, but I don't always have the best instincts there, hence the 6 months in high school spent dating Jaymes the president of the Barry Manilow fan club. Desi brings me back to reality. "I'm going to be your assistant."

"Upon your approval of course," interjects Kellie the theme park Voldemort. "He's been a dancer with the company since 2004. He was appearing in BINGER'S MILLENNIAL BASH until he injured himself during the PARTY LIKE IT'S 1999 section of the show."

Binger's Millennial Bash? How can that still be running? Should I tell them the rest of the country has been living in the twenty-first century for quite a while now?

"Here's a copy of his injury report and his personnel file." Homerun Kellie! If I don't accept him I'm a bitch. If I do I am stuck training someone while I'm learning my own job. It's my first decision and either way I lose.

There is a heavy silence in the room. Everyone is waiting for my response.

I look at Desi. It must be hard to give up dancing and get stuck behind a desk. I bet he needs the money.

He looks like a nice guy.

"Let's give it a shot."

His relief is tangible. "Thank you very much. I appreciate the opportunity."

"And hopefully his dyslexia won't be an issue." Kellie's eyes narrow as her smile grows. Desi looks mortified.

"I'm sure it won't. We all deal with challenges in one way or another, don't we Kellie?" I didn't think it was possible for her smile to get bigger, but it does. "I can help him proof things and he can help me remember my nametag."

"*Si*. Teamwork," says Desi with a sincere smile.

Kellie regains control by changing the subject. "I saved the best for last."

"Hello. I'm Matt," he looks at Kellie, "Matthew O'Connell. Welcome to the team." He looks to be almost forty, maybe just a little older. The hair is thinning a bit, with dashes of salt in the pepper. Where have I seen that tie before?

My heart sinks. I bought a similar one for Paul the last Christmas we were together. Don't give in Frances. Breathe through it. I make my way to his face. Nice teeth. Full lips. An easy smile. Firm jaw. Sad, blue eyes. There's a story behind those eyes.

I put out my hand. He grabs it. His hand is warm. I know I'm blushing. I can feel the heat in my cheeks as I smile. "So nice to meet you.

Thank you very much for the gift basket in my room last night. It was lovely."

His smile grows. "I thought I smelled lilacs."

This news does not appeal to Kellie who quickly steps between us wearing an even bigger smile. It's like the Mason-Dixon Line, separating the north and south of her face. "That's our Matt, very thoughtful. He does those kinds of things for *everyone*. Just the other day, the office cleaning girl Terry…"

Petra looks up. "You mean Tammy."

"Whatever." She looks over toward the twins, her eyebrows raised, "Tammy?"

They nod.

"Of course, Tammy. Tammy had a fallopian cyst removed and Matt insisted on sending flowers. He circulated the card himself. It had a funny monkey on the cover. Remember everyone?" She ends with a forced little giggle.

So Medusa does have a heart. Desi gives me a quick glance, which confirms it. Kellie likes Matt. She thinks I'm competition; the new single woman on the team. That's why she was being so snarky.

"Listen, today is really just about introductions. Matthew is going to be tied up with these budget meetings all day so I figured we could help you with relo … that's HR talk for relocation. I arranged for a company car. Desi will be your tour guide. Spend the day exploring Orlando."

"Thanks," I say with surprised sincerity. "I'd love to get started on finding an apartment." I try to keep my eye contact with Kellie but

I can't. Matthew keeps staring at me. Is it my imagination? He hasn't taken his eyes off me.

We start to exit when I see Joy entering through the door on the other end of the conference room.

I double back and excuse myself as I take three oatmeal raisin cookies, one for me and two for Desi. I say, "Thank you Joy."

The last thing I see is her smile.

CHAPTER
THREE

I can't believe I'm working for a company with its own motor vehicle fleet, but here we are looking at a parking lot full of cars. They are, of course, labeled. Someone has written PLANET BINGER all over most of the autos. The ones that are sans label are really boring in a single soccer Mom on a budget kind of way. I was kind of hoping for something with a little more style.

"Hola, Doug," Desi says with heavy eyelids as he saunters over to the older man behind the counter. Evidently they know each other from a nightclub in an old hotel called the Parliament House. Sounds British.

Introductions are quickly made and Desi plays this guy like a *maraca*. Four flirting minutes later, we are pulling out of the parking lot in a wonderfully logo free vehicle, a candy apple red Fiat 500 with twelve miles on it.

"If I'd made out with him I could have gotten us a convertible."

I laugh for the first time in weeks. Desi is so gutsy. I never would have said that in front of my boss. I want to be the kind of boss that people would feel comfortable saying things like that in front of.

Wow. I'm someone's boss. I have a cat. I have to buy a car. I'm on a collision course with adult living. I haven't felt like this since I was married.

Two or three miles later we're in front of something called The Vinings of Lake Buena Vista. It's like a resort but evidently people actually live here. You'd think everyone would be older, but they're not. Most of them are younger than me. I am, after all, now officially a ma'am.

The buildings are Pepto-Bismol pink stucco and gushing fountains. I hate it immediately so we move further east, and look and look and soon all these simple complexes and their model apartments and their amenities begin to blur.

We break for lunch at a Pizza Hut on Kirkman Road near Universal Studios.

I haven't eaten at a Pizza Hut since I worked as the salad bar girl at one on Long Island. It's comforting. Here I feel rather free from the pressure of being Manhattan fabulous.

I order a Meat Lovers Supreme personal pan style pizza. The mammoth anti-Bloomberg Diet Pepsi cuts through the grease very nicely. The iceberg lettuce from the salad bar is glorious; so crisp and devoid of any nutritional value. I'm glad we chose this restaurant. "More bread sticks please," I say to no one in particular and then turn my attention toward Desi.

Watching someone eat who used to be a dancer no longer living under that body perfect pressure is revelatory. Desi is savoring every single bite. If he isn't careful that thin and crispy crust is going to make him thick and chewy.

"So what do you think of Orlando - happy to be here?" he asks between bites.

"Sure."

"That sounds like something you think you have to say."

"Well, frankly, I just never expected to end up working for a giant Bunny that can speak."

"Dreams come true."

"Really?" I say so incredulously that a half chewed piece of pepperoni falls out of my mouth and onto my chin. "This wasn't exactly my dream."

"When I was a little boy growing up in Cuba, I..."

"Where in Cuba?"

"Ciego de Avila." He lets out a throaty laugh. "Heard of it?"

I start laughing too. "No..."

"Most people haven't. It's in the middle of the country. We grow pineapple and sugarcane. I'm the only boy in my village that grew up to be a dancer. Very macho, my village..."

"That had to be hard."

"A girl who is a few years older than me got to visit the United States. She was a gymnast; beautiful girl with these long, long legs. Fifteen years old and she got to see the world. I was so jealous." He chews for a moment and then wipes his mouth with a paper napkin. "When she came home, she brought toys for all the kids in the village." He is silent for a second.

"And?"

He makes a disgusted face. "She got knocked up by one of the guys in town. She works in the pineapple factory now."

"Oh," I say, surprised at how sad I could feel for a stranger.

"She started drinking a lot. People brushed her off. Not me."

"That was sweet."

"Not really. I knew what I was doing."

It suddenly strikes me that although we ended up at the same Pizza Hut, Desi and I grew up in totally different worlds. I never had to have a strategy when I was a kid. Who knew that was a luxury?

"She'd have too much rum and want to talk about her adventure in the States."

"She'd reminisce?"

"When you're staring at a brick wall, you turn around and look in the other direction, right?"

"You mean if you don't like the present, you think about the past?"

"*Si*, the past or the future. That's it." His eyes glaze over for a second as he relives the memory. "She would get loaded and start talking about her trip. I *memorizado*, excuse me, I memorized," under his breath he repeats the English translation, "…every word because in my heart I knew someday I was going to be here and I wasn't going to ruin my chance the way she had. I wasn't going to end up in a pineapple factory."

"What's the girl's name?"

"Maya."

"Do you know how she's doing now?"

"Five kids." He throws down his slice of pizza. "My mother's letters say she got really fat."

The waitress returns with my credit card receipt. I sign it. We rise to leave. "You never told me which toy Maya brought for you."

"A stuffed animal."

"What kind?"

"Binger Bunny."

Our tour of uninspired architecture continues.

We are near a theme park called, Holy Land - a thrill ride through Jerusalem or a virtual tour of the Stations of the Cross I guess. I bet the water flume turns into wine.

We pull into an apartment complex called Oakwood near a mall. There are no oaks to be seen. Ironic. I can get behind that.

The rental clerk seems nice enough. Emily, according to her nametag is dressed nicely with beautifully lacquered nails, which she uses like a laser pointer as she points out the property's features.

Her tour lacks adjectives, which is refreshing. A kitchen is just a kitchen and not, "a state of the art cuisine center designed to feed your entire family tastefully and efficiently." The grout in the bathroom is simply grout and not, "a look featured in *Architectural Digest*, June of 2012."

Emily shows us a cute one-bedroom apartment with a nice view of the pond in the back for $850 bucks a month, or less than half of what I was paying in New York and for twice the square footage.

"Free theme park tickets if you sign a one year lease today," chirps Emily, the Oakwood Hospitality Representative. I look outside.

There's a little family of ducklings living right beneath what would be my balcony. That would drive Katzenberg crazy and provide me with hours of free entertainment.

"Where do I sign?"

She whisks us to the clubhouse/workout center/office of the Oakwood Friendship Team to take my application. She hears where I work and tells me I am entitled to a ten percent discount on my rent, which suddenly goes from $850 to $765. I love this place! My debt to earning ratio, while high, is fine. I'm approved and we start wrapping up the deal. I have just grabbed the Binger Boroughs pen I swiped from the hotel to sign the lease when Emily asks, "Do you have any pets?"

"A cat. Is that a problem?"

"No. We do however, for future reference, have a twenty five pound limit on all dogs."

"That doesn't apply to cats, does it?" Emily laughs. I don't. Instantly the deal is off.

"You might want to discuss your options with a veterinarian. Perhaps the animal is an appropriate candidate for feline gastric bypass surgery. If you opt to have the procedure done you would both be welcomed to the Oakwood community with open arms." She moves us toward the door. "Enjoy these complimentary Oakwood canvas shopping totes." Just as my hand starts to twist the doorknob Emily clears her throat.

"Could I please have the theme park tickets back?"

We are back in the Fiat before I fully comprehend what just happened.

"They are clearly biased against cats of size. That's a class action suit just waiting to happen."

"Girl, we are stopping by Petsmart to get you some Science Diet *Light*. Your cat needs help. Pretty soon you'll be buying collars at Lane Bryant."

I ignore that gibe against fat cats everywhere and count strip malls as we head toward some part of town called Metro West, where it appears the 90s came to die. Seven shopping centers later and we're on something called Hiawassee Road. There are apartment complexes everywhere. They all look like the ones that we have already seen.

Just when I think all is lost, I see a sign that says, "Guest House for Lease." An arrow on the sign indicates a left turn, which we make. The scenery changes. We are on a dirt road with eroded ruts and branches sticking through the surface.

The landscape looks completely natural between the houses, which are few and far between. There is moss hanging from the trees and huge prehistoric looking tropical plants bending toward the road. All the houses are unique, not like all the cookie cutter subdivisions we have driven past today. The road starts to loop back toward civilization before we see the home we're looking for. To the left of gates that look like they haven't been closed in quite some time is a sign that reads, "Guest House for Lease. Inquire Within." I get out my iPhone, but there is no phone number listed.

We park in the driveway.

The house has a charm, actually kind of an aged glory that I wasn't expecting in the land of prefab. It has a tile roof but I would guess it was built in the early fifties or late forties. The color is creamy beige with just enough yellow to make it cheerful. The roof is at an angle of roughly forty degrees and there are heavy wooden shutters on either side of many windows, which seem to be of several different eras. They don't match. The original house is at the center and it is clear that several additions have been put on over the years.

A small burst of wind carries leaves that swirl around us. "Please join me out here in the back," says an elderly voice. "The screen door is unlocked." We enter the backyard pool area and are greeted by the outstretched arms of a slightly frail looking woman with wispy white hair surrounding a face remarkably free of lines. If we were in New York I would think she had work done but first impressions say she isn't the type. She's wearing a hostess gown that must have cost quite a bit in its day. The purple and green of the paisley has only gotten richer with age. "How do you do? My name is Gladys Nelson." She smiles and offers both of us her hands.

We return the introductions and compliment her on her home. She's pleased. I can tell. "May I interest you in a cocktail?"

We hesitate. "It's a little early," Desi explains.

"One of the pleasures of a shaded yard is that you can pretend it's already dark. Have a drink. I promise not to tell."

Ms. Nelson starts to pick up a pitcher of Manhattans, but it is too heavy for her. Desi, such a gentleman says, "Allow me to bartend." As he pours, we take our seats around a very old, wrought iron patio table that has been taken care of beautifully.

"The flowers are lovely."

"Thank you dear. I arranged them myself from the beds here at the house. My husband planted the perennials several years ago, just before he passed away."

"I'm sorry."

"Emphysema," she says as she lights up a Capri Menthol Ultra Light.

Desi brings over the libations, a word I never would have used before meeting the lady of the house, and sits down. Drinking two days in a row is not my usual habit but this is too good to pass up.

"Were you expecting guests?" Desi asks.

"Well, I do think it's good to be prepared, but in all honesty since the sign just went up this morning, I figured I might have some callers. I find that a Manhattan or two loosens the whistle a bit. People let down their guard and show their true colors. That helps when interviewing potential tenants."

I promise myself that I will only have one of these bourbon truth serums.

"My first husband had too much to drink at our wedding reception," she says, shaking her head at the memory. "He was such an angry drunk. Where's the fun in that? I left the party and never looked back." She sets her knowing eyes in my direction. "Sometimes a girl has to move on even if she doesn't know where she's headed."

I decide not to pursue that line of conversation. "Is the guest house still available?"

"You're the second person who has stopped by today. The first one, however, was a Yankee. He won't be moving in here anytime soon."

"Well ma'am," finally another ma'am, someone older than me, "I'm from New York and …"

She interrupts. "No dear. Not a Yankee of geography, a Yankee of *philosophy*. No one can help where they were born but we all have freedom of thought. The young man of whom I speak seemed terribly rigid. I couldn't possibly rent to him." She rises. "Follow me please; the guest house is this way."

She leads us away from the pool and down a slightly overgrown path. On the way I give her all the pertinent information, age, job and such.

"Forgive the condition of the trail. I shall speak to the lawn man. The house hasn't been rented for several years but I woke up today with a wild hair and decided it was time. I've had the windows open all day to air it out a bit."

I take one look at the house at the end of the path and know that it's my new home. It's like a miniature version of the main house. Handmade tile mosaics flank either side of the French doors that open into a living room with wide plank, dark wooden floors. Gauzy curtains float through the air. There is a fireplace with a wide, simple mantel of roughhewn wood. Tile matching the exterior mosaics surround the fireplace. The kitchen is small, but has wooden cabinets with a finish that matches the floor. Old spoons and forks make the handles for the doors. The appliances are either retro or actually from the fifties but there is a dishwasher, thank you Lord. I've never had one of those before. Maybe I'll actually cook.

I want to cry when I see that a cat door is already installed and is waiting to be walked through. The Formica counter is a powdery country blue. I hate it but appreciate the flaw; otherwise this place might be too perfect.

The bedroom is basic but large and has plenty of closet space. I can finally get my parent's bedroom set out of storage. The room won't get morning light, which is terrific. I'm not by nature an early riser. The other bedroom is small but who cares? There's a second bedroom. I've never had one of those before either!

The bathroom is huge considering the age of the house. It has a shower and a separate tub with those old fashioned claws that you only see in romantic comedies. The tile design that is found throughout the house is on the floor of this room. The pedestal sink is huge and deep. There is a linen closet and plenty of shelves for storage.

"It's heaven."

"I'm glad you think so. You see this is the original house. My husband and I built the main house after living here for several years. Once the children started coming we simply had to have more room."

"What about the garage?" asks Desi.

"It's included. There's a room above that's yours too." Oh my. Maybe I could actually set up a real studio.

Here comes the deal breaker. I take a deep breath.

"I have a cat."

"That's wonderful. I adore cats. My little grey tiger passed away only a few months ago. Her name was Pal."

"This one is really huge from what I hear. More like a bear cub," adds Desi, who must be a dog person. There is just no other explanation for his behavior.

"All the more to love," says the landlady. "My late husband weighed over three hundred and fifty pounds when he passed away. We had eight pallbearers. One of them ruptured a disc."

"I hate talking about money, but…"

"That's good breeding dear."

I smile and roll my eyes.

"Never dismiss a compliment Frances."

I blush. "Very well, thank you Mrs. Nelson."

"Gladys. Please call me Gladys."

"How much is the rent?"

"Well now, this does include all utilities since the entire property is on one meter. And you have use of the pool too." Crap. Mrs. Nelson is a good businesswoman. She knows exactly what this place is worth.

"Perhaps it is more than I can afford."

"Perhaps it is." There is an awkward silence broken only by the smell of the jasmine and orange blossoms growing near the house. I love orange blossoms.

"$850?"

"Darling, that wouldn't be fair." I frown and nod. "I couldn't possibly take over $725 for the place, one year lease; get me the security deposit when you have it."

"But…"

"But nothing. I like you. That's all that really matters. You and this house belong together. I can tell. Besides you haven't heard all my terms."

Uh-oh. There are always terms.

"You'll have responsibilities."

"Excuse me?"

"Keep this old lady off the streets. I'm 79 soon, God willing, to be 80." That probably means she's closer to 90. "On occasion you'll need to help me with my errands. Liquor and smokes do not magically appear."

"Amen sister," says Desi, who takes a swig of his drink and quickly lights up a cigarette of his own.

"It's a deal."

The sun has begun to set. The sky becomes a lovely mix of pink and purple. I'm surprised to hear myself say, "How beautiful." I seldom notice the sky.

Gladys smiles. "I like to think of it as being God's compensation for putting us between the Gulf and the Ocean."

"We should get going. We've kept you long enough."

"Oh dear. I was hoping you two would stay for supper. I have some lovely cold chicken from yesterday's Canasta party. It won't be a bother to make you each a plate."

I look to Desi. He's the one with a life here, not me. "We'd love to," he says as he drinks another sip of his second Manhattan.

Perhaps I'll drive when we leave.

As we make our way up to the main house, a burst of fireworks lights our way.

CHAPTER
FOUR

Katz is waiting for me when I get back to the hotel along with the remnants of a pillow he ripped into while I was gone. I smile in spite of myself and start to clean up when my cell phone starts playing HAVA NAGILA. Teresa is calling. She programmed the ring tone herself. I pick up. "Call me at the hotel number."

"I already did."

"I just got back."

"Did you check the voice mail?"

"No Teresa, I didn't. I literally just walked in the door."

"You didn't respond to any of my texts today either. This is why you're single almost three years after your divorce."

"Listen you …"

"It's just as well. I want to give you the good news in person … I mean myself … over the phone. You know what I mean…"

"Okay."

"I bought you a car!" and she disconnects.

I'm overwhelmed by this news and run over to the bedside phone, waiting for it to ring. And wait. And wait. Then I wait some more. When I'm done with that I wait a little more. Finally she calls. "What took so long?"

"I wanted to conference in Tommy."

"Hi Frances."

"Hi. Have you heard about this car thing?"

"Yeah, I …"

"He was with me Frances. What do I know from cars? Tommy checked it out before I bought it."

"And?"

"It is in re …"

"He says it is in perfect condition," interrupts my sister Auto Maxie. "Larry is driving it down to the Auto Train tomorrow. The shipping is a gift from us. The car you're paying for."

"Thank you, I guess. What kind of car is it?"

"A steal."

"Of course, it's steel, it's a car."

"No, no, no," barks my sister. "The car. Such a bargain. Let me tell you the story," she says, as though either of us have ever been able to stop her from talking. "I went to a service today for Mr. Kleinschmidt, my friend Tova's father, Bernie the Kosher butcher. You remember him. He told bad jokes and always patted your rear end when he hugged you goodbye."

"Sorry to hear he passed," I say by rote, instantly reliving the sensation of his arthritic hand on my ass.

"Don't be or you wouldn't have this car."

"What?"

"I bought Mr. Kleinschmidt's car today at his funeral. His widow Phyllis has macular degeneration. She was thrilled to be rid of the burden. She even threw in four steaks. Very tasty."

"What kind?"

"Porterhouse."

"Not the steaks! The car! What kind of car is it?"

"Maroon, not a scratch on it."

"Not what color," which would normally be my priority had I chosen the vehicle. "What *kind*?"

"It comes with snow tires."

"That will be a huge help here in Florida Teresa. What kind of car is it?"

The used car broker starts laughing. "You really want to know, don't you?"

"Yes."

"Good! It's a surprise! I'm not going to tell you."

Memories of Teresa fixing me up on a blind date for my junior prom flood my brain. She didn't want to tell me then either and that story did not have a happy ending. Again I am reliving someone's unwanted hands on my ass.

"Tommy, what kind of car is it?"

Silence.

"Tommy!"

"Tommy you ruin this mitzvah for me and never again will I talk to you. I swear to God," threatens Mrs. Goodwrench.

"You're both nuts. G'bye." Tommy disconnects.

"Listen little Miss Visa-Debt, the car only cost two grand and it even has a full tank. According to the Internet it is worth much more. Let me surprise you."

"I love it when we pretend I have a choice."

"Me too! It's cute, isn't it? Auto Train, Sanford, FL day after tomorrow, 8:30 in the morning. I've emailed you the directions. The train station is on Persimmon Drive. Such a pretty name…"

"Very."

"Great! Now I am craving fruit which is not on my Atkins." There is a crash in the background. "Dammit, would you two settle down? Listen, I have got to go. I'll talk to you soon."

She's already gone. I hang up the phone and the second, literally the second it hits the cradle it is ringing again. I jump. Katzenberg gets startled and runs into the bathroom. Unfortunately the door is shut. I hear a thud. I am concerned until I see him stagger back into view.

"Hello?"

"Hello Frances."

I can't place the voice.

"This is Matt O'Connell. I was wondering if you'd like to meet me in the lobby for a drink."

CHAPTER
FIVE

"I'll be right down."

I have to change my outfit.

Dammit all to hell everything in my closet is either too much or too little. I left all the right clothes with the movers. I compromise on a nice black skirt and a fitted white cotton shirt from H&M on 34th Street. I pull my hair back, apply a fresh coat of lipstick, put on my new sandals from Macy's, pet the cat, grab my purse and head downstairs.

I go back into my room, grab the Jo Malone, spritz the air, walk through it, pet Katz again, grab my purse, and start to leave, come back in, turn on the music channel so Katz has company and finally escape. As I head to the elevator I check my watch. Ten minutes. Not bad. Really. It could have been much worse.

The lobby bar is not as nearly as simple as its title implies. It's a scaled recreation of what some would call the best of Manhattan. The entrance is Times Square.

A host dressed as the Phantom of the Opera asks if I'm meeting anybody. With a flourish of his cape he leads me toward the faux Winter Garden Theater. Matt is waiting there in what would be considered a box seat reading some official looking report. He's still dressed in his suit from earlier today.

The Phantom speaks. "The show starts in fifteen minutes. Remember to," and then he starts singing, "listen to the music of the night."

With another sweeping gesture of his cape he vanishes. Softly. Slowly. There is a moment of silence.

"Hello."

"Oh, you're here," he says awkwardly. He stands and makes a gesture toward the empty chair across the cocktail table. He grimaces as if to punish himself for a lack of manners and crosses to pull the chair out for me. I sit. As he goes back to his own seat I see that he has tucked a napkin into the pockets of his trousers.

"Nice to see you," he says with a smile.

He sits down and almost meets my eye. I'm sure it's not his intention but he is staring at my breasts. I arch my back just a little bit, maybe more than I intended. He quickly looks up. "Thank you … uh, for joining me."

"We can celebrate. I found a place today."

"Did you say Celebration?"

"Pardon?"

"Celebration, it's a little town just outside of Kissimmee on Hwy. 192."

"Oh. No. My new place is right outside of … uh, Metro West, that's it. It's a cute little guesthouse. Celebration sounds like a town obsessed with Kool and the Gang"

"Actually it was built by Disney."

"Oh my God. How frightening. Bet you it's considered corporate espionage to run over a chipmunk." He doesn't laugh.

"That's where I live."

"And I'm sure it's lovely."

Silence.

The Statue of Liberty stops by and tells us tonight's drink special is The Wall Street. The price is tied to the current prime interest rate. Matthew orders an international beer sampler called The Ellis Island. I order a chardonnay, which according to the menu is an Upper West Side White Whine. Anyone who has ever been to New York City knows the typo was deliberate.

"I was driving past the hotel and thought you might like a little company." He looks handsome in the moonlight. Much better looking than I first realized. "How was your day?"

"Great. Thanks again for the time off."

"Oh, that's a company policy. Anyone moving to Orlando gets seventy two hours of personal time."

"But Kellie…"

"…is in HR. She doesn't get to deliver good news often so when there is an opportunity…"

"She grabs it," I finish stopping just short of asking him if he realizes that could apply to her grabbing him as well. He's a nice guy; too nice for his own good. I bet he is from the Midwest.

"The company car was her idea. She didn't have to do that."

An Ed Koch look-alike delivers the drinks.

Matthew raises his glass, "To new adventures."

"You made a very good impression on everyone this morning."

"That's nice to hear."

"Joy actually smiled twice today."

I choke on my wine. "I noticed that too!"

Matt laughs. "I've been keeping track of her smiles since we started working together."

"And the total is?" I ask.

"Counting today, it's three."

"There was another time?"

"Yeah. I remember because it was the one time Kellie called in sick."

He doesn't seem to get what he just implied so I stifle a laugh and there is a short lull. Our eyes meet and suddenly we both become very self-conscious.

"Listen, would you mind talking shop a bit?"

"I thought we were."

The smile returns. "Actually I wanted to talk to you about a project to which I am going to assign you. I was looking at your portfolio..."

"Which pieces specifically?"

"The documentation from your UN Project. Incredible images. You really captured the diversity."

"The Hunger Summit?"

"Yes. I'm just a numbers guy but the way you portrayed the cultural stereotype versus the truth of what's going on. Really inspiring."

"Thank you."

"Are you familiar with Tiny Planet?"

Who isn't? It might as well be the poster child for love/hate relationships. A little research will tell you Tiny Planet was originally designed by Art and Mary Binger for the 1965 New York World's Fair. It's a trip through an idealized vision of our world - windmills and piñatas and happy Eskimos ice-skating on a glacier with their best friends the polar bears, who despite their natural programming don't eat any of the little children playing nearby. No cultural integrity. It's the kind of thing grandparents adore and teenagers find totally stupid. The worst part is the redundant, innocuous song that is played over and over and over as you take your trip through the land of stereotypes:

We all see the sunrise
We see the sunset
We all love someone
we haven't met yet
Though mountains divide
It can't be denied
It's a tiny planet after all

Smiles are bright
Tears can be shiny
As our hearts get bigger
The planet gets tiny
Oceans keep us apart
But we know in our heart
It's a tiny planet after all

I've always thought they should play that song at an Arab-Israeli summit. They'd finally agree on something and ask someone to turn off that song.

My parents took us to Binger Village when we were kids. My mom never completely got that song out of her head. She complained about it for years afterwards. We loved to torment her by singing it over and over and over.

I look Matthew straight in the eye and banish all memories. "You're talking about the boat ride where …"

"Actually, it's an attraction. Attraction. We don't call them rides. People associate the word ride with a carnival. We prefer the term attraction, meaning that it is something that attracts our guests to come visit us."

"Okay."

"I'm sorry if I sound like a stickler. It's our standard operating procedure or SOP."

"So, let me get this right, our SOP is to call Tiny Planet an attraction, not a ride."

"Right!" he says with the pride of a teacher who has done his job well.

"So this meeting, getting together for a drink, is about an attraction?"

It goes right over his head. This guy is all business. "Exactly!"

"Can I be honest?"

"Of course."

"I really don't care for that ride," his eyebrow rises, "attraction."

"No one does. We get hate mail. That's why this is so exciting! It's a chance to make a real difference. Our team is going to update Tiny Planet for the first time since 1965 and you're going to be the Art Director!"

He starts to pull out charts and schematics just as the lights begin to dim. An Ethel Merman impersonator comes out and starts singing "525,600 Minutes," from *Rent*. Somehow I suspect it will be lasting even longer.

"Maybe we should get out of here," I suggest.

"You wouldn't mind missing the show?"

Here's the chance to earn a couple of points with the boss. I bite my lower lip and say, "Business first."

We take our drinks and head to the patio. It's a lovely night. There's just enough breeze to be comfortable and we have the place to ourselves. Everyone else is watching the show. In the background you can hear the Merm singing a sanitized song from *Book of Mormon*.

Matthew is set up again. Blueprints cover the table. "The rehab is on a fast track for the 47th anniversary celebration of the Florida operation."

"We celebrate forty-seventh anniversaries?"

"Marketing does. Just pretend it's the fifty-first anniversary of the World's Fair, okay?" he smiles. "I have been pitching this project for two years and it is finally going to happen. Everything has lined up perfectly. I think you might have been the last piece of the puzzle; a good luck charm."

The waiter shows up with another round of drinks. "I took the liberty," says the considerate man in front of me. He raises his glass. "To your first day."

"To a tiny planet."

We each take a sip. It's quiet for a second, but comfortable. I notice his ears have been pierced but have healed over. I bet he hasn't worn an earring in years. It's nice to know that he went through a bit of a wild phase. "You know," says Matthew, "When I was a kid growing up in Madison …"

"New Jersey?"

"No. Wisconsin."

I *knew* he was from the Midwest! Where else could those good manners and that slightly nasal voice come from?

"I used to watch *The Wonderful World of Art* every Sunday night. I remember them taking about Tiny Planet on TV when I was a kid. Now I'm here working on it. That amazes me."

"Matthew..."

"Please call me Matt. Kellie introduces me as Matthew because she thinks it gives me more authority."

"Okay, *Matt*," I raise my glass again, "Congratulations on having a dream come true."

"Thank you."

"So we start tomorrow?"

Again he grimaces and then slaps his forehead. "I almost forgot. You aren't in the office tomorrow."

"Why?"

"Report to Binger University ..."

"What's that?"

"Orientation. It's just for one day." He rolls his eyes, "It used to be three. Class starts at eight in the morning." He checks his watch. "And it's almost eleven now. I should let you get some rest."

We down our drinks quickly and Matt walks me to the elevator. We hear a Carol Channing impersonator sing, "And I Tell You I'm Not Going," from *Dreamgirls*. I remark that I believe her. Matt laughs. He's my *boss*. I need to keep that in mind.

We arrive at the elevator. He pushes the button. It arrives immediately. Of course it does. Everything runs very efficiently around here.

"Thanks for a nice evening," he says.

"You too," I say as the doors start to shut.

"Oh by the way …"

"Yes?"

He grins like a cat. "Don't think I didn't get your attraction joke." And the door shuts.

Now normally this is the kind of thing that I could dwell on all night long if given the opportunity. Life, however, has other plans. Just as I start to realize what he said, my iPhone vibrates. I grab it from my purse and check caller ID.

It's Paul.

CHAPTER
SIX

The Binger Transportation Network did not make getting to Binger University any easier this morning. I had to take the Binger Train thingy to a Binger Ferry Boat, walk to the Binger Cast Member Transfer Center and catch a Binger Bus. I'm a frazzled, sweaty mess in real danger of being late by the time I arrive.

The building almost defies description. The entrance features the characters from a very successful underwater animated film from several years ago called, "Goin' to School," in which a little fishy named Verne risks life and gill to get the education that his family thinks is only for fancy air breathing landlubbers. At the end of the film he graduates Magna Cum Tuna and has a cross species affair with a dolphin. It made a lot of money and now it's a Broadway musical.

I walk in through a door disguised as the portal into a wrecked ship and it happens again. The interior is completely bland. Evidently if the public can't see it there is no need to make the space at all interesting or energetic.

"Can you tell me where the class for new hires is being held today?"

The woman behind the information desk, who has been smiling up to this point, gets a very stern look on her face. "Nametag?" she says in the most patronizing tone possible.

I open my purse and magnetically attach the mandatory ID to my blouse. Order is restored to Binger Universe. The smile returns immediately.

I am in one of eleven "Cultures" classes for new employees - forgive me, Cast Members, being taught today. Directions are given and I frantically climb three flights of stairs and slip in through the door that was just about to be shut. My momentum nearly causes me to collide into several desks. I stop, but my purse does not. It falls off my shoulder and onto the floor. The contents spill out. Everyone scrambles to help me. Soon everything is being given back. The last item retrieved is one of my tampons handed to me by a boy named "Bradley" who appears to be seventeen or so. He looks mortified and sort of excited at the same time. He spies the Tampax label and giggles.

It's going to be a long day.

I grab a seat as the lights begin to dim. Two people in the back are holding flashlights in each hand and shining them toward a red curtain in the front of the classroom. A man and a woman, both in their fifties, emerge dressed very corporately a la JC Penney. They try to pull off a certain Vegas-like flourish but don't quite manage.

"Hello class, I'm Shelaylee Ward," says the woman.

The man, a bit on the short side but good looking says, "And I'm Louie!" The woman looks at him as if to prod him. He holds his pose for a beat, and says, "Graham. Hello class. I'm Louie Graham!" and then puts his arms up in the mirrored version of her pose.

Together they say, "Welcome to "Cultures", the Planet Binger New Hire Training Seminar!" The woman, Shelaylee if I heard correctly, starts to fan herself as though the choreography really took it out of her. Her partner, Louie, starts applauding with his arms outstretched, leading us to follow his action. The flashlights are turned off and the fluorescent overhead lights start to hum. I guess that means class has begun.

Shelaylee starts critiquing our adherence to what she calls, "the Binger Dress Code," while Louie explains why it is a violation as he refers us to the information packet that was waiting on each of our desks. They keep saying that it's the first day and not to worry. "We're not going to send you home but we could! HA HA!"

One man from the Finance Division gets busted for wearing a tie with the Gucci logo. "We don't wear the logos of other companies unless they are a legally approved sponsorship partner of Planet Binger such as British Petroleum which proudly presents The Eco-Responsibility Film at The Planet of Progress Pavilion," says Louie without any sense of irony.

"Where is that?" asks a girl named Helga who is actually taking notes. What a kiss ass.

"That's at BVOT, our permanent World's Fair!" chimes Shelaylee. "That stands for Bingers Vision of Tomorrow, B-V-O-T, which offers our guests a permanent technology expo and a worldwide walking tour around the Global Lagoon of Diversity. BVOT.

It's Educating and Entertainment at the same time."

"That's Edutainment!" sing speaks Louie. "BVOT opened on September 30th, 1982. It was the second park of the five we currently operate here in Florida," he adds, playing quite the infomercial host. He should have a toll free number.

While he passionately gives us trivia and history lessons, Shelaylee walks up and down the aisles pointing out grooming violations. She stops in front of one woman of color and inquires about her dreads. The woman says it is cultural. Ms. Ward backs off quickly and moves on to the earrings of a teenage girl. "They're too big," she accuses. The girl, named Carly, gets very defensive. I want to tell her to relax. There's no winning the earring wars.

Louie who clearly loves his job plays diplomat. "No one is saying that your taste is bad. All we are saying is that it fails to uphold nearly fifty years of corporate policy."

They stop at my desk.

"We cannot put enough emphasis on the importance of choosing natural color when d-y-e-i-n-g our hair," offers Louie, the Mr. Blackwell of Theme Parks.

"Excuse me? I don't color my hair. This is real." They look at each other as if to say, "Yeah, right."

There is an awkward silence. Shelaylee looks at Louie and motions for him to speak. She starts mouthing something along the lines of, "Go. It's your turn to talk!" Finally she gives up and says, "Introduction time!" in an exasperated voice.

"Hello, my name is Jackie and I'll be working as a hostess at the C-Span Presidential Palace."

"My name is Lars and I'll be selling Churros at BVOT."

"Hello my name is Daniel. I am going to be a hydraulic mechanic at the Ford Pinto Racetrack Inferno in Retroland."

We continue until everyone in the room has spoken.

Then class really begins. They start with the historical background of the Binger Dynasty. They cover the heritage of the five parks that make up Planet Binger: the Kingdom of Enchantment, BVOT, The Binger Orion Studios, The Peaceable Kingdom Animal Park and Binger's Baby Boomer Playground a park for geriatric adults meant to capitalize on the graying of America, which is co-sponsored by AARP.

In addition to the parks there are twenty-five hotels of various prices and themes, an evening nighttime entertainment complex called Isle of Delight which has ten nightclubs and live music, the Binger Vacation Club, a shopping mall called Bingertown, two water parks insensitively called Tsunami Cove and the Polar Icecap, and a miniature golf course based on the animated film *Sad Ol' Gilmore* about a fatherless little boy who ends up winning the Masters.

The scope of this is place is mindboggling. They go onto explain that Planet Binger is its own tax municipality. We engineer and maintain all the roads and infrastructure. We generate all our own power, have the world's largest laundry facility on property and own other parks in California, Japan, China and Spain. They, or we I guess, just announced a new park to be built in Australia. Helen Reddy is going to have her own concert hall. It sounds kind of like Celine Dion in Vegas meets Branson, MO.

Evidently the company isn't content to dominate only on land. "I just got back from a lovely trip to Nassau in the Bahamas on Binger Cruise Line," says Louie. "We had an inside verandah room with a virtual porthole on the Binger Enchantment." After confirming there are no allergy issues, he passes us each a mini Toblerone purchased Duty Free at the Sanford Executive Airport.

"While there are over sixty thousand people working at Planet Binger Resorts International in Florida, we shouldn't underestimate the importance of each cast member's individual contribution to the magic," says Shelaylee.

"It is Binger Philosophy that one person can make a difference, and two can build a Kingdom," says Louie, as he looks at one of the many photos of Art and Mary Binger that adorn the beige walls. Shelaylee nods in agreement with total conviction.

As if on cue, the overhead lights go out and a documentary on the whole Binger Family, of which I am now evidently a member, starts to roll. It's meant to be very inspirational. I guess it is. I find myself wondering what the Michael Moore version would have to say.

While the video is playing I'm left alone with my thoughts. I think I did the right thing by not answering Paul's call last night. It had been such a good day. It was all about the future, my new life. I didn't want to be grabbed by the past so I ignored the call. That makes sense, right?

He didn't leave a voice mail.

I know that because I've checked six times.

Oh great. More tears. I immediately feel very self-aware. I look around. Almost everyone in the room is weepy too. My eyes move up to the screen. There's a ghosted photo of Art and Mary Binger with rays of sunshine behind them. Binger Bunny is running in slow motion, a choir is singing and a narrator that sounds just like James Earl Jones says, "And to think it all started with a rabbit." Everyone in the room applauds as the lights come back on.

Louie's big doe eyes are welling up. He is too emotional to speak. Shelaylee takes over. "People that is what we are talking about - the heritage that we honor each and every day working here at Planet Binger. You should all be proud …"

"Proud … " repeats Louie, who manages one word before becoming overwhelmed again.

"… to make the enchantment happen for our guests."

Louie has recovered. "The important thing to remember is that we are all part of one show, one experience."

"One ENCHANTED experience," interjects Shelaylee as she holds up a bumper sticker with the slogan written in red against a white field, Berlin Sans FB type, 72 point. She begins to hand them out with military precision. "Enchanted."

"The better we all do our jobs, the easier it is for the rest of the team to do their jobs well. Frances," all eyes turn to me, "the more eye-catching and clear the signs your team designs, the easier it is for them to find The Dutch Family Robinson Treehouse of Terror, where Fern works at the Binger Orion Studios. The better Guthrie gets our guests through the gates, the easier it is going to be for Zoey when she waits on them at Ye Olden Golden Fries of France at BVOT."

"It all boils down to being there for each other, for being the best Bingerphile you can be at any given moment," says Louie.

"Being *in* the moment," nods Shelaylee. "And that can be challenging sometimes. We all have problems that can distract us." Her eyebrows rise, "Louie, do you have a problem?"

"Yes!"

"What is it?"

"I love my job way too much!"

The suck ups laugh like it is the funniest thing they have ever heard. Shelaylee wipes a tear away from her eye. "Now Louie, let's get serious. Do you have a problem?"

"Yes, I do," he takes a breath. "I suffer from Acid Reflux Disease."

"Does it do you any good to think about that while you're at work interacting with our guests?"

"No! None at all!"

The suck ups nod in agreement.

This is starting to feel like a church service.

Sister Shelaylee then asks, "Does anyone have a problem that is preventing them from being here one hundred and fifty percent?"

Shelaylee does. She doesn't know that it's impossible to do anything one hundred and fifty percent. I make the mistake of rolling my eyes.

She sees me and goes in for the kill. I can see my shock reflected in her bifocals. "What about you Frances?"

"What about me?"

Louie closes the deal. "Do you have a problem your new Binger buddies can help you with?"

"No I don't," I say emphatically.

"It's fine not to share but it's also fine to open up and let people in," says Dr. Shelaylee, my latest therapist. "This is a new start for you. Perhaps the best choice is to embrace that and let go of some of your old problems."

"No offense but I could tell the minute I saw you from behind the red velveteen curtain that we weren't going to have your full attention," tag teams Louie.

Maybe they're right. What do I have to lose? They can't call Paul and tell him anything I say. I'm one of them now. Maybe Timothy the new square dance caller at the Neon Porcupine on Isle of Delight can give me some advice. Sure he looks to be about twenty-two and during his introduction he mentioned that he's been in jail and has five kids, but still, he's lived a lot of life. Who am I to judge?

"I just moved just here from New York," several people grimace. I chose to ignore that and continue, "without calling my ex-husband to tell him. Now I wonder if I did the right thing. I struggled with that decision but in the end decided that if I didn't know whether or not to call that I shouldn't, so I didn't."

"You can't change the past. You made a decision. Let it go Frances," says Bradley who is remarkably mature for his age. I only wish he hadn't licked his lips while he was saying it.

"But there's more…"

"There always is," says Ruth who told us in introductions that she has been married three times and took this job so she and her severely diabetic husband would have health benefits. "Sweetie, you left him and New York for a reason. Don't look back."

"But last night he called me."

Several people gasp.

"I didn't answer," I admit. "Today I've been wondering if I did the right thing. It's all I can think about."

"Louie," Shelaylee commands, "get the trouble bucket."

Louie goes behind the curtain and returns with an old steel pail. "Frances, close your eyes and visualize the problem. Visualize your ex-husband being able to fit in the palm of your hand. Now pick him up and throw him in the trouble bucket."

"Trouble bucket?"

"Yes! Write this down everyone," Louie advises. The suck ups already had their pencils out. I hate them.

"At the beginning of every work day visualize putting all your troubles in a big old bucket. They'll be there waiting for you when you have time to think about them."

Shelaylee raises her glasses for emphasis, "Let them go people. Let your problems go."

People start applauding. Tina who was just hired to work at the Motorized Cart Race Track at Binger's Baby Boomer Playground starts making a whooping sound and waving her fist in the air.

"Good work Frances. Thank you for trusting us," says Louie.

Shelaylee comes over to me, gives me a quick hug and whispers in my ear, "For what it's worth dear, I think you were right not to take that stupid bastard's call."

I return her hug, which surprises both of us.

CHAPTER
SEVEN

I can't wait for the movers to get here this afternoon with my Bose alarm clock. No more stuttering cows. That's a victory right there.

What shall I wear for these sure to be burly men? I'm thinking overalls and something kitschy. How about my new Peaceable Kingdom t-shirt!

I kicked ass in the Binger trivia contest yesterday.

Before I know it I'm out the door.

Then I come back, kiss Katz, put on some lipstick, a splash of perfume, my mom's earrings and take off for real. At the faux Automat in the lobby I buy two cups of coffee, grab some Equal and a stir stick and head outside. Desi is waiting for me in the parking lot.

"Sanford ho!" I say with gusto.

"Who you calling a ho?" says my assistant wearing tight white jeans and a plunging tank top that briefly exposes what appears to be a pierced nipple.

Traffic is horrible going in both directions and a forty-mile drive ends up taking about ninety minutes. "Get used to it," says Desi.

By the time we arrive, the Auto Train has come and gone. The parking lot is nearly deserted. We pass some really cute cars on our way into the building. One of them has to be mine. I wonder which one it is.

"Hello," I say with my best new Binger smile that I learned how to make in class yesterday.

"Mornin'" says the older man behind the counter who appears to be slipping into a coma. Energetic, he is not.

"I'm here to pick up my car. My brother-in-law Larry Teitelbaum of Teaneck, New Jersey faxed over the papers yesterday. It should be under the name Fiore. Frances Fiore." I hand him my New York driver's license for ID.

"The picture isn't great. I just moved here."

Why is he staring at me?

"I'm looking forward to getting the new one taken."

"Be sure to stop by and show all of us the new one," he says with a raspy chuckle.

What feels like twenty minutes later, he locates the paperwork, which as it turns out was in front of him the entire time. "Here you go young lady," says the walking dead as he slips me the key.

"I don't know which car is mine."

"Now how's that possible?"

"My sister bought it for me." I nearly go into the full story but somehow I instinctually know that Mr. Jim Roberts according to his Amtrak nametag isn't all that interested.

"Well you're lucky," says the man with two first names. "I did the inventory check as they unloaded the train. It's a surprise, you say?"

"Yes."

A smile crosses his very dry lips. "Guess which one is yours."

"The cute red one?"

"You mean that Volkswagen?" Jim Roberts says with a big smile.

"Yeah."

"No. That's not it."

Desi decided to get in the game. "The Chevy Cobalt over there? The light green one missing one of its hubcaps?"

Fireball shakes his head. Evidently that's not it.

Which one would Teresa chose? "The lavender mini-van?"

"Nope."

Desi points to a Geo Metro with a cracked windshield. "That's mine," says our man Jim. Desi points to a rusty pick up truck with Lawn Service written on the side.

"Why do you keep choosing the ugly ones?" I shriek. Desi giggles. We both look in the other direction. Desi, trying to top himself, starts to laugh and points to a huge old maroon Buick with a white vinyl roof and white upholstery that must get about six miles to the gallon. "Stop it!" I scream. "I am not a pimp."

"That's your new car," says Jim Roberts in a monotone. "Surprise!" He slowly waves his arms over his head as he walks away.

"That looks like a car some old guy would drive," says Desi, who looks like he wants to laugh. "Did someone die or something?"

"As a matter of fact someone did."

We walk out toward the car. What was Teresa thinking? The car takes up two and a half parking spots. It has a CB radio antennae and a bumper sticker from the Atlantic City Tropicana. The Saint Christopher Medal looks new. No way that belonged to the Kleinschmidts. My Jewish sister must have bought that.

She likes to cover all the bases.

"There isn't a scratch on her. The tires are in good shape. And GM has always made a killer V8," says Desi revealing a totally unexpected side of himself. He must be a top.

I look at the keychain for the little remote thingy. There isn't one. However it has been engraved with, "A Sister's Love is Forever." There is a big red bow on the grille. I smile in spite of myself. I unlock the passenger door to let Desi in. I am winded by the time I make it around to my side. I slide in and turn on the engine, which kind of purrs actually. The seats are comfortable. There's a posh armrest between the seats.

Desi laughs and points to a cassette player, which has a box of tapes next to it. I grab the first one I see, put it in and soon the Ray Conniff Singers are harmonizing "Moon River" for me, and my huckleberry friend. While grabbing the tape I also discover half a bottle of Viagra and a pair of Granny panties. Please let them belong to Mrs. Kleinschmidt. I don't want to consider any other options. Desi grabs the Viagra and throws it in his bag.

He hands me an envelope. "What's this?"

I rip it open and start to read. "It's a letter from my sister."

Dearest Frances:

It's a great deal. It's in great shape. Now drive somewhere and find a man offering the same virtues.

Love you more than you know.

Sister Teresa

PS — Larry got you a great deal on auto insurance from Manny at Temple, who thinks you're very pretty...

In the glove compartment, along with three faux Giorgio air fresheners, I find the owners manual, which I guess I now own.

According to the booklet this horseless carriage is a 1992 Buick Park Avenue Ultra. As I recall the early 90s was a classic era in the history of American automobiles. What else does this little book say? The interior has wooden trim with a rosewood finish. The spare tire lives in a wheel hub outside of the car, attached to the trunk. There's an electric warmer under the driver's seat.

That's another great feature for a Floridian.

I look up. It's hard to see over the dashboard. Perhaps I'll just sit on one of the snow tires that are in the trunk. Then I spy a magic button. I touch it and my seat rises up about two inches. Instinct tells me to drive directly to a dealership and sell this thing, but I should keep an open mind.

I promised Desi breakfast. He's being very subtle. I can hear him chanting, "IHop! IHop!" under his breath. Luckily Central Florida doesn't suffer from a lack of chain restaurants. He drives his own cute, late model, car. I follow him at an appropriate distance behind. He warned me not to get too close.

"I don't want anyone to know we're together," were his exact words.

I hate to admit it, but this thing handles very nicely. I feel safe in this car and God knows I should. It's bigger than my apartment in New York, more comfortable too. Oh my God. The seats adjust electronically and offer lumbar support. If they vibrated, I'd propose.

I want the Stuffed French Toast at the International House of Pancakes but I can still taste that Pizza Hut. Better to go with an egg white omelet. Desi goes for the Belgian Waffle, which is kind of fun to hear ordered with a Cuban accent. Between bites small talk gets a little bigger. We go through family stats and work stories.

"So are you seeing anyone?" I ask.

He rolls his eyes. "No. Still looking for the right guy I guess. But there are other reasons too…"

"That sounds like an excuse."

"No it's not. I'm kind of waiting for my divorce from my wife to be final," he explains.

I nearly choke on my wheat toast.

"Yeah."

"You're married to a woman?" I say trying not to sound as incredulous as I feel.

"It's an immigration thing."

"Things like that really happen?"

"Yeah. I'm married to a Lucille Ball look-alike from Universal Studios."

"Desi and Lucy."

I can tell by his reaction that he's heard that joke before.

"What about you?" You're divorced, right?"

I nod.

"What happened there?"

Just as I start grasping for a way to evade the question, fate provides me with the perfect distraction. Desi gets a call he has to take.

We finish up and I pay the bill. Before I know it I'm back in the car and looking for a diversion to avoid thinking about Desi's question. I shove Dino Martini's "Italian Songs of Love" into the player, turn up the tunes and enjoy the smooth ride. I'd turn on the radio but it only has AM.

I pull up to Gladys' house and see a Trans American Van Lines truck. The movers are here! It looks like they are nearly done unloading. I missed most of it.

Yay!

I run out back to my place. Mrs. Nelson is holding court wearing a turban, a plum colored bathing suit and a Maude-like vest that would dust the floor if she weren't wearing high heels.

"Join us for mimosas, dear?"

She has obviously charmed the three men. They finish unloading what is left in the truck and when I offer to tip them they shake their heads. The oldest one, who has to be in his late sixties, takes off his hat, bows toward Gladys and says, "The pleasure has been all ours."

"Darling, unless you need me," says my landlady, "I think I'll lead these gentlemen to the garden gate."

I smile, and wave goodbye. They leave and only then do I realize I have been left with a lifetime of boxes waiting to be unpacked. It's exhausting just to look at them. What I have always dreaded seems be true.

I'm a girl that comes with a lot of baggage.

CHAPTER
EIGHT

I take a second to enjoy being alone. Pretty soon the place will be cluttered up with the debris of my life. You can actually hear the silence. That never happened in New York.

I cross to a box, take a deep breath and open it. The red deco phone that I bought on sale from Pottery Barn is right on top so I plug it in. The minute I do, it begins to ring, which is odd because I haven't even told anyone I got a landline with my Internet package yet.

"Hello Teresa."

"Hello Miss Park Avenue!" says my laughing sister. "You got the car, right? I wouldn't know for sure because you haven't called. According to the tracking number we were given by a stranger it was picked up a couple of hours ago."

"Yes, I did. Thank you very much."

"Do you love it? Do you absolutely love it?"

"Let's just say I'm infatuated"

"Okay, Ms. Pragmatist, that's good enough for me. God forbid you should commit to anything or anyone."

"So - uh, how did you get this number?"

"I tried you on your cell, and it went straight to voice mail. It was off. NEVER turn off your cell phone Frances – not in a movie theater or on a plane, even when they say you have to. You never know who is trying to get a hold of you."

Yes I do. That's why the phone was off.

"So how did you get the number?"

"I remembered that one of my sorority sisters from Rutgers is now a big wig at Verizon. PS, she never married. Big time career gal. Always going to fiber optic seminars or something. She got me your number. End of story."

My sister should work for the Department of Homeland Security. She can get through any defense system, including mine. "Well listen, everything here is fine but I am staring at a lot of boxes that aren't going to unpack themselves."

"Put on upbeat music. Save the things you are looking forward to seeing and/or use for last. It helps motivate. Start with the room you use the least." There is a pause. "In other words, the kitchen," says my life coach.

"How did you come up with that little system? You haven't moved in years."

"It was on Martha Stewart before she went to prison. It made sense, so I remember."

"Thanks for the tip. I guess I should get started."

"Okay, I'll let you go."

Good.

"But before I hang up…" damn I was almost off the hook, literally. "Tommy called me today. Something is wrong. I'm not sure what it is but if he calls see if you can get him to talk."

"Come on Teresa, a speech therapist with a pound of meth couldn't get him to talk."

She sighs. "You with the jokes. Listen to me. If he calls get him to open up. Something's going on and he needs his family."

My sister. She watches over people. "Okay, Teresa, I will. I promise."

"That's good enough for me. Thank you. Goodbye Franc … Rachel! Put down that *Rugelach*. I got some nice salmon for dinner." I hear Teresa growl. "Frances, I have got to go. I have a crisis on my hands. A crisis! Goodbye."

"Goodbye."

I hear her say, "Rachel, don't you dare eat another bite of that," before I hang up.

I did my tour of duty. It's my niece's turn now. Better her than me. That's my last thought before walking toward the kitchen to unpack.

Pots and pans first. Glasses. Mugs. Spices.

Memories are what really weigh down boxes. I open the next corrugated scrapbook and there it is, our china. I remember the day that Paul and I found it. We were on 5th Avenue. Rain was coming down in thick sheets. The storm drains were flooding and we had to jump over huge puddles of dirty water on every corner. We were both exhausted. We'd spent the day registering for wedding gifts at Bloomingdale's, Crate & Barrel, all of the usual places. We couldn't agree on patterns. I wanted something bold and colorful. Paul said that his mother wanted us to go with Wedgwood. How trite. Frankly it was typical of his family.

My cell phone rang, and this was way back when people were very precious about using their cell phone minutes. It was my friend Shari and her girlfriend Aimee.

They were nearby and did we want to meet them at an art show at Flatiron Clay? We practically ran to get there. We were looking for a distraction from each other and the wine was free.

Just before we left the art show we met a ceramicist named Mariko. She was Japanese but had just moved to the City from somewhere in Canada. She was showing these totally gorgeous, handmade plates and bowls with pink cherry blossoms that kind of faded into a light blue sky. We bought twelve sets without thinking and ended up having to pay rent a week late. Now I have place settings for six, except for a soup bowl that broke a while back.

Holding the plate makes me feel as though I am in two places at once; here, today, unpacking and in New York on that rainy day when everything still seemed possible.

I stand there for a minute. Not moving, just standing there feeling the weight of one plate. I'd like to throw it on the floor and watch the cherry blossoms smash but I can't. It's not my nature.

I remember what Desi said. If you don't like the view from where you are turn around and move on. Unpack another room. That seems like a good idea to me.

The master bedroom unpacks quickly and is gorgeous. I'm impressed. I stare at it for a moment or two. It's so nice to be able to use my parent's bedroom furniture.

I think I'll put my friend Victor's painting up in the dining room. Huge abstract palm leaves and birds. It was too tropical for New York. It never fit. Here it has a home.

I make good time and watch the boxes dwindle with the sun in the sky. I light a few candles and put on some Joni Mitchell. I've already learned that you don't go for irony here in Orlando. Just give in to the obvious. I can hear the fireworks keeping time with "Urge for Going," but "Big Yellow Taxi," drowns them out.

It's time to deal with the box that's been staring at me all day long. I tear it open and start to rummage through. What have we got here? It's my jar of smashed pennies!

Grand Canyon.

Philadelphia Zoo.

Times Square.

There's one from every touristy place I've ever been. Those should be easy to come by around here. "Time to get a bigger jar," I say to no one in particular.

Here's my t-shirt from Cher's farewell concert. My souvenir program from the next time it came to town, a bunch of disposable memories.

Underneath them all, buried deep, is what I have been thinking about all day long.

I wish I still smoked. I'd feel stronger if I had a cigarette in my mouth. I take a sip of the tea that one inevitably brews for these occasions and start to peel away the layers of jewel toned tissue paper that protect the heavy silver frame holding my parents wedding picture. I start to run my fingers across the photo. The pink polish on my fingernail contrasts with my black and white parents.

Dad was so handsome. His hair never changed. He was wearing it that way on the day of the accident.

Mom was a beautiful bride. Look at that gorgeous spray of orchids. I want to tell the girl in the picture that both her daughters wore that dress to their own weddings. The material, "Brussels lace," she called it, so delicate.

Mom, you had the perfect veil, very Jackie Kennedy, very sixties; a pillbox hat with shoulder length tulle spilling out of it like wings.

"You were an angel, Mom. You are an angel."

I stare at the picture for a while, smiling, which is not easy; then I take a deep breath and turn the frame over. You can still see where the felt wore away the last time I opened it. It's time to look underneath. I wipe away a tear, and start to push aside the little brass hinges that hold the back of the frame in place.

Then there is a knock at the door. Thank God for distractions. I gently put the frame down on the bookcase and run to the door making my way through the maze of discarded boxes.

Its Kellie's depressed assistant. What's she doing here?

"Hello Joy."

"Hi." She looks nervous. "I never do anything like this but I was on my way home to a night of *Big Bang Theory* reruns on TBS, all of which I already have on DVD, and I just decided to see if you could use some help. Normally I'd call and see if you minded the company, but I didn't have a number to call."

Of course not - she isn't a member of the Teitelbaum spy network.

Joy continues. "I stopped at Winn Dixie and got Diet Coke, those oatmeal raisin cookies I know you love and three kinds of chips." She reaches into the bag. "And medium salsa because I didn't know if you liked mild or hot."

"Please, come in."

"Really? Because I could just drop these off and leave if you're not in the mood for a visitor." Joy hands me the package and starts to leave. "Happy housewarming."

"Joy, get in here."

She smiles, which counting the three smiles Matt mentioned, brings the grand total to four. This lady is on a roll!

"I'm so glad you invited me in because I called everyone from work. A few of them are going to stop by too. I figured if I was going to be pushy, I might as well go all the way." She comes in. "Wow! What a cute place."

I hope her nervous energy sustains for unpacking.

I give Joy a quick tour. Just as we make our way back to the living room, there is another knock at the door. It's Gladys, carrying a pitcher of Tom Collins cocktails, "with appropriately, tall, frosted glasses," as she points out. Joy drinks hers rather quickly. I stick with my green tea.

Soon we are all sitting on the floor organizing my old CDs. Gladys grabs an Air Supply album and says. "This reminds me of my late husband…"

"Why?" Joy asks with eyes wider than one of those doe eyed kid paintings from the seventies. "Did you make love out of nothing at all?"

The silence is loud. After a very withering look Gladys finally says, "No. He died of emphysema. Air Supply indeed! What an insensitive name." Gladys stares at us long with anger in her eyes before starting to laugh. We join in. "Frances dear, how can you listen to this trash?"

"It belonged to my ex-husband." I throw it into the garbage bag.

"Well, no wonder the marriage didn't last," says the suddenly saucy Joy.

Gladys grabs a Nat King Cole disc. "Now here is some real music. My husband and I saw him in person at the Sands in Las Vegas in 1964, the year before Mr. Cole passed away. We were there for a milestone birthday. We had cocktails with him and his wife after the show."

While I'm wondering whether or not to believe her, she reviews the songs.

"Play number seven, please." "Sentimental Reasons," fills the room. Gladys sings along, sipping at her Tom Collins while Joy and I slow dance. One song and the three of us are left alone with our thoughts of what I'm guessing were three very different men. The only thing they have in common is that they're gone.

The song ends. Number eight begins. Joy keeps dancing, Gladys keeps singing and I go with the flow. When "I Wish You Love," ends Joy gives me a little hug. "Thank you. I haven't danced in a long time."

"You're very good."

"I know! But get this, my ex wouldn't even dance with me at our wedding."

"Some men are like that," says Gladys.

"He had gout. Thank God we didn't have children together. They probably would have inherited all of his bad qualities." She takes another gulp of her Tom Collins.

We can barely hear the pizza guy at the door over our laughter. We open the door and see that Desi and Gratciana are right behind him carrying a ton of Chinese take-out, just as my cell rings. I nod toward her and Joy answers.

"Thank you both for coming over," I say to the newest arrivals.

"Oh good," says Desi. "There's still work to do." He insincerely adds, "See Grats? We didn't get here too late after all."

Gratciana beams. "I don't care. When my husband offers to take the kids for the night, I go. I am happy to help. Give me the dirty work."

"So your little boy is feeling better?"

Gratciana looks surprised. "Yes, he is. Thank you for asking."

Joy hangs up the phone. "It was your brother. He said he'd call back later." She hugs Desi and kisses Gratciana on the cheek. "Anyone else coming?"

"We invited Matt," says Gratciana who is breaking off a stringy piece of cheese from the pizza.

I must be hungry because I get a little pang in my stomach. "Is he coming?"

"That's between him and Kellie," quips Desi as Gratciana hits him. "They're working late."

"Time to eat," I announce to the room in spite of my dwindling appetite.

We dig in. The food is delicious. So much for Teresa, who told me to kiss good Hot and Sour

Soup goodbye. This is hot. It's sour. They got it right.

As the meal starts to wind down Gladys asks, "Are you spending the night here darling?"

"I'd love to."

"Oh good!"

"But my cat," I see Desi mouth the word "huge" as he stretches out his arms, "is still back at the hotel and I've got so much to do here."

Joy wipes her mouth and takes charge. Suddenly she's a blonde commando. "We can make this happen everyone. Here's the plan. Frances, you go to the hotel and finish up there. Gratciana, you're an office manager. Manage the office in the small bedroom. Gladys, grab that pitcher of Tom Collins and follow me. We'll finish unpacking the kitchen."

Desi poses. "And I can make everything pretty."

What feels like ten seconds later, I'm at the hotel packing. I check the room three times before I remember to look behind the shower curtain. Thank God. I almost left without my Lady Gillette and Nivea Moisturizing Sesame Oil. Katz saunters up to me and I pick him up. Outside we can hear kids playing in the pool we never used.

I grab the faux Louis Vuitton cat carrier, which I'm always proud to remind people I bought cheap on 6th Avenue, and open it. Katzenberg jumps right in as though he is ready for another adventure.

I gather my bags, balance Katz on my shoulder and leave the room without looking back.

We make our way through the lobby of Binger Boroughs. We walk through Manhattan and Queens before we get to the parking lot, which is just outside of the Bronx. When Katz sees the car for the first time, he looks at me as if to say, "What the hell is this?"

Even though I know I shouldn't, I let him out of his carrier and he quickly makes himself at home on the ledge of the rear view window.

I head down the hill, through the security gate and just before turning left onto the main road, I put the car in park and look back. With quiet certainty I say goodbye to New York City.

CHAPTER
NINE

Desi keeps pretending not to be able to lift Katz. People laugh. People nosh. People yawn. People start to get tired. Gratciana is the first to leave saying that she needs to get home to her kids. Gladys starts to fade. Joy and Desi walk her home before leaving themselves. Soon the cat and I are alone in our new home.

Katzenberg goes from room to room exploring. I go from room to room seeing what got accomplished while I was away. The little office looks great. The futon that Gladys gave me looks wonderful in here; as good as a futon ever looks I guess.

The kitchen is organized to the point of absurdity. It probably will never be this clean again. Joy is amazing. She actually inventoried and alphabetized my spices. The next time I want cilantro, which I personally hate and don't know why I own, I will find it right between chili powder and cinnamon. She even posted a little list on the inside of the cupboard.

Better yet, in the morning I shall throw the cilantro away. It was probably Paul's anyway.

After a quick stretch and yawn, it hits me how tired I am. I blow out the candles and make my way toward my brand-new bedroom anticipating how great it will be to sleep in my own bed. The new sheets are the perfection that Bed, Bath and Beyond promised. Who knew a higher thread count could change your life? Katz is curled up next to me, purring.

Just close my eyes and drift off to sleep. That's the only thing left to do today. Everything else actually got done. Soon I am feeling it, that great moment when your body starts to let go and cares fade away.

My phone rings.

The cat gets startled and runs away across my chest, snagging the formerly perfect sheets as I stumble for the receiver with only the aid of the 2 watts of light provided by my clock. This had better be important.

"Hello?" I say doing my best to sound as though I was dead asleep. A guilt trip needs to begin somewhere and I have always found this to be a very effective start.

"Oh geez, Frances, I'm sorry. I forgot all about the time change," says my brother in Queens, New York, EST.

"Tommy, we're in the same time zone."

"But you're in Florida."

"Yeah, but time zones generally go North South, not East … Listen, Tommy, I don't think you called to talk about time zones. What's up?" Then I get a sinking feeling in my stomach. I'm wide-awake and remembering Teresa's warning earlier today.

"Something is wrong. Get him to talk.

Then I remember his call that I forgot to return. It's not like my brother to call.

He pauses for a long time.

"Tommy, you're not using again are you?" My brother used to find a little too much recreation in recreational drugs, especially after the accident. To the best of my knowledge he left that behind him a long time ago.

"No Frances. I'm clean."

"Okay then, what about Cousin Tony?" I pause waiting for a response.

How my Aunt Josie and Uncle Nick, two of the sweetest people you would ever want to meet could be the parents of that loser is beyond me, absolutely beyond me. When we were kids Tony was always pulling Tommy down, getting him in trouble all the time. Making messes that the rest of us would have to clean up.

"It's the garage, isn't it?" More silence. Another answer.

Our father had always worked for his older brother, Uncle Nick, at the garage he and Aunt Josie had in Floral Park on the edge of Queens. I can still hear their voices. He'd answer the phone, "J and N Garage." She'd answer the phone, "N and J Garage." The always put each other first. It was sweet, confusing for the customers, but sweet.

Aunt Josie died from uterine cancer about a year after my folks were killed. Uncle Nick didn't last very long without her. Their stupid ass son, my Cousin Tony inherited the business and Tommy has been working there ever since. My quiet, dopey, loyal brother could have written his ticket at any garage in town. He's an amazing mechanic and so trustworthy, such a good man.

Hardworking. Honest. And he hitches his wagon to our idiot cousin.

"It's bad Frances. I think he's going to lose the place. My last two paychecks bounced. Creditors are calling all the time." Poor Tommy. It's got to be like losing Daddy and Uncle Nick again. That garage is his home.

"He's doing coke again, isn't he?" No answer. "Dammit Tommy did you call me at one o'clock in the morning to talk or to listen?" Still nothing. He starts to talk but he can't. He's too emotional. "Okay then, listen, okay? You've got to talk to Larry about this."

"No."

"Why? Why can't you talk to him and Teresa about this?"

"Larry already lent Tony money and Teresa doesn't know."

Oh no. She's going to have a fit.

"Besides, Tony already hit him up for more. Larry said no."

"Larry's no fool. It would just go up Tony's nose."

"You don't know for sure Frances."

"Oh don't I? Don't I just. This is the third time he's pulled this."

"Now listen …"

"No, you listen Tommy. You can't pay your bills with bounced checks. No money is going to come into your pocket as long as it is going up that bastard's nose."

"What if I …"

"What if you put yourself first for a change Tommy?"

"I can't make rent this month."

Crap. I should have bought the cheaper sheets.

"You know Teresa and I will do whatever we can for you. Anything. You don't even have to ask. You need it, it's yours. We'll find a way."

"Thanks."

"For you. Not Tony. Just remember he's the one who put you in this position." Silence. I soften my tone. "Tommy you deserve so much better than you've gotten from him. Do you know that? Please tell me that you know you deserve more."

"Frances, I've got to go."

"Okay, Tommy, sure. Hey…"

"Yeah?"

"It's going to be alright. Whatever happens, it's all going to be alright."

"Yeah right," he says, not believing it for a minute. "Thanks for listening."

I want to say, "but you barely talked," but I can't. He has already hung up. Alone in the dark, images start coming to me: The big, giant fans that cooled the garage, the car washes Teresa used to organize in the parking lot before holidays so we'd have money for presents, catching Uncle Nick steal a kiss from Aunt Josie in the storeroom, my Dad covered in grease lifting me up onto the hood of a car during summer break and buying me a cold 7 Up from the old-fashioned machine that sold glass bottles. My Dad's smile.

If he was here he could fix this. My Dad could fix anything.

CHAPTER
TEN

Why do people who never cook insist on setting up a kitchen? They go out and buy all the nonperishable stuff they think they need just in case they cook and it sits there until they move, then they throw it all out since they never used it and then the minute they are in their new place they go out and buy it all over again never to be used.

I wish someone would explain this phenomenon to me because then I'd know what I'm doing in this grocery store.

Publix they call it according to the sign out front. It's amazing. Nothing like Gristides or Food Emporium back home. This is more like a Fairway on steroids. It's huge, huge, huge — that's how I hear it in my head. It echoes. And for some reason it's really bright in here. I guess they don't have any dirt to hide.

There are old ladies in freshly laundered starched smocks and little white paper hats handing out samples of different foods. So hygienic. I've had a tiny pizza roll, a cube of watermelon, a sample of Boar's Head luncheon meat and a little slaw. I'm stuffed.

"Crab rangoon?" offers Betty Crocker's Grandma.

"Don't mind if I do, thanks."

Clamato juice to wash it down. Lovely.

It gets even better. The prices are crazy cheap. The staff is actually *smiling*. Can it be they enjoy selling clean, affordable food in a well-lit environment? This is a system that works.

I'm off my game. When I entered I turned to my left and started in frozen foods. I got my sugar free popsicles first. I better put them back or they'll melt. I think I'm going to be here for a while.

Or not.

Kellie Holden is standing in the middle of the snack chip section. She hasn't seen me yet. Maybe I can get away without her noticing. Stare at the floor and move away from the Cool Ranch Doritos Frances.

"Frances? Frances Fiore?" It's Shelaylee from Binger University, running up the aisle and causing a commotion. She's wearing sherbet orange colored Capri pants with a matching top, a crotched white cardigan and white sandals with a matching bag.

"Oh my gosh," she moves to hug me before tensing, "oh look, it's Kellie Holden."

"Hello Shelaylee," says Kellie with an "I'd rather be getting a mammogram" subtext.

"Frances. What a … surprise," adds the inhuman Resource Director. Please note that she paused where most people would have said the word, "pleasant." She is passive aggressive without being passive. That's the worst kind of evil.

"You two gals work together, right?"

We both nod without enthusiasm.

"I'll tell you, that is what I loved about my year as the Planet Binger Ambassador. I got to know everyone."

"Ambassador?"

Kellie gets a funny tone in her voice. "The Planet Binger Ambassador represents the company to various organizations and serves as the media spokesperson."

Shelaylee the theme park diplomat continues, "I held the position two years ago. It was a wonderful experience and now I know almost the whole durn company between being Ambassador and my training work." It is clear that she's overwhelmed by her own good fortune.

"That's nice," I lie in an effort to be nice. Sounds like hell on Earth to me. Why would a theme park need a media spokesperson? Insane. CNN cutting to Shelaylee for an update on the line in front of a frozen lemonade stand.

A very tight smile and raised eyebrows flood Shelaylee's face. "Kellie also ran that year. Lady, you were some serious competition."

Kellie looks, I don't know, deflated. "I was first runner up." Something in the way she says it makes me take note. Kellie Holden is sick of coming in second.

Small talk is exchanged until Shelaylee looks at her watch. "Oh my golly, I have got to run. My husband Terry is a magician. He has a performance tonight at the Leesburg Elks Lodge."

"Sounds like fun," I say, unsure how to respond. I suppose on some level I knew that magicians marry, but I never expected to encounter the spouse of one.

"Well, tickets are still available if you don't have plans. There'll be some single guys there!" She and Kellie exchange polite nods. She then comes over and gives me another hug.

"I'd watch out for that one Frances. She'll shove a knife in your chest and watch you bleed." She turns away and smiles at Kellie and then says between gritted teeth, "Kill her with kindness. That's how you win."

She starts to walk away. "Nice seeing you both. There's a great price on Swiffer on aisle three. Check it out ladies."

Kellie and I quickly part company and go our separate ways. I casually cruise each aisle picking up the things on my list. I grab a couple liters of Diet Coke. I watch a Glad Wrap demonstration while eating a Hot Pocket sample. I get cat food for Katzenberg which costs about half of what it does at the Petland on 9th Avenue. I retrieve my sugar free frozen popsicles and head toward the check out where I read *The Enquirer*, which I did not know was still being published. Before I can find out what's going on with the latest Kardashian, I'm offered a choice of paper or plastic. When I leave they actually thank me for shopping at Publix and unlike Manhattan grocery stores I am not given an implied go to hell glare when they have to break a large bill.

I'm leaving the store when I see Kellie at the curb looking very frustrated. She's screaming into her pink phone and her French Tip manicure is being ruined as she chomps on her nails. "But

I ordered the cab half an hour ago!" Her eyes get wide the minute she sees me.

"Kill her with kindness. Kill her with kindness. Kill her with kindness," keeps going through my head. "Kill her."

"Hey Kell," please note I shortened her name. What's up?"

"It's not important. Never mind."

Deep breath. Swallow. "Do you need a ride?"

She pauses to consider. "No, that's okay. I'm fine." She pauses again. "Unless you're heading my way." It's killing her to accept help. That makes me feel better. "Stupid car. My sister sells Chevrolets and talked me into buying a brand new Spark and it has been in the shop for the last three days. I couldn't put off shopping anymore because I'm out of dog food."

I knew she was a dog person.

"I can take you home. My sister got me a car too."

"Oh, your sister is in sales?"

"No," I say picturing Teresa flashing her credit card. "My sister buys."

The garage flashes into my mind. I hope I can pay Teresa and Larry back quickly. They might need the money.

Kellie looks shocked when she sees the car. "Your sister bought you this?" I nod. "I thought perhaps you inherited it from your grandparents or something."

"At least mine runs," is on the tip of my tongue but I keep my mouth shut. I just think it really hard. My knuckles turn white while clutching the padded leather steering wheel.

We pull up to Kellie's place in a condo complex called Middle Brook Pines. I offer to help bring the bags inside. She resists. I insist. No way am I missing a chance to see the inside of that condo.

As she unlocks the door, I notice that she still wears her high school class ring even though it causes her finger to indent.

I can see into one of the bags I'm carrying. Swear to God it wasn't intentional. I just have incredible peripheral vision. She got a *Ladies Home Journal*. What is she, Amish? Her paper towels have powder blue geese on them. I prefer the classic simplicity of white.

I'm hit by an overwhelming blast of potpourri. I look up. The door has been opened and my eyes are burning.

"Don't just stand there. The AC is on. Come in. Come in!" she urges. The first thing I notice is the pink carpeting on top of the white ceramic tile with dark grout.

The love seat, there is no sofa, is covered with a fabric of dark red roses tangling through a field of light blue. The tables on either side are glass and that silver plastic meant to look like chrome that fails to fool anyone. The walls are covered with awards and commendations from grade school on. The dinette set, is just that; a dinette set at which two people could sit. A room that was clearly designed for a full dining room set swallows the small table.

I set the bags down on the counter that leads to the kitchen. There are geese *everywhere*. I guess the Bounty is meant to complete the theme. I glimpse inside the refrigerator as she puts away the groceries. Even though she claims she hasn't been able to shop its fully stocked. She opens the freezer. She has an entire week of lunches already made and labeled with the appropriate day of the week.

"There's a powder room under the stairs in case you need to freshen up," says Kellie, trying to be a good hostess. I go to splash water on my face, really, it's not *just* to gauge the hideousness of her bathroom. Surprise, there are more geese. Evidently it's a flock that migrated from the kitchen.

On a little shelf to the left of the toilet are an affirmation book and a can of English Tea Garden air freshener.

Kellie is waiting for me with a plastic cup of Diet Pepsi with a slice of lemon on the rim. The tour continues upstairs. Her home office looks more office than home. It has one of those Office Depot work centers that are more about productivity than style. There's nothing personal in the room, just a PC flashing the Planet Binger homepage and a stack of manila file folders next to some boxes from Avon.

"I'm a representative. You'll get a catalog every Monday in your mailbox at work just in case you'd like to order," she explains. "Recycle afterwards!" Her faces frowns a little bit. "I also send out the information on Facebook, so be sure to accept my friend request!"

Sure. That's going to happen.

The master bedroom is huge and gets great light but there's hardly any furniture. There is a balcony that overlooks a courtyard. It's a nice view. Kellie crosses into the room, toward what

I imagine is the bathroom when I notice that her bed is a twin, not a full, not a queen. No headboard. She sleeps in a single bed with white eyelet sheets and very ruffled pillow shams. The bedspread itself has little Binger Bunny silhouettes woven into a solid pink background.

Kellie gasps as she opens the door to the bathroom. "Bad girl. Mama's toilet paper cozy is not a toy!" I hear whining, from both Kellie and her dog. As she walks back into the bedroom, she is followed by a longhair Chihuahua with three legs. "Frances, please meet my best friend Tipsy." The dog barks and dances in a circle on her two rear legs. Kellie runs to her bedside table and throws her a treat. "Good girl," she says. "Good baby!" She looks up at me with eyes full of pride. "The doctors didn't know if she'd ever be able to do that after the cancer."

Watching her scratch Tipsy on the belly as her three legs pawed at the air, it's easy to imagine doing the same thing if God forbid anything should ever happen to Katz.

Look at her down on the floor playing with her dog and massaging the nub where its leg used to be. Okay, so that's disconcerting. It's also sweet in a horrible kind of "can't stop looking at it" way.

Five more sips of Diet Pepsi and some trail mix that tastes vaguely of potpourri, and I am out the door.

"Thanks for the ride! Here's a trial size bottle of Skin So Soft!"

"Oh I couldn't," I protest.

"I insist," she says as she and Tipsy wave goodbye.

CHAPTER
ELEVEN

I wish I could say the first few weeks at work have flown by, but that would be a lie. They have dragged by slowly. A minute has felt like an hour. An hour felt like a day. A day felt like a month. No need to turn decades into centuries; although I could.

I have yet to turn in one piece of artwork for review, much less see it finished. I doodle through countless meetings, but I don't think that counts. Everything has been about obligation and introductions and learning more corporate policies than I ever could have imagined existed. Desi is getting the office set up and frankly it's a mixed blessing. Having an assistant has taken away most of the projects that would normally distract me.

I now know which forms to fill out in the event that I get a paper cut and have signed many forms stating that my intellectual property is no longer my own if inspiration strikes within ten miles of the parks. Binger Bunny now owns my ideas and me.

So, the fun of relocating appears to be on the wane. I go back to my cute little house and only see what it isn't. The bedroom is really dark. The front door sticks because of all this damn humidity. My adorable post-divorce Jennifer Convertible sofa that I bought on Broadway and 55th is swallowed by the living room. It looked so much better in my apartment in New York. The scale worked. Here, not so much.

New York. Manhattan. It still feels like home but I'm starting to get it. Frances doesn't live there anymore. Frances lives in Orlando and she's starting to talk about herself in the third person. Industrial warehouse complexes have replaced Rockefeller Center. The department stores on 5th Avenue have been replaced by Wal-Mart. Theme parks have replaced Central Park. Freelance has become corporate.

A small part of me likes these changes. I actually seem to like getting up to a day that offers very little in the way of surprise. I don't want anyone to know what an irrational mess I can be. So I have developed a very clever strategy. I smile and do my work.

Today I've worked on a couple of logo presentations. No one asked, but I did it because some of the work is in desperate need of updating.

Tiny Planet has yet to start. Budget approvals and all that corporate nonsense are holding things up. Professionally there are no real diversions yet.

Personally things aren't much better.

I'm avoiding Teresa because I know the minute we talk she's going to grill me about what's going on with Tommy who, by the way, I have not heard from since his late night call that laid all of his troubles in my lap. I don't know what the hell is going on with the garage or my brother and that makes me feel even more isolated.

I am in desperate need of a distraction.

"Hello Frances," says the handsome distraction entering my office.

"Hi Matt."

"Got a minute?"

"What's up?"

I get mad at myself for feeling a little giddy around Matt but that doesn't mean that I'm willing to stop myself from feeling giddy.

"I wanted to get a couple of things on your calendar."

They'll be lonely.

"Schedule away."

"We are going to have our first meetings on the Tiny Planet project next week."

"That's what I was told last week."

"Well this week it's firm." He looks up from his notes. "We're on for Monday, unless of course something changes." He looks up from his notes and smiles. "There's more. Tomorrow we are going to have a work session with our partners in the Signage Department to discuss some of the challenges we are experiencing in guest routing and the potential impact to this year's fiscal bottom line should we implement enhancements."

Silence is followed by my best blank stare. He doesn't seem to be picking up on the point I'm trying to make here. I open my mouth slightly and cock my head to the left.

His eyes narrow, "Is there a problem?"

"My vocabulary. I'm still fairly new to corporate speak. Could you please translate?"

"We need some bad signs replaced cheaply."

"Thank you."

"We could have dinner tonight and discuss it."

"Really?"

"Yeah," he says quickly. "It'll be a business expense."

"I have plans tonight."

"Oh," he says in this totally cute crestfallen way. "I understand."

"Of course, I could always watch *The Real Housewives of Hell* tomorrow night instead."

"I'll do my best to make giving up your big night worthwhile. Where would you like to go?"

"I'm new in town. Surprise me with anything that isn't a chain."

"This is Orlando. I'll do my best."

"Make it seven thirty. My landlady is serving Coconut Lime Rickey's on the lanai. We'll leave after the cocktail hour."

The distraction walks out of the room after taking down my address, which I can now recite by memory. A hint of his spicy cologne lingers and I'm smiling.

Desi ducks in. "I'm leaving for lunch."

I swirl around in my chair. "Take your time!"

"Someone is in a good mood," says Assistant.

"Just watch out for Miss Holden the walking stop watch," I warn.

"Why?"

"She monitors how long people take in the restroom."

Desi shrieks. "You're lying!" he says as he exits giggling. He turns around. "Aren't you?"

I shrug. Better to maintain the mystery.

Maybe it's actually time to do something quasi productive. I could finish MY 401K enrollment.

Open up Affinity and play with a few sign layouts. That would look good if Matt stops by again.

I could check my e-mail.

My in-box has been inundated. A lot of it is just spam that has been sent to everyone in the company. BVOT Cast Member watches are in at the Binger Emporium. Bingerteers, the company Volunteer Action Council, is having a Junior Achievement Bowl-a-Thon. Kellie is trying to organize a team. *Delete.* There's also an invitation to a mandatory meeting regarding graphics and the Americans with Disabilities Act. Since "not another one" is not a response option, I click "accept" and wonder how many of these things I will have to go to in the course of my career. I take an online computer tutorial about Binger Computer Policies. Primary colors and fluffy animated characters caution that it is against company policy to download porn, which just makes me want to download porn even though I have never done it in my life.

Close Outlook.

I've got time to check my personal account. It has been a while since I've checked my email. I've been avoiding it and now it's crazy full. A few girlfriends have sent notes asking how things are going in Florida. I respond but keep it brief.

In the last few years I've created distance between a lot of my friends and me. As far as I'm concerned Paul got most of them in the divorce settlement.

Paul. My heart sinks. There are two emails from him. Subject lines: "You're GONE?" and "No goodbye?" I stare at them for a long time, too long. Just as I am moving the mouse to open the first one Matt sticks his head in the door.

"See you at 7:30," he says with a quick smile before he exits. Easy. Breezy. No hassles. Just in and out. Simple. I look at Paul's email again and can only see disappointment and complicated history.

I remember the exact moment that I first saw Paul. He was wearing khakis that were way too big and a shirt that had to be a hand-me-down. It was pink and totally threadbare. Translucent almost. I could read the writing on the Blink-182 t-shirt he was wearing underneath. His tie was very thin, black with little penguins on it, tied loosely.

It was a hot night, right after I graduated from NYU but he wasn't sweating; at least in my memory he isn't. I was having that glorious summer when everyone with a Studio Art degree is thinking, "What the hell do I do now?"

I needed money so I was working as a cocktail waitress at the Time Café above a band bar called Fez on Lafayette Street, by the Public Theater. Paul had an internship in their offices. He was in grad school at Columbia for Art Administration. After one summer of the non-profit lifestyle, he switched to the MBA Program. He thought it was a better choice for a guy who wanted a family. It impressed me that he was thinking that far into the future; considering the needs of people that weren't even here yet. It seemed like something my dad would have done.

The bar had a great outdoor cafe, perfect for checking the street scene and hanging out, which

Paul did. A lot. He always seemed to find an excuse to be there. Always during my shifts too, as Rodney the pre-op trans bartender pointed out.

"We're just friends," I kept saying, hoping to be wrong.

By Labor Day we were dating.

We had our first kiss in Central Park. We were playing Badminton. There had been some rain, but we had a picnic and played a few games anyway. I won the first one. He won the second. We were evenly matched.

The third game almost ended in a tie. I kept Paul running but he spiked and I just missed it. I fell trying to get the return. Paul was being a gentleman, a good sport, and came over to help me up but I pulled him down onto the ground. I fell into his arms laughing. Our eyes met and I got shy. I looked away for a second. Paul grabbed my chin, turned my face toward him and kissed me while we were both still out of breath from the game.

I remember thinking I'd just had my last first kiss.

For Halloween that year we went as Eleanor Roosevelt and FDR because his mother Michele had convinced herself that Paul and I were related to each other. Turns out my third cousin twice removed had been briefly married to someone in Paul's family. His Dad thought it was funny but his mother was frantic. She kept trying to convince us our children would have two heads or something. She even talked to her doctor about it. I'm sure she was disappointed to discover genetics were not going to be the issue.

I'd bet good money she celebrates the anniversary of our divorce. We never got along. She thought I wasn't good enough for her son. Divorce does have some advantages. I never have to see her again.

The Halloween party at his parent's pretentious little country club ended early. Paul drove me back to the City. We hooked up with some friends at a party on the Lower East Side and then headed uptown to my apartment. I was sitting on his lap in the wheelchair that we had rented for the FDR thing. He kissed me and made his way down my neck.

I pretended to be demur and collapsed into his chest. "I'm a little scared."

I expected him to say something perfect, the kind of thing that I'd remember the rest of my life. He took off his glasses and looked me dead in the eye.

"The only thing we have to fear is fear itself.

We were laughing as he wheeled me to the bedroom.

We used to laugh a lot.

We made love for the first time that night. In honor of that evening I guess, we used to talk about sex in a First Lady, President kind of code. I'd talk about Harry S. Truman carrying a big stick, always willing to drop the big bomb. We'd be out for drinks and Paul would say, "One more of these and I'm going on a trip to Betty Ford." Mary Todd Lickin', that kind of thing. It was dirty and sweet at the same time. I loved it. Hillary Clit-on. Dwight D. Eisenboner. Tricky Dick. Lyndon B. *Johnson*. Jackie Oh Oh Oh my God! We never made a Bush joke.

By Thanksgiving of that year I had all sorts of new things for which to be thankful. I had found a job at Landvik and Pehl, a small advertising agency run out of Landvik's Brooklyn Heights townhouse. Our big client was the Sun Block Council of America. I was the Art Department, the Office Manager and the Notary.

Paul is still the only man I've ever said, "I love you," to. I said it for the first time on December 24th. I wanted it to feel like a gift.

"I love you too Frances."

Merry Christmas.

Happy New Year.

By Memorial Day we were living together, which my parents hated even though they thought the world of Paul.

He loved them too. He really did.

He must miss them. He lost something when they were killed. It wasn't just me. I wish I could have been that generous when it all happened.

My folks helped us move into our apartment on 51st Street despite the fact they weren't thrilled that I was going to be living with Paul. I can still hear Daddy muttering, "Your mother and I never lived together."

When we got to the apartment it was a mess. It was like a maze that we had to make our way through from the front door. Paul was waiting in the center of the living room with a bottle of champagne and four glasses. He looked so cute in my t-shirt from BAM. He was down on one knee. In his hand there was a blue box from Tiffany's that held the most beautiful ring anyone has ever bought from the Paramus Zale's. My parents were in on the whole thing. My mother took a picture of the exact moment. I remember because it was the last time anyone ever took a picture of me using real film and a flash. There was a blinding flash of light the exact moment he asked me.

I can't describe how I felt when he asked me to marry him. There are no words. I just knew we were going to be together forever.

My attention goes back to my email. I take a deep breath and delete both messages from Paul. Then I delete my deleted messages file. Delete temptation.

What a powerful little button.

CHAPTER
TWELVE

Sheer is fine. Lime green is fine. One would think they would work well together but one would be very wrong.

Screw it. Lime green it is. And the pink camisole stays too. Tie back the hair and meet him on the lanai. Walk out the door, lock it, return, splash some Chanel, let the hair loose, shake out the head, pet the cat, and leave. It's simple.

"Darling, you're late," says my landlady the geriatric flirt. "I've had to entertain Mr. O'Connell all by myself."

"Thank you Gladys."

"The pleasure was all mine, believe me."

Matt smiles. "Did you know that Gladys was one of the June Taylor Dancers on the Jackie Gleason Show?"

"No, I didn't."

"Oh it's hardly worth mentioning," she says with a giggle. "I was living in Miami and went to the audition on a lark. My father arranged it. I got the job but when Mr. Gleason got a little grabby, I turned him down and lost the job. End of story."

"Wow."

"Now Mr. Art Carney was a living doll, a little moody, but very kind. We exchanged holiday cards until he passed a few years back. It was he who first introduced me to this cocktail in the Grove."

Gladys hands us glasses garnished with orchids from her garden. Matt goes to sip his immediately. I catch his eye and caution him. I have come to learn that Mrs. Nelson always enjoys making a toast.

"To the honeymooners," she says with a wink, before taking her first taste of Coconut Lime Rickey, which while delicious, is as potent and about as subtle as my landlady. "So is this a business meeting or a date?"

I nearly choke on a hunk of coconut. I am about to spin diplomatic when Matt's phone rings. He checks his caller ID. "If you ladies will excuse me, I have to take this phone call." He walks over to the other side of the lanai and out of earshot.

"Is this a date?" I challenge with all the incredulous energy I can muster.

"Dearest some things just need to be out in the open."

"Come on!"

"I am an old woman; I don't know that I'll be around for the ending. Let's cut to the chase."

HAVA NAGILA...

Oh my God. Now my phone is ringing.

"So is it a date or not?" asks Teresa.

"I can't talk right now. I'll call you later."

"Don't worry about calling too late. I'll be up ... waiting."

I disconnect and go in for the kill. "Gladys that was totally inappropriate. For all I know he has a girlfriend or something."

"Well, what do you think?"

"It's complicated. We work together. He's handsome and smart but he's also sort of my boss and," Gladys' smile grows bigger, "and, he's right behind me, isn't he?"

"Yes he is," he says in an uncomfortable tone. I guess he isn't used to speaking of himself in third person. He gulps down the rest of his drink. "We should leave if we want to make our reservation."

We share a quick goodnight with Gladys and head out the door. I offer to drive. He looks at my car and says something about gas mileage, environmental responsibility and protecting the ozone layer for future generations. We take his car, a late model, light blue something or other.

The radio isn't on. No music is playing. There's no competition for the conversation. The fireworks slow down traffic around Universal Studios, but Matt doesn't freak out. I like that.

As we make our way closer to downtown Orlando, he plays tour guide. We are headed east on I-4 and as we pass exits he tells me what to expect on the roads not taken.

We go past something called Orange Blossom Trail, which sounds lovely. Turns out it isn't. "That's where the hookers hang out," explains Matt.

Orlando has hookers? That's like hearing that the Vatican has an S & M bar in the catacombs.

Okay, so maybe it isn't that implausible after all, but how does Matt know about these prostitutes?

"The guy I replaced was a regular with one of the boys down there. He got busted and left town."

"Sad."

"Yeah, especially for his wife."

That's one thing I never had to worry about with Paul. If anything, he was too heterosexual, too much man for one woman – in his own mind at least.

Maybe that's too harsh. I can't pretend that I didn't turn him away long before he started looking elsewhere. What did I expect?

Delete.

I've never been downtown before and it isn't what I expected at all. "This is Lake Eola," says the Orlandonian - Orlandite - Orlandophile? - to my left. It's charming. Not a tourist in sight. There's a beautiful fountain in the middle of the lake. There are people riding swan boats and there's a string quartet in the band shelter. Around the perimeter of the lake is a little path with Japanese gardens and an ice cream stand.

We park the car and head toward the restaurant. "A little jazz club called Dexter's. Great food. I thought you might like it."

"Really? Why?"

"I noticed you ordered the Thai chicken salad at the cafeteria last week."

"Oh, do they have a good one?"

"No. I don't believe it's on the menu. But you had chips with it."

"Right. Fritos."

"Oh."

"So this place has corn chips?"

"No. Homemade potato chips. I thought you would like the potato chips."

"That's sweet. You chose a restaurant because of the potato chips?"

"Yeah." Silence. "We could go somewhere else," he says with a contrite smile as he opens the door. "There's a great place in Winter Park that makes its own Funyuns."

A girl who reminds me of myself at her age seats us. Brown hair, too much eye makeup, she's trying very hard to be her own person. No nametag. What a rebel. She stares at us with a removed, bored look; but who am I to judge? It has got to be rough to be a nonconformist in a town like Orlando. The only road is the one in the middle. She'll be a soccer mom before she's thirty-five.

"Enjoy your meal," she says in monotone.

The place is nice and intimate. Personal. Good artwork on the walls. Colorful. The jazz is present without being overpowering. I order a pressed veggie sandwich with a small salad. Matt orders the obligatory potato chips for the table and a steak for himself. He must workout. That diet isn't showing on his body. As he excuses himself to go to the men's room I let my eyes wander down to his jeans. They fit nicely.

He returns and I take a deep breath.

"About what Gladys said," we say in unison. I blush. We both smile and look away.

"Ladies first," says my potential date.

"Don't think that I put her up to that."

113

"Gladys strikes me as the kind of woman who will say and do whatever she wants. I don't think you could put her up to anything."

"Very observant."

"Yep. Just like you."

I smile in spite of myself. "Oh really?"

"That's right, and you're not sure which answer you'd like to hear."

"To which question?"

"Is this a date or not?"

"There's nothing wrong with a little mystery." I try to sound cocky but inside I know he's right, dammit.

Two baskets of homemade chips, dinner, and a bottle of wine later, all the shoptalk is out of the way. A comfortable glow settles in. The band, Groove Logic I think they're called, starts to play "Spring Can Really Hang You Up the Most." Slow. Sexy. Sentimental. Couples get up and Matt leads me to the small dance floor.

It starts off awkwardly for both of us but we find the tempo. His arms are strong. We fit together well. His cologne smells spicy and masculine. The crisp cotton of his shirt feels good brushing across my cheek.

It ends too soon. Matt's hand lifts my face towards his and I begin to anticipate being kissed. Instead, the beat of the music changes. "Let's get out of here," he says.

Soon we are walking around Lake Eola. Couples holding hands walk past us, rollerblades zoom ahead, a dog runs between us with his frantic owner following. The dog ignores him and keeps running at his own pace enjoying the chase.

Matt doesn't seem to notice. He's quiet and looking at the ground, lost in the pattern being made by his own two feet. For a long time he says nothing. Then he stops.

"There's something I should tell you."

There is a pause and he looks away.

He turns back and smiles. He puts his hands in his pockets, kicks around a rock and alternates between looking at me and the sidewalk.

"I was married."

"You're divorced? So am I."

"No, I'm not divorced."

"Not divorced? You're still mar…"

"My wife died three years ago."

Oh.

Her name was Thia, short for Cynthia. They met while working at an ice cream shop when they were both students at the University of Wisconsin. They married right after graduation. Matt went to Graduate School in Chicago while Thia taught school. They moved around a bit, going from town to town before ending up in Orlando. They were just starting to try to have a baby after concentrating on their careers. They figured they had all the time in the world.

Matt pulls out his phone and shows me a picture of a woman that will always be young and beautiful. Her blonde hair will never turn white and her hazel eyes will remain unlined. In the photo she is either waving hello or goodbye. Her engagement ring catches the light of the flash. It's a snapshot and meant to be casual. It is anything but.

"It was an accident."

Those words stab at me. I'm no stranger to the consequence of accidents but this isn't my moment. I say nothing and am relieved to have the excuse to hold onto my secrets for another day.

"Her grandfather, his name was Dean, he had Alzheimer's. It was getting bad. I mean, when is Alzheimer's good, right? He lived on a little Christmas tree farm in a town called Montello … between Madison and Milwaukee. Thia's Mom and her sisters were taking care of him, so he wouldn't have to go to a nursing home."

"It must be hard to watch your father slip away like that." I fight the impulse to add that losing him quickly isn't any easier.

Matt continues. "I suppose there are just things we can't prepare ourselves for … things that are meant to be hard. Something would be wrong if they weren't."

I touch his arm. "You're right," I say.

He smiles as he looks at me. It lasts longer than I expect it to. I can tell he's lost his train of thought.

"You were telling me about your wife's grandfather…"

"Right. So anyway," he says in an exasperated tone, "he was sick. Thia offered to go to Montello to give the ladies a break. I didn't want her to go because she'd be gone while she was ovulating; we were trying to have a baby. Did I mention that?"

I nod and smile. He returns the smile and continues.

"I made plane reservations to join her for the weekend. It was October. The sisters all came here and Thia went back to Wisconsin to take care of Dean. I remember them laughing by the edge of the pool. They were reading the weather report in USA TODAY. There was a cold snap in Wisconsin. Unseasonably cold, it said."

It's hard to watch him relive this.

"The furnace hadn't been serviced yet and when Thia, at least I've always assumed it was Thia, went to turn it on she had no way of knowing that the vents were blocked."

"They passed away in their sleep. Asphyxiation. Some old lady stopped by my mother-in-law's house with a casserole and said something about Dean needing an angel to lead him to heaven. Karen, that's Thia's Mom, told her to shut her fucking mouth and then thanked her for the hot dish."

Matt and I resume our walk around the lake.

"Thanks for telling me."

"Yeah, well I just wanted you to know why I'm not rushing into anything. I went out with another woman about six months ago and it was a disaster. It was either too soon or she was the wrong woman. Take your pick."

"Kellie?"

Matt looks at me like I'm crazy. "Oh God no. That would be like dating my sister."

"Really? You should tell her that."

"Frances, Kellie was Thia's best friend. She's just being protective."

"Of you?"

"Of Thia."

We walk for a while sharing stories. He tries to get details out of me but I'm not forthcoming. I am a woman of mystery. I like not being defined by my past.

We park up the street so as not to disturb Gladys. Even though it could lead to a spectacular mistake it feels right when I invite him in for a drink. I've dwelt on my old mistakes and disappointments for too long. Maybe it's time to make some new ones.

We reach my front porch. As I fumble for my keys Matt gently turns me around to face him. He grabs my face and kisses me. It's slow. It's relaxed. It's perfect. I feel like a teenager, shy and excited at the same time.

The glow of the porch light gives landlady a chance to spy. Better to move inside. I turn and find the door is already unlocked.

That's strange. I'm usually good about that. Matt senses my concern and walks in ahead of me checking out every room. "Nothing is wrong," echoes in my head.

He turns the corner heading into the guest room. I hear movement, and a hit connecting to someone or something. Oh my God, someone is here.

Matt's voice, deeper than usual demands "Who the hell are you?" I hear mumbling and someone getting to their feet. I grab a candlestick and instantly feel like Miss Scarlet from Clue. I'd laugh at myself if I weren't so scared. I head toward the guest room to see what's happened, and run right into my intruder with a thwack. I fall to the floor in a move that hurts my dignity more than my tailbone. A rough, callused hand reaches down to help me up.

I look up and see it belongs to my brother Tommy.

CHAPTER
THIRTEEN

"Who the hell is this guy?" Matt demands.

"Who the hell is *this* guy?" asks my brother who has always made it monosyllabically clear that he wishes Paul and I would get back together.

"HAVA NAGILA, HAVA..." my cell phone rings. For once in her life my sister Teresa is the path of least resistance. I answer call.

"What?"

"This is how you answer a phone? Hear that sound? It's Momma spinning in her grave. Where are your manners?"

"Teresa? Hold on." I cover the phone to make introductions forgetting that my sister has super hearing. "Matt this is my brother Tommy. Tommy this is Matt."

"Oh yeah when your landlady let me in she said you were on a date."

Teresa is screaming over the phone. It is after midnight. She is sure to have awakened her entire family, several neighbors, and blown out two or three T-Mobile towers. The girl is loud.

"WHAT? TOMMY IS THERE? WHAT IN THE HELL IS TOMMY DOING THERE? AND, WAIT ONE FREAKIN' MINUTE! YOU INVITED YOUR DATE IN?"

"Well Frances," says Matt with a weak, crooked smile, "it looks as though everybody else has decided it *is* a date."

"HELLO? CAN ANYONE HEAR ME? THERE IS A PERSON ON THE OTHER END OF THIS PH…" I disconnect the call and walk over to Matt.

"I've got to figure out what's going on here."

"With me or your brother?"

I just smile. Sometimes silence is the best response.

"Okay. See you tomorrow." He kisses me, on the cheek, which is either a mixed signal or the most gentlemanly thing ever. He starts to walk away and turns back to Tommy, and shakes his hand. "Welcome to Orlando. Sorry about slugging you before."

"No problem. Thanks for looking out for my sister." There is promise here. That's the longest sentence I've ever heard my brother say to someone he just met.

Matt leaves. I take a deep breath and turn around to face my brother who is no longer in the room.

"I'm in the kitchen."

I follow him and see that he is making coffee. Evidently it is going to be a long night underscored by HAVA NAGILA playing in the background.

I slowly drag the details out of Tommy. No surprises, Tony the terminal asshole was still spending money on cocaine and bouncing payroll checks. Tommy finally called him on it. He marched into Uncle Nick's old office to confront him and caught Tony, doing a line. That was the last straw, seeing his rent money go up that loser's nose. Tommy finished up the car he was working on, "It wasn't the customer's fault," and walked out the door.

He just wasn't sure where he was headed when he left. Tony was calling nonstop. Teresa was calling nonstop. He had enough, packed up his pickup truck and hit the road. Two days later he was here.

That was over a week ago. Now *my* phone is ringing nonstop. Teresa and Tony are both tenacious. It's got to be genetic. Through voicemails I have been able to figure out that Teresa found out what is going on. She's livid. She needs someone to blame for the money she and Larry lost and somehow has decided it is *my* fault. Teresa thinks if I had told her what was going on she could have saved the day.

So, in a role that many middle children find themselves in, I'm in the middle. It's been like this ever since we were kids. Teresa thinks it is her job to keep things under control; hence, she is controlling. Thank God she is busy planning Christian's Bar Mitzvah otherwise she would be on the next plane down here.

Tommy on the other hand is easy … almost too easy. He doesn't make decisions so much as wander into his choices. It's no surprise that he didn't take off from the garage until things reached critical mass.

My brother has a charm that is hard to ignore. He sort of radiates decency. Tommy was the kind of kid that brought injured birds and lost puppies home. He'd stay up all night taking care of them.

You can just tell by looking at him that, although shy and quiet, he doesn't have a mean bone in his body. Women have always found him very attractive so I wasn't shocked to hear Gladys say that as long as he mowed the lawn with his shirt off, he could move in. In fact that's where he is right now. The sun is shining through his thick brown hair. He is sweating and shaking his head with a big smile on his face. He kind of looks like that Diet Coke commercial that everyone was talking about years ago. You know, that construction worker one? It's not easy to admit, but my brother is hot.

Katzenberg is running alongside him totally and blissfully unbothered by the sound of the lawnmower. This is a cat that grew up on the streets of New York. Noise he understands but freshly cut grass is exotic and never before seen. He looks so happy rolling around in it. It sticks to his coat and looks like a fun faux fur that you'd see in the window of Bendel's on 5th Avenue.

Joy has just pulled up into the driveway to pick me up. We're going to do a little spa pampering today. I'm looking forward to it. I think Joy and I are going to be good friends but the girl could use a makeover. Her gorgeous blonde hair has no shape and falls into her face thanks to an exceptionally poor posture. She needs highlights. Her outfit doesn't really work either. Maybe I can get her to hit a couple of shops today.

"HAVA NAGILA..."

I throw my iPhone on the couch and walk out the door. I can't take Teresa right now. She treats Tommy and me like we are her little pet projects. That is so incredibly arrogant.

Hm. Joy could use a new purse too.

On our way out I bring Tommy a glass of lemonade.

"Tommy, Joy. Joy, Tommy."

"We talked on the phone…" says Joy.

"That's right."

She must be allergic to grass that is freshly cut. She's breathing a little funny.

"Let's get out of here," I say for her own good.

We are off to the official Planet Binger Spa, which I'm very excited to see. It's almost worth going on property during a day off. "On property," that's what we insiders call being anywhere Planet Binger.

Orbit Drive, Docking Station, Parking Alien, all the stuff that seemed bigger than life doesn't even capture my notice anymore. We drive past the Binger Wedding Pavilion and the nondenominational church our guests visit for weekly services.

Bunny ears form the cross on the top of the building.

Okay that was a lie, but it sounded plausible didn't it? If they can find a way to get those ears on a surface, they do it. I think some of these people have Binger ears tattooed on their ass.

The spa is themed to a Binger Studio film called *Furry Friends*. Actually I am rather surprised that they used that one - spas are kind of anti-furry with waxing and all.

It's also sort of infamous. During the movie a rooster named Raymond (alliteration always) opens a barbershop that becomes very successful.

He quits crowing at dawn, which throws everyone in the farmyard into a tizzy. When the kindly but gruff farmer oversleeps, the cow's milk curdles so he confronts Raymond, whom everyone no longer loves. The rooster's line, never to be forgotten is, "I couldn't cock-a-doodle-do. I was up late shaving a beaver."

Needless to say the overt vaginal allusion gave late night comics a field day. Feminists too. They charged that the curdling of milk and the victimization of the cows were both clearly anti-woman and anti-lactating statements. The company claimed it was a coincidence.

It's kind of hard to believe that no one stopped to think of how that might be interpreted …

Joy and I walk through the heavy, ornate doors. The décor is gorgeous in an over-the-top rural, dried flower, feminine way. Alabaster animatronics cherubs flank the door and shower fairy dust on us.

The entire glob of cheap red glitter lands in my mouth. A woman with huge hair that has got to be a wig walks up to greet us as I gag and spit. Her accent is as thick as her ankles. "Hey girls, y'all got an appointment?" Krista, according to her nametag, has a huge smile and her teeth are exceptionally white except for the slash of lipstick running across the front two. She must notice my reaction because she pulls a compact out of her baby blue smock and immediately rubs her left index finger across them until the red stain vanishes.

After a sea salt exfoliation and a Shiatsu massage, the tension I have been carrying in my shoulders is gone. Teresa, gone. Tommy, gone.

Matt, Paul, where the hell is my career going, gone. I rejoin Joy who has had a pomegranate aromatherapy pore-shrinking facial and a hair consultation that led to a new hairstyle (Thank you God!) with high and lowlights. Two women speaking Korean are giving us pedicures. Their conversation blends in with the new age sitar arrangements from the Binger Songbook.

"Give her a manicure too," squeals Joy. "She's got a man in her life now."

It was probably a mistake telling Joy about my date with Matt but I had to confide in *scmeone*. Teresa is off limits. Tommy is worthless. You can't tell a man about a man; especially when their first meeting involved physical violence.

"So then he hit Tommy and left."

"Matt hit your brother?" says Joy, little Miss Recap.

"Yeah."

"Poor guy."

"Matt?"

"No. Tommy. What a horrible welcome."

Joy keep up. I don't want to talk about my brother. Maybe this is making her uncomfortable. She keeps trying to change the subject. Joy keeps asking me questions about Tommy and what's going on at home. What's he like? Is he happy here? Did he leave a girlfriend back in New York? Would the two of us like to come over to her place for dinner some evening? Honestly, I know it sounds a little self-loathing, but women can be so thick sometimes. A little support please? I am trying to talk about a potential relationship here.

"Sure. Tommy and I will come over to dinner sometime."

"Thursday?"

"Well, I'll have to ask him." He has no job. He knows no one here except Gladys and I. He's broke and personally I would love to see someone else throw the man a meal. Just to make it look convincing I bite my lower lip and pretend to review my calendar. "But I'm pretty sure we can work it out."

"I could invite Matt too."

I totally lose the relaxation buzz I have going. "No!" I exclaim which causes several of the women in the spa to look our way. I slink down into my chair and start whispering as though I could still protect my privacy. It's kind of like putting on sun block after the sunburn. I know these things. The Sun Block Council used to be a client of mine.

"Why not?"

I pause looking for the justification for my reaction. After an eternal ten seconds or so the best I can come up with is, "We can't be too open about this."

"Why?" says the suddenly bold Joy. You know, I think I liked her more before the highlights. Even though it was only twenty minutes ago I yearn for that simpler time.

"There are lots of reasons."

"Such as?"

"We work together."

"And?"

"And he is still dealing with his wife's death."

"Oh please. Is that the best you've got? That was almost three years ago. It's time to move on."

The Next Happiest Place on Earth

"Help me out Joy. What are you looking for here?"

"Just admit it!"

"Admit what?"

"You're not over your ex-husband yet."

I laugh a little too loud and roll my eyes a little too much the way people do when they're not ready to face the truth. She can't be right. I've taken charge of my life. How much more do I have to do? I've made new friends, I took a new job, I moved to a new city. I bought a car.

What else do I have to do?

Wow.

I know exactly what I have to do.

"Do you offer waxing services here?"

CHAPTER
FOURTEEN

Things are quiet and just a little tense in the changing room. Joy has a nice figure - not that I look at those things. Not in a sexual way at least. It's more like checking out the competition - not that I think of Joy as competition. Damn, girlfriend is in great shape.

She is, however, covering up what God gave her in some really horrible lingerie. If in fact one could call those men's boxers and sports bra "lingerie." The next time Joy and I hang out I'll take her to Victoria's Secret. Right now I'm guessing she gets her underwear at Sports Authority.

But I digress.

"Frances, I'm sorry."

"About what?" I say with pursed lips and an arched eyebrow.

"I think you're doing a great job getting on with your life. Better than I did."

Okay, so that was sweet. But still...

"I know how hard that can be."

"Well then, maybe you need to take your own advice."

"Maybe I do," she says with resolution, "but we're not talking about me. I didn't say what I said because you're not doing enough. But maybe," she bites her lip, "maybe, you could do more."

As we drive back to my place Joy tells me a story about the first time she caught her husband with another woman. "He said she was a dog walker as if that explained everything. Of course, the problem was we didn't have a dog so he went out and bought a pit bull. The first day we had him the dog pulled a pair of lace panties out from under the bed. They weren't mine."

That might explain the boxer and sport bra look.

"Sounds like my ex," I say, testing the waters of fuller disclosure. "Toward the end of our marriage he developed an allergy to pants. Couldn't keep them on." I consider saying more but am interrupted by Joy's laughter. It's shy and a little out of shape, but it's laughter just the same. What a wonderful way to deal with sadness. Laugh and move on. But some stories aren't funny. Sometimes it's impossible to laugh, no matter how hard you try; no matter how badly you want to.

I look at Joy's sweet face and for a second I want to continue with the rest of the story. Part of me is ready to spill my guts and be here, right now, with a friend that obviously cares; but in my heart I know I'm not going to say another word. Better things stay the way they are. I like not being defined by the past. I like that very much.

So I look at Joy and swallow my impulse to say what is on my mind and in my heart. I just smile. Secrets are safe for another day.

We pull into the driveway. Tommy is near the garage working on my Buick. He found some doohickey on the Internet that guarantees a 10% increase in gas mileage. If it works I'll actually get one mile per gallon. That car guzzles gasoline the way that Katz guzzles Friskies.

Katzenberg too is outside and chasing a blithe butterfly that manages to stay just out of harm's way every time his paw swipes at it. I'd stay and watch but I've got work to do.

"Just think about what I said, okay?" Joy asks.

A quick hug and I am out the door.

I run into the house and check my phone. Caller ID says that Teresa called five times. God knows that can wait. I walk over to the kitchen window. Joy's car is still here. Tommy is checking under her hood. Perfect. She'll keep him occupied.

I run to the bathroom to brush my teeth and do the upside down, head flip, hair refreshing ritual. Better I look my best. That will help. I pick up the phone and start to dial.

God, I hate that we have to include the area code for local calls. It's so damn annoying. I should put these new numbers into my phone. Sometimes I think - oh, the phone is ringing!

"Hello?"

"Hi Matt!" I say, sounding way too perky and a bit desperate. Relax Frances. One deep breath later I brilliantly think to add, "How are you?" I use a deeper voice, trying my best to sound casually sexy.

"I just got back from volunteering at Give Kids the World."

Oh my God. I'm the whore of Orlando, trying to seduce a man that does charity work for sick kids. I resort to using some very rusty flirtation skills, feminine wiles that have been in mothballs for far too long. My mind references a *Self* article from a couple of months ago. The headline was, "Let Him Think It Was HIS Idea…"

"You just popped into my head … while I was in the shower." That's good Frances. Get him thinking about you naked. All soapy. Nice move. Very smooth. "I thought I'd call and see how your weekend was going."

"Oh, it's fine. I got my septic tank cleaned out."

I give him the image of me naked and he returns with that lovely image.

"That doesn't sound like much fun."

"True enough."

"You should be good to yourself tonight. It's Saturday night in Celebration, Florida! Surely there's an ice cream social or a taffy pull in the Town Square."

I can hear him smiling which makes me smile. "What is it about you and Celebration?" he asks. "You're awfully critical of something you've never seen."

I go in for the kill. "Is that an invitation?"

Mission accomplished.

I spend the rest of the afternoon prepping for Tiny Planet and finding source images so I won't second-guess myself; but my mind keeps wandering. I look at the purple irises from Gladys' garden that I've been sketching and they're not really all that floral. They're more like penises … tall, thin, leafy penises blowing in the wind.

I do my usual routine of getting ready too many times. Outfits are thrown on the floor and fast become a Cristo-like fence of assorted fabrics. I put the orange colors in one pile in honor of The Gates.

I start to leave but remember that Katz is still outside. I'd leave him out, but Tommy is nowhere to be found. I spend the next five minutes chasing him around the yard. We finally get inside but now I need a quick touch up. I splash on a little more Jo Malone and walk out the door. Gladys is waiting by the car with a bottle of Merlot and a Cheshire grin.

"See you tomorrow."

Driving through Celebration, Florida is like being in a Norman Rockwell knock-off. It's derivative. It's as though it knows what it was inspired by but it can't quite manage to become it. It's one of those places that people move to because they don't want to think about what color to paint their homes.

I can't believe I'm here to seduce someone.

I'm having dirty thoughts in a very clean town.

CHAPTER
FIFTEEN

I barely knocked on the door and we were on our way to the restaurant. We're at The Columbia, which specializes in Spanish-Cuban cuisine, according to the menu. I'm guessing it is the only Spanish or Cuban in Celebration, Florida.

"I'll have the *Arroz con Pollo*," Matt says with a mid-western twang. He must have studied Spanish in high school.

"I'll have the 1905 Salad please. With shrimp,"

Matt looks so handsome in the candlelight … like the boy you want to get when playing "Who Will I Marry?" with your girlfriends. His smile is easy, innocent, and totally unaware. He has no idea that I am a seductress; one who seduces.

Please let it be good. It has been a long, long time since I've had sex. I *deserve* good.

"Would you like a glass of sangria with that?" says our blonde, southern waitress at the Spanish-Cuban restaurant in Celebration, Florida.

"A pitcher," I respond, assuming that seduction will be easier for both of us if we are just a little toasty.

The dinner conversation is pleasant. We talk about work. I tell him about my day at the spa. Then I remember that while I was being pampered he was helping sick children. I'm so shallow. Before I realize what I have said I offer to volunteer with him sometime.

More sangria.

I start to feel a little glow going. Good. It's doing its job.

Distract yourself Frances. Think about food. Chew. Hmmm. The pressed Cuban bread is hot and salty. My salad is delicious. So is the shrimp. Oh God. What if he's small and I have to pretend not to notice?

Enough. Look around.

I'd recommend The Columbia to anyone back home in New York. But there's something about this joint that cracks me up. It's themed. It's not real. Not much in Florida is, I suppose. It's meant to look like it was built at the turn of the century but I'm guessing it's about twenty years old. Justin Bieber is probably older than anything in this town.

Why is it they keep tearing stuff down to build new stuff and then when it is done they try to make it look as though it is the age of the thing that was originally there? It's architectural plastic surgery. In New York we just slap on another coat of paint and hope that it passes the health inspection.

We order flan and *cafe con leche* because what else are you going to order at a Spanish-Cuban restaurant?

I smile, grab my bag, excuse myself, and make my way to the ladies room which is filled with

Mexican tile, stucco plaster and silk plants. I nod to the Irish looking restroom attendant at the Spanish-Cuban restaurant in Celebration, Florida and choose a stall.

I close my eyes, enjoy the cool air and sober up just a little bit. That's better. Relax Frances. The mariachi music is good, considering it's mariachi music. My toe starts taping in rhythm with the beat. It's nice to be alone for a second and away from all the pressure of imaginary sex.

HAVA NAGILA…

"What?" I say in a voice that tries to minimize the inevitable echo that goes along with taking a call in the bathroom. "What do you want?"

"This is a lot of attitude from someone who I have left over two dozen voice mails for," says my sister the travel agent for guilt trips.

"I'm sorry. How are you?"

"Forgiving. I've decided you can't be responsible for that asshole Tony blowing our money on blow. What he did, he did and if I can't upgrade the linens at Christian's Bar Mitzvah, so be it. If we have to downsize the gift bag, the world will not stop spinning. Hershey's or Godiva. Chocolate is chocolate. That shouldn't come between me and my sister."

"Chocolate is chocolate? Wow. Today you are a woman. So grown up."

"We cut the guest list on Larry's side of the family so maybe it's a blessing in disguise. Cousin Tony is not coming so the bar bill is sure to be lower. More Jagermeister for Aunt Mary Caruso." She pauses for a laugh. "Hello?"

"Hi."

"You're echoing. What's with the echo? Why is there an echo?"

"It must be the connection," I say too loudly.

"Are you in a public restroom?"

"No."

"Liar! You totally answered the telephone while you were in the bathroom. Who or what are you trying to avoid?"

"Nothing. No one!"

"More lies. I'm hanging up."

"Teresa, don't make me go back to that table."

"Where are you?"

A few minutes of catch-up follows. Teresa is up to date and my *con leche* is probably as cold as my libido. "Teresa I don't know what to do."

"It's not like it's changed since the last time you did it sweetie."

"Don't joke."

"Okay, you want serious? Here's serious. When you were a little girl, you took a bad spill on your roller skates."

"I don't see how this applies …"

"Patience. You were about eight. Look at your left knee. See that little scar in the shape of a crescent roll?"

"I would have said crescent moon, but yeah. I see it."

"It's from that fall."

Sure as hell, there it is.

"You loved roller skating. It was so annoying. Mama and Daddy made *me* go out with you so *you* could skate. You fell and then bam, the door shut. No more skating."

"It really hurt."

"Life does that sometimes."

"Laurie Fuller's birthday party…"

"Riiiiiiight. They went skating. You refused to go. We all begged you, but you wouldn't go because you were scared." She pauses for effect. "How many more parties are you going to miss, Frances?"

"I haven't thought about that in years."

"Of course tonight's party will be in your pants."

"Teresa, what if I fall?"

"Stay on the bottom. You'll have nothing to worry about."

"I cannot believe my sister is telling me to go back out there and have sex."

I hear a door shut. She's whispering. "Frankly I've always regretted that I didn't do more skating before I got married."

"Really?"

"A girl only gets so many invitations to the roller-rink."

"What if it's bad? What if I disappoint him?"

"What *if* you actually lived life instead of thinking about it so damn much? Go have some fun." Another pause. She's considering her words. "My darling sister, sometimes you forget that life is for the living. Go live your life."

I wash my hands and use the complimentary Chanel knockoff provided by the Irish looking restroom attendant at the Spanish-Cuban restaurant in Celebration, Florida. She looks at me, smiles and hands me a stick of Wrigley's gum.

"Go screw his brains out."

He must have an idea of that I want to do. We get back to his house really quick.

Matt unlocks the door and gives me a sweet little kiss before we go inside. No expectations. We're holding hands but I withdraw in the foyer when I start to imagine his dead wife picking out the color scheme.

Then I hear Teresa's voice in my head.

Life is for the living so I reach out for him and we kiss again. One kiss leads to another. Foyer leads to living room to staircase to his bedroom door to a long look and a smile.

The door opens and we walk through it together. Joy was so wrong. Look at me. I'm going to have sex.

I'm skating on air.

CHAPTER
SIXTEEN

I wake up more than a little disoriented. Thank you Mister Sangria. I look to my left and see Matt sleeping in a tangled mess of sheets. Content. I kiss him on the forehead. He gives me a sleepy smile. For a second I feel warm and safe. One sweet second; then I gather up my things and leave. I manage to get out the front door without waking Matt up.

There's a slight breeze. I stop to look around. The sun is starting to rise in Celebration, Florida. I'm not a morning person, but the light at this time of day certainly is pretty. The dew is burning off and there is just a touch of mist in the air.

I pray that no one noticed I was out all night; but evidently God isn't listening this morning. Gladys is waiting for me at the top of the driveway. I feel totally busted. I'm nineteen again and my Mom just caught me trying to sneak in after an overnight date. The inner voice says to relax. I am, after all, an adult. I'm an adult who just got busted trying to sneak in after an overnight date.

You can stop going to church. You can even convert to Judaism. Catholic guilt is still Catholic guilt.

"Come in! Come in!" she says. I shake my head and make a big show of yawning. Gladys gives a withering look and adds, "I have coffee." I don't move. "It's French Vanilla."

French Vanilla means getting to put off having to deal with my brother and there might be a muffin in the deal too. Landlady has kick-ass muffins.

Gladys wins.

Whenever I walk into her house I notice a new little treasure. This morning that would be a gorgeous bracelet that has been left out on the table in the breakfast nook. Art Deco. I'm guessing it is from the 20s. I pick it up. "This is lovely."

Gladys gets a twinkle in her eye as she pours the coffee into two mismatched china cups with chipped saucers. "It was Daddy's wedding gift for mother. According to family stories he could ill afford it. This was right after the crash. He went ahead and bought it anyway. Faith and love paid for that bauble."

"How did your parents meet?" I start to say.

"I won't have that bracelet being used as a delay tactic. Now put down the pretty jewelry and tell me all about last night."

I try to be coy. "I'm sorry. What do you mean?"

"What do I mean? What do I MEAN? Don't waste the time of an old woman. I'm nobody's fool. You had sex."

"Pardon me?"

"There's no point lying. I can smell it on you."

"Really?"

"No, of course not! You can't smell things like that." She starts laughing. "You really thought I could smell sex? That's delicious."

I take a large sip of my coffee, burn the roof of my mouth and rise to leave.

"Don't get mad. I'm just having fun with you."

"This is fun?"

"I don't get many thrills like this. I'll pay if that's what you want. Take the bracelet. Whatever you want, it's yours. Here, have a muffin." It's blueberry, so I sit back down. Gladys tops off my cup and settles into her chair.

"How was it?"

"It was different."

"Different. That can be good Frances. That can be mighty good." She gets a quizzical look on her face. "What did he do? Take you from behind? My husband liked that … until he gained all that weight. Then it got too hard because he was too soft." Gladys laughs at her own wordplay. I just stare at her. She settles down. "Okay. Okay. Just tell me what happened."

I struggle to find the right words. None come. "We were kissing. Things started heating up. We went into his bedroom and…"

"And … and … what?"

"Let's see," what's safe to tell her? "He unbuttoned my blouse."

"That's all you're going to give me?" She looks so disappointed.

"Slowly. He unbuttoned my blouse slowly. Then he slid it down past my shoulders. My bra strap fell to the side, the way it always does but this time I felt it, you know? It sent this little shiver down my spine."

I must be blushing by now. I can feel the heat.

"Shivers are nice. I always liked a good shiver."

"It felt kind of sexy, I guess," embarrassed to say that aloud. "That was nice. It had been a long time since I felt that way."

"Well Frances, congratulations! The drought has ended. Hallelujah!"

I hope I'm like her when I'm her age. Hell, I wish I were like her *now*. She's still sexy. I bet she's always been that way. Gladys Nelson was born sexy.

"You know that feeling of someone's skin rubbing up against yours?"

"Yes I do. I know it well. Like it. Like it a lot."

"I wanted to feel that again. I wanted to feel that really badly."

"You were horny."

"Okay. I was going to try and be a little more poetic."

"No need. Horny. Two syllables. Says all you need to know."

"Okay. Uh – okay. I started undoing his shirt. One button was kind of stubborn and I accidentally ripped his shirt."

"There are no accidents Frances."

"This was! Nothing major, just a little tear. I was out of practice."

"What did he do?"

"He laughed and ripped the shirt open."

Gladys starts to say something and stops. Instead she fans herself.

I tell her some of what happened, but I'm careful not to say too much. I don't want to be indiscreet. That wouldn't be fair to Matt; so I just give her the cliff notes. The only two people who need to know the whole story are Matt and I me

We were sitting on the bed. Face to face. I could feel his breath. I was nervous but I didn't want him to know. He started to take off my bra. My breathing got shallow. I think Matt mistook that for passion. My face tightened. So I smiled hoping he wouldn't notice my clenched jaw. Then I whipped my hair over the front of my shoulders thinking that it might make me feel less exposed.

Matt gently pushed it away and smiled as he cupped my breasts with his hands. I heard a deep breath escape from his chest. He looked at me and smiled before he began kissing them. Then he took my nipples into his mouth. I giggled, which luckily Matt mistook for pleasure. Paul used to do that too. It felt like I was nursing a baby.

I loved watching him undress. He was so confident. It made me feel less insecure. By then his shirt was already off. So I could see the muscles in his arms as he took off his pants. My eyes followed as his jeans landed on the floor. That's when I noticed his socks didn't match. They were both black, but they weren't from the same pair. One had been washed more than the other, so it was faded. It made me want to cry. Evidently I wasn't denying any of my impulses last night. So I did. I cried.

"What's wrong?"

"Your socks…" I started to say, chocking on a sob.

"Oh," he said, looking down twisting his ankle to get a better look. "They don't match do they?"

I stifled a sob.

"So you're crying about my socks?"

I wrapped myself up in his flat sheet, which didn't match the fitted sheet and then the dam opened further. I couldn't have shut up if my life depended on it. Matt, God bless him, he listened to every word.

"I'm not crying because of your socks." Matt sat there and shrugged his shoulders, kind of dumbfounded I suppose. I looked at him and took a deep breath. "The socks made me think of your wife."

"Thia is the socks?"

"Right," I say relieved to be understood.

"Um - I'm not getting your analogy."

"No woman would let a man out of the house with mismatched socks."

His voice got very small. The corners of his eyes got moist. "Oh." He looked away from me, and I let him. I didn't want to meet his gaze.

"Look, I haven't been with anyone for quite a while. This isn't easy for me," I admitted.

"Me either."

"I know." I kissed him twice and pulled away to look him in the eyes. "I know."

"This bed is crowded," said Matt through one of his sad smiles.

"Yeah. It is."

"Your ex-husband just grabbed my ass."

I smiled as I was wiping away the last of the tears. We were both silent for a moment or two.

"What are you thinking?" Matt asked.

"I'm sick of feeling this way. I'm sick of feeling like my life is on hold and that the past is more important than the present or the future."

"I could take off my socks…"

I laughed out loud, which after crying is kind of messy. Matt handed me some Kleenex in a box that didn't match anything else in the room, which made me start crying again.

Matt held the tissue while I blew my nose. "Frances, what do you want?"

"Let's just keep things simple. It's just sex."

"Come on Frances. It's never just sex."

"It can be. It doesn't even have to be good."

"Really? Thanks very much."

"I didn't mean it wouldn't be great. The foreplay was really nice. Superior even. I just I meant that I don't have any expectations."

"Shhhhh, you don't get to talk anymore." He kissed me on the lips. "Let's review the situation. There is a beautiful woman in my bed.

I smile. He thinks I'm pretty.

"Who just wants to have sex. No expectations."

"Yeah. But if that's hard for you. I mean I know you've been through stuff too and …"

"I've only got one question."

"Yes?"

"Why are we still talking?"

He kissed me and stood up as I pushed aside the sheet I was using to cover myself. His underwear, brand new Calvin Klein black boxer briefs by the way, slid down past nicely toned thighs and calves. There was a light dusting of golden hair on his legs. The light from the candles we had lit gave me the chance to see the parts that don't need to be described.

Matt laid me down on the bed, careful to look at me. I arched my back and then he began to remove my panties. It's funny the things you think about at a time like that. I could see my feet. They had tan lines from the straps of my sandals. The last time I remember noticing that was on my honeymoon with Paul. We were on Fire Island. Robert and Lil McKiernan, good friends of my parents, had lent us their beach house on Kismet as a wedding gift. It was off-season and it was just the two of us for an entire week. It was as though we owned that island.

But here I am with someone new.

My eyes returned to Matt's face. His smile got bigger. As he made his way down my body he surprised me by softly kissing the scar on my left knee.

I never expected to enjoy myself last night. It has always taken me a while to lose my inhibitions enough to really let go. It wasn't like that last night. I kept shifting my weight to give Matt guidance. I met each of his thrusts with one of my own. That encouraged him to push harder and harder until we both exploded. We fell asleep right away. I slept great.

"After-sex sleep is the best," purrs Gladys.

"Until I woke up."

"You see dear, that's where you're wrong. That's when the fun begins again. Morning sex can be wonderf…"

"No. No morning sex. I left before Matt woke up."

"Why in the world would you do something like that?"

"I didn't want things to get complicated."

"Oh. So, you were thinking like a man!"

"I was selfish."

"Like I said…"

"Here's a guy who hasn't been with anyone since his wife died."

"You don't know that."

I pause and get anxious, jealous almost.

"You're right. I don't."

"So relax. Forgive my language but you were just screwing with your head."

My jaw drops. I couldn't have heard that correctly. "What?"

"Screwing with your head." Gladys takes a big gulp of coffee. "We've all done it."

"Done what?"

"Your mind needed to have sex so you found a way to make that happen. That's all, sweetie. You found a man to make that happen. That's more than understandable."

"Really?"

"Now you just have to decide if you want to go back for more."

Gladys makes it sound easy, but it's not. Matt was right. Pretend all you want to, sex is never simple.

CHAPTER
SEVENTEEN

I wake up Monday morning, not feeling at all well. Son of a bitch! What a rotten time to get my semi-annual cold. For a second or two I indulge in the fantasy of calling in sick but then I remember the phone call I got from Kellie Holden the night before.

"Hello Frances, this is Kellie Holden, HR Specialist from Planet Binger."

She sounded so official I wanted to throw up and I don't have the flu. I have a cold. "Hello Kellie, this is Frances Fiore, Art Director for the same company. What's up?"

She pauses to purse her dry pink lips. "My Outlook was down on Friday. That means the notice for Monday morning's meeting never got sent out."

"Oh. Is there a meeting on Monday?"

She doesn't respond. "Once again, you want something done, you've got to do it yourself."

She can turn anything that happens to anyone anywhere into a lament about how it affects her. Get some perspective Kellie.

"Kill her with kindness." That's what Shelaylee said. The first half sounds really good. It's the kindness part that will be difficult.

I try really hard to sound sincere. "What a hassle Kel." Oh no. She hates having her name shortened. "*lie*. Did you have any plans for tonight?"

"Uh – no."

"Well, um, of course not." Recovery mode. Think. "You can't make plans on Sunday night and do a good job on Monday.

"Right."

Homerun. Thank God, Tommy walked through the door and gave me an excuse to hang up. "Gotta run Kellie. My brother is home. Give," Nipsy … three legs … Tripod? No, Tipsy. That's it! "Give Tipsy a hug for me. See you tomorrow."

"Goodb," click.

It was a weird evening. Tommy was surprisingly chatty. He whistled a lot and never asked me where I had been the night before. We watched *The Bodyguard* on BET. Swear to God toward the end of the movie when Whitney Houston gets on the plane I saw him tearing up.

Poor Whitney.

Congestion is really all I can think about right now. Even though the non-drowsy Dristan has an expiration date from 2011 I give it a shot and hope for the best.

Getting ready for work on Monday isn't fun. I go for big hair hoping that it will give my head more room to pound and go heavy on the eye makeup to make up for the red, runny nose. I spritz a little extra Jo Malone to compensate for the Vick's Vapor Rub. The smell confuses Katz. He backs away from me with a scrunched up face and then starts batting my keys toward me in kind of a get-the-hell-out-of-here way. I forget

149

to grab my sunglasses but by the time I realize it I'm closer to the car than the house. To hell with it, I can wear the huge cataract sunglasses I found in the glove box. They look very Jackie O - in a geriatric way.

God bless Desi. He must be psychic. He's already brewing coffee in the Hello Bunny coffee maker, which is a total Hello Kitty rip-off. It's kind of a Japanime thing that I think was meant to compete in the Asian markets.

I throw Desi his Monday morning bagel that I picked up on the way to work. We both say thank you in unison. That, methinks, is teamwork.

"Anything special happen this weekend?" he asks.

In hindsight I really should have seen the trap being set.

"Not really."

"No dates or anything?"

"Nope. Spent the weekend working around the house and hanging with my brother."

"Because my sources tell me you were seen with Matt this weekend." I stop mid sip and look at him over the rim of my Binger Peaceable Kingdom Cast Member coffee mug. "At the Columbia in Celebration. You had a 1905 Salad, a pitcher of sangria which you pretty much drank by yourself and were last seen leaving the restaurant heading toward his house."

"What did Matt supposedly have?"

"Chicken."

"You don't know that it was him I was with."

"Credit card vouchers don't lie."

Desi's laughter is out of control. "Girl, if you are going to try and keep secrets, you got to be careful where you go. My friend Scottie saw you."

"Scottie?"

"Yeah. He works at Columbia as a bartender when he's not performing - he didn't charge you for your sangria. Check the receipt." His eyes get wide. "So how was the big date?"

Before I can answer a blur of red hair, brown roots, and pink florals whizzes down the corridor. The scent of potpourri lingers. It must be really strong if I can smell it with this cold.

"Meeting people!"

My heart sinks. I'm about to see Matt for the first time since this weekend. Nothing to do but try to take a deep breath, wheeze and get it over with. Desi hands me a box of tissues and follows me into the conference room.

One by one everyone files into purgatory wearing shoot-me-now looks. Joy, the twins Petra and Pauline, Gratciana looking very tired, everyone but Matt enters. I know Desi is watching me so I'm careful not to react.

Kellie stares at her watch. Her toes are taping. She has one of those frozen smiles on her face. With a deep breath she says, "Okay. Let's get started."

She begins this truly crazy presentation about the importance of the new computerized time clock system, which was just imported from our division in Germany. Evidently it is the most important thing facing international entertainment conglomerates today, perhaps the entire world. According to Kellie the scope of this issue is overwhelming.

Thank God for the caffeine in non-drowsy Dristan. Just as she starts in on the accountability of punctuality Matt finally enters. My heart sinks.

He's sneezing.

I hand him a tissue. Behind me I hear Desi quietly chuckling to himself.

"Grab your new IDs everyone." She waits for us to do so. Now raise them in the air where I can see to make sure you're doing it right. The magnetic strip should be facing north…"

Sixty molasses minutes later, the meeting is over. People rise to leave. Petra is walking as though her legs fell asleep. Kellie gathers her notes with a smile and hugs them to herself in a masturbatory job-well-done kind of way.

Matt catches my eye as the room empties out. "Frances, could you stay behind? There's something I'd like to talk to you about."

As he leaves I can see Desi's shoulders moving up and down. That boy is too smart for my own good.

Matt follows the crowd and shuts the door behind them.

"Hi," says my handsome one-night-stand.

I smile to buy time. Please let me think of something perfect to say. "Hi back." Trite. The pause would have been longer if it weren't for the sneeze that followed.

"Sorry about that. It's probably my fault. I volunteered at Give Kids the World and some kid gave me a cold while I was there. Give the world, get a cold. Same old story."

"I've caught less worthwhile colds."

He moves closer to me. "Really?" He puts his arms around me. I start to move away. He follows.

"Matt, we're at work."

"I bought in some of those mini things from Dunkin' Donuts. They're all in the break room inhaling them. We've got ten minutes easy."

"I don't want to get you sick…"

"I'm already sick."

He pulls me even closer. I tilt my head, ready to be kissed and can feel my sinuses draining. His lips are half an inch away from mine when his approach stops. "But maybe you're right. Perhaps this isn't appropriate workplace behavior." He starts to back away.

Without thinking, I grab his tie and pull him back to me. His weight collapses against mine and pushes me against the wall. I can feel his body through the thin linen material of the suit he is wearing today. One part of his body is making itself especially known.

"Munchkin."

"What?"

"Munchkin. That's the name of those mini donuts."

"Oh. Okay." He bites his lower lip. "Just for future reference, that's the last thing a guy wants to hear at a moment like this."

I roll my eyes.

"At least compare me to a Long John."

"What's a Long John?"

"They're like long donuts with icing. They usually have a cream filling … or jelly."

"Okay – this is no longer sexy."

We both start to laugh. This time my weight collapses into his. He catches me with no effort.

I feel as light as a feather … and carefree too.
I could get used to feeling this way.

"Should we talk about the other night?"

"No," I say too quickly. That must have sounded
awfully adamant. I blow my nose as seductively
as possible to buy time and collect myself. "Why
ruin things by talking? Let's just enjoy the way
things are now." I kiss him. "There's always time
for talking later."

"Wow. You're like a fantasy."

"Oh come on!"

"Really. It's been so long since I just
had fun."

"Me too Matt. Me too."

For a second it looks like he wants to say
more. "Frances, the other night was great." He
continues. "You were incredible."

Suddenly I feel so bold. "You think I'm good
in bed?"

His eyebrows get higher and his voice gets
lower. "Yeah Frances, I do."

I move to lock the door while he blows his
nose.

"Wait 'til you see how I do on the conference
table."

CHAPTER
EIGHTEEN

The rest of the week has been seen through a stuffy head, runny nose blur. I'm so sick of being sick. Eyes watering, decongestant, Nyquil and Zinc under my tongue until my mouth tastes like metal all the time.

Kellie gave me a coupon for some cold medicine inside a greeting card with a picture of Aunty Body, a character from an animated film called *Outside In*, about the battle against cold germs. The exchange ended with a lecture about coming into the office not feeling well. I guarantee she didn't talk to Matt that way.

She also told me my 120-day probation period is over. I passed with flying colors and am now a fully vested cast member.

I've been working from home, which has been a great chance to jump on the Tiny Planet renderings. I've got a good foundation but something is missing. If there was more time I'd like to do more research. But that's life in the corporate world - you wait and wait for something to get started and then it's hurry, hurry, hurry. Matt makes the big presentation for the money people in two months. We've to get everything done before that deadline. It's going to be a real crunch.

"Frances?"

I make my way toward the staircase through the jumble of sketching paper and art supplies on the floor of my studio. "Yeah Tommy?" I scream just as he is rounding the landing coming up from the garage.

"You're sure you don't want to come with me to Joy's? She's making her own sauce. Homemade pasta too."

I start coughing theatrically and shake my head no. Tommy hands me some bottled water since tap water in Orlando sucks and the coughing subsides. He catches my eye to make sure that I'm okay and then notices the drawings I've been working on.

"Hey, these are good. Which country are they supposed to be from?"

"Spain."

"Really? This is supposed to be Spain?"

"Kind of as seen through the eyes of Picasso. I'm trying to define each countries contribution to the visual arts. Picasso, Spain. Van Gogh, the Netherlands."

"Cool! Who'd you choose for the United States?"

"Not sure yet." Not sure I want to talk about work. Better to change the subject. "How's the new job going?"

It took Tommy all of one day to get *three* job offers. The guy is a great mechanic; but he surprised me. He took a job at Jon Ron's in the front office. It's a local shop that specializes in foreign cars. The owners seem like really nice guys and they're being really good to my brother.

It's got to be so much better than working for that ass Tony.

"Today we renegotiated with this debit card company they use and I managed to talk them down on their charges. We saved like 25%."

Wow. That's amazing.

Tommy *talked*.

I'll look it up later but I do believe that's one of the first signs of the apocalypse. "Good for you. I'd hug you but I don't want you to catch my cold." Instead I slug him on the arm.

"Hey Frances, thanks."

"For the slug? Here's another one!"

"I'm telling Mom and Dad." The mood changes the way it always does when their names come up. Tommy shifts uncomfortably. "I just meant thank you for everything you've done."

"It's nice … you being here."

We hug despite the germ factory that is me. Tommy pulls away and makes the mistake of continuing to talk.

"It's great to see you doing good."

"Please don't…"

Maybe he didn't hear me.

"Frances, I wanted to say this to you for a while." His eyes look up as though he's going to find the right words on the ceiling. "Don't feel bad. You know, because you're still here."

I start to protest but he continues. The guy finally starts talking and now he won't shut up. "Mom and Dad would tell you the same thing."

Okay, they were his parents too. He can say that; but then he goes too far.

"I think Sam would too."

There it is. No matter how hard you try to leave things in the past, behind you so you can get on with your life, other people won't let you. They won't. Not even your own brother.

I can feel my face get tense and my lips narrow. I know Tommy had good intentions. He opened the door because he cares about me. He just went too far. He went too far. Now it's my turn to look at the ceiling.

"You know what Tommy? You're right."

"Yeah?"

"Yeah. Things have been going really well."

"You deserve it. After everything that hap…"

"You know what's helped?"

"What?"

"Not talking about it. Not being surrounded by people who define me by all the rotten stuff that happened. Not being reminded about it everyday."

"Oh. Okay Frances. I get it."

"Don't talk to anyone else about this."

"Not even Joy or Gladys?"

"Why do you say that? Have you already talked to them?"

"No. But they'd probably be good people to…"

"No." My voice is adamant. "No one."

"Okay," he says without hesitation. "I won't."

Cold be damned. I kiss him on the cheek to ease the tension and show there are no hard feelings. He starts to leave. I go back to my drawing. As Tommy reaches the stairs, he turns around.

"Frances, I don't have to go out tonight."

"Yes you do. Go. Please?"

"Come on…"

"Now Tommy, Joy was expecting both of us. It would be rotten to totally cancel."

"Okay. You're right. I'll go."

"Do you need directions?"

"No, I know how to get there. I'll see you later."

There are times when you see people differently; as though it's a person you've never met before. I usually look at Tommy and see a sweet little boy with a shag haircut and a heart of gold. Today I see him as a man, a very good man.

I walk to the window to watch his truck pull out. There are flowers next to him on the passenger seat; a little grocery store mixed bouquet. That'll make Joy happy.

I spend most of the night working on Tiny Planet. Gladys stops by with some art books she and her husband bought back when they could still travel. She points out various places they stopped. She talks about her kids and family vacations. Her stories make it much more real to me; gives me deeper images. They'll be great source material.

As she says goodnight I stare into her eyes. I want to believe Tommy hasn't told her anything but I need to be sure. By the time she leaves, I relax. He hasn't said anything to her. She doesn't know.

Later I get on the Internet and make my travel plans for my nephew Christian's Bar Mitzvah. It feels odd to be making plans to go back to New York. I wonder what it will feel like, staying at a hotel in my hometown, seeing so many of my relatives again.

Well, I love my nephew more than I dread facing that.

I go to the window to open it up; air the room out a little. It's gotten dark out. I go outside on the little balcony and sit down. I can finally feel my breathing begin to relax.

The night air is clear and full of possibilities. I can smell the jasmine that borders the yard. Off in the distance the fireworks turn the sky lavender, silver, red, and green.

For a second I review all that has happened to me since I came to Orlando. I've got a new home, fairly rewarding work, new friends and Matt - whatever that ends up being.

Normally this would be a perfect moment. Not tonight. Tonight my mind can't help but drift back to everything Tommy said. Don't feel guilty.

But I do. I think I always will.

CHAPTER
NINETEEN

My mom always said that colds take ten days to get over. So, that means I'm an overachiever. I can breathe again and it has only been eight days. Each breath is an accomplishment.

A weekend of rest and I am ready to go back to work.

By work I mean Theme Park Administration's Annual State of the Planet; a day spent evaluating the guest experience at the various parks that make up Planet Binger. Some of us are going to BVOT, Binger's Vision of Tomorrow with the permanent World's Fair theme.

We were all told to report in time for the Opening Ceremony. So I arrive at the front gate at 8:58 dressed as a guest...which is what we call our customers.

Gratciana always says, "I'm going to have some guests over next week. Does that mean I can charge them $90 to get in?" She's a pistol, that Grats.

I have my unwashed hair pulled back into a very sporty ponytail. It looks gorgeous with the thick coat of zinc oxide that I have all over my nose. No one better give me any grief about that. It was already red from the cold. I'm not risking sunburn.

Please remember, I used to work for the Sun Block Council of America. Safety first. Block harmful UV rays.

I'm wearing a University of Wisconsin tank top that Matt gave me, and a really comfy pair of cargo shorts. I bought them yesterday with Joy on a girl's day at the Mall of the Millennia, which is Orlando's version of high end. It's supposed to be very fancy. The folks from Windermere shop there. Very *fuh, fuh.* You know decent chain restaurants like the Cheesecake Factory, Nordstrom, Macy's, Crate and Barrel, that kind of thing.

The Dollar Store costs a buck twenty-five.

It's right by the Orange County prison on 33rd Street. When you shop on the higher levels you can see the guards patrolling the perimeter of the jail.

Joy is wearing a short sun dressy thing that she picked up on Sunday. It's very breezy. The strap of her new, pink, lacy bra sticks out just enough to be appropriate. "You look cute," I mouth in an exaggerated way.

Matt didn't take it as far as the rest of us; he looks like he's dressed to go golfing. His shorts are not short at all. They're long and very plaid. He's wearing a polo shirt from a company Habitat for Humanity build. It's got a little hammer embroidered over the pocket. It's faded and doesn't fit very well.

Next time he's coming with me to the mall.

Kellie is the only one who didn't get into the touristy spirit. She's wearing a shapeless silky, pink dress with a drop waist. Shoes dyed to match. I think I remember Betty White wearing something similar on the *Golden Girls.*

"No one told me we were going casual today," she says.

"Oops," says Joy with a huge smile.

Desi walks up and says, "Don't worry Kellie. You look fine." He raises his knock-off Versace sunglasses to show me that his eyes are rolling. Then he slowly turns around to give us all a full view of his outfit. Somehow he has managed to make a very tight kind of semi-cropped top and the shortest pair of shorts I have ever seen on a man work.

Desi's legs are amazing.

You could cut paper on those calves.

We're all sharing morning hellos when Kellie shushes us. "Focus people. It's time for the BVOT Parade of Participating Partners."

Triumphant music floods the front gate courtyard and some kind of chemical fog starts to roll in. I guess it camouflages the entrance of the choir. Suddenly, singers wearing costumes from what I'm guessing are supposed to be their countries of origin surround us. There's a big strapping lumberjack from Canada, Queen Elizabeth and Prince Charles look-a-likes on a horse representing the U.K. There's a girl in a red and white striped blouse and a tight black skirt wearing a beret from France and someone dressed like the Pope representing Italy. I can see someone in lederhosen. He must be from Norway. Germany has a couple that looks like they fell off a cuckoo clock. A man, on a burro, wearing a sombrero, represents the people of Mexico.

It's a total stereotype.

I'm including that in my evaluation.

There are acrobats from China. Moroccans come in wearing flowing robes. The Russians are in heavy furs, gorgeous, but heavy. Those poor people! It must be more than 80 degrees out here. I'm on the outlook for PETA when Australian Aborigines enter. They look much more temperature appropriate.

They perform "I'd Like to Teach the World to Sing," in perfect harmony. Right around, "For peace throughout the land," I realize I haven't seen the USA yet. The song ends and I am still seeking, which is ironic because the New Seekers originally performed the song in a Coke commercial. I look around. Sure as hell, there it is; a sign saying the show is sponsored by Coca Cola.

Then an even more triumphant swell of music is heard. The countries, now in a straight line, split in half to make way for some sort of an entrance. Lights cut through the fog and lasers fill the courtyard. A melting pot of Americans enters. A Cast Member (if it was India it would be a caste member) from each of the fifty states, delineated by the t-shirts they're wearing enters. They form a cluster that reflects the map of the United States; Minnesota is next to Wisconsin, Texas is next to Louisiana, and so on. DC, Puerto Rico and some other municipalities are off to the side looking slightly dejected. They're all singing "America the Beautiful," as American icons such as the Statue of Liberty, the

Grand Canyon and for some reason a Denny's flash on the walls around us. At the end of their song the fog gets thicker, the laser-show crescendos, and the audience's attention is drawn to the sky.

When the smoke clears all the singers have disappeared. Vanished. They have been replaced by poles flying the flags of the countries of BVOT in the Global Lagoon of Diversity. The crowd goes wild. One veteran in a motorized scooter salutes the flag while his wife wipes away a tear. A Japanese family beams and takes a photo near their flag. So does a very Nordic looking family that is either from Germany or Norway. I can't tell which flag they're standing by.

Evidently the rest of the crowd is less than overwhelmed. They storm the gate and don't look back. We are staring at an international array of backsides leaving us in their dust. It's like the beginning of the New York City Marathon with a far wider assortment of body types.

"Wow," says Kellie. "They must be in a hurry to get to their first ride."

I catch Matt's eye and feel very smug. "You mean attraction. We call them attractions."

We start at the BVOT Permanent Technology Expo at the front of the park. Perhaps by permanent, they mean outdated. The first display is a multimedia presentation about?called "The Wonders of the World Wide Web" hosted by the cast of TV's *Fraiser.* We keep walking past the other displays; Jennifer Lopez and her second husband demonstrating an iPod, stuff like that. We debate getting on the Nokia World of Wireless Telecommunications Attraction but the line is too long.

Dancers on Segways circle a gorgeous fountain gushing water about forty feet into the air. In a mirror suspended above that you see the dancers weave in and out of patterns like a flower or a snowflake. The music corresponds to whatever shape is being built. "Let it Snow! Let it Snow! Let it Snow!" "Raindrops Keep Fallin' on My Head." The show ends with them forming into the shape of a Binger Bunny silhouette. Desi is muttering something in Spanish.

"That could have been so much better," he says to no one in particular.

He's so good at his job that sometimes I forget he's a dancer at heart. As the performers exit a very cute boy gives Desi a small wave. Desi beams. He responds by blowing the guy a kiss. It's sweet … no big deal.

Kellie disagrees.

"Desi, don't call attention to us. We're here as guests."

No wonder that woman has no life. She's too busy monitoring the lives of others. Sad, sad, sad. She doesn't give a damn about Desi blowing a kiss. She's pissed off because she hasn't blown a kiss for a long, long time.

Desi looks as though he's getting ready to tell her off. Again I mouth my words. "It's not worth it." Desi smolders but takes my advice. As we walk away I see him looking wistfully at the stage.

I get the sense Matt wants to talk to me, but we're never alone. Lunchtime finally arrives but the group cannot reach a consensus about where to eat. Joy and Desi make overtures about splitting up but I shoot them a "don't you dare stick me with Kellie," look that cuts that off at the knees.

Ms. Holden makes a presentation to the group. I'm sure she wishes she had access to Power Point. "Kids, our eight dollar meal vouchers, loaded onto our Enchantment Bands," she says, ~~indicating~~ *pointing* to the gray bracelet/tracking devices we are all wearing, "Won't cover most of the restaurants in the park … even though they are a terrific value for our guests."

Keep talking Kellie. I'm quickly losing my appetite. She, of course, obliges.

"According to last year's fiscal stats, the average price of lunch at BVOT is twenty-three dollars." All of us look at her dumbfounded, with open mouths. She senses she may have gone too far.

She tries to recover. "I'm just saying if we go backstage and eat at the Cast Cafeteria, I'll bet we can bank two dollars each, at least. You know we're free to keep whatever we don't spend." Thinking that doing things her way will shut her up, we agree.

We're wrong. She keeps talking about company policies all the way to the restaurant.

We enter. It's clean but as always, without much color. There are lots of flyers announcing company policies. Copies of the company newsletter, *The Binger Report*, lie strewn about. People in an array of costumes make their way through the place.

We look up at the menus. There are a lot of choices. Desi heads for the salad bar, Joy chooses the International Steam Table Buffet featuring three kinds of Lo Mein, and Matt gets into the burger trough. Finally. I can talk to Matt while we're in line. I step next to him and tap him on the shoulder.

"Hi."

In unison we both say, "Can we talk?" Then we both laugh. I'm still laughing when he abruptly stops. Something in his eye changes. I don't even have to look. I already know. Kellie is standing behind me.

She's trying so hard to be one of the gang today. It's really kind of pathetic. "Hi you guys. Good choice on the burgers. I cannot believe that Joy and Desi went for the weigh your own entrees. What a rip-off!"

Only then do I realize what a long line we are in. Matt and Kellie are talking about some people that I don't know so I tune out. The noise of their chatter in the background, I'm left to my thoughts.

What does he want?

I get to the cashier line with my cheeseburger, onion rings, large Diet Coke and frozen Snicker Bar for dessert. The total is six dollars. The cashier hands me back two bucks from my voucher for eight. In the corner of my eye I see Kellie smugly tilt her head to the left in a, "See I was right after all," kind of way. I smile back and pretend that there are death rays shooting out of my mouth.

Finally, a way I can kill her with kindness.

Lunch is eternal. I keep trying to catch Matt's eye but I can tell he's not looking at me on purpose. He doesn't want to drop any clues about what is going on between us away from work.

At work too, counting the time in the conference room.

After returning our dirty dishes to the conveyor belt by the door, we head back into the park and start evaluating the Global Lagoon of Diversity.

Matt and Kellie explore the attractions. Desi, Joy, and I evaluate the shopping in each country. I just found out that I get a 40% discount with my ID now that I'm permanent. How cool is that? Get this; they have a service where you don't even have to carry your bags. No kidding. They send them to the gate and you pick them up on the way out. It's like Amazon Prime without the waiting.

My evaluation scores just went through the roof.

I was doing pretty well with my credit card until now but today my Visa gets a workout. I buy tea in the UK, with matching cups and saucers for Gladys. Joy points out a really cute sweatshirt that she thinks would look good on Tommy. She's got a good eye. I snatch that up right away. So now I am on a roll. I get Christian a gorgeous ring for his Bar Mitzvah from a small Israeli kiosk they have set up near Mexico where I get my niece Rachel, not a small girl by any stretch of the imagination, a really cute poncho. For Teresa and Larry I get a DVD of the first season of *The Wonderful World of Art*.

I wonder why it's just his name in the title. What about Mary? What about her wonderful world?

We're in France buying perfume when I bump into a friend wearing a matching sweater set and sniffing the Angel Perfume that she has just sprayed into the air.

"Hello Shelaylee."

"Well, Frances Fiore as I live and breathe! How are you, honey?" I haven't seen her for months, since that morning at Publix. She still remembers my name. Amazing.

I tell her about finding the guesthouse and working on the renovation of Tiny Planet. I tell her about Tommy moving here. All the details just spill out. As I'm talking I realize how happy I sound.

"Sweetie, you sound t-riffic!" Then she pulls me away from Desi and Joy. They're too busy loading up on free samples to notice.

"Is there a man in the picture?"

I smile but offer no details. Matt's not really my boss. I don't report to him or anything but it's still kind of murky. For all I know we are in violation of some kind of Binger-too-involved-in-your-private-life corporate policy.

Shelaylee smiles back. "You and your ex back together?"

The smile evaporates and turns into laughter. "Oh God no!" I pause to realize that I haven't been thinking about Paul much at all. "No, it's someone else. But it's new; too new to know exactly what's up."

"But you jumped in the pool!" She hugs me and then pulls away to look me dead in the eye. "Good for you. Good for you!" She hugs me again. Then I feel her tense up.

"Uh-oh. Here comes trouble. Eighty-six the personal talk."

I don't even have to look. I already know. Kellie is standing behind me, *again*.

"Hello Shelaylee."

"Hello Kellie. Oh golly. Would you look at the time? I gotta pick up my step father from adult day care." She shakes Kellie's hand and hugs me goodbye.

Before she leaves she whispers in my ear, "That bitch is stalking you. Get a restraining order!" She walks out of the store laughing. She turns back to grab a package the Parisian clerk was wrapping up. "Bye girls!"

Kellie looks deflated. "Why does that woman hate me so? I never did anything to her…"

I go into middle child placate mode. "Kellie, she doesn't hate you. I think…"

Kellie checks her watch. "It's 5 p.m.. We're off the clock. Let's get a drink."

"What?"

"A drink. We've earned it. Schlepping around here all day long."

Schlepping? Kellie Holden uses Yiddish?

"Do they even serve liquor here in the Park?"

"Uh – yes. We're in France, Frances. The theme wouldn't be complete without a wine bar."

I invite Desi and Joy to join us. They both look at me like they'd rather have a colonic.

"We're going to keep shopping Frances," says Joy.

"Have fun," adds Desi, working hard to suppress a giggle.

Matt is nowhere to be found. Crap. I'm on my own.

Kellie leads me toward a hidden little corner of the French Pavilion. There are tables with white linen tablecloths surrounding a small cast iron fountain. The rushing water gives the air a nice chill. The waiter arrives to take our order. I ask for a Chardonnay.

Kellie orders a gin martini, up with a twist of lime.

In broken English the *S*ommelier, Dana from Champagne according to her nametag tries to explain. "Pardon Madam, but *notre policie*, rather, our policy is wine only. No hard liquor until sunset."

Kellie shoots her a look I've not seen before. "It's 3 a.m. in France. The sun has set *there*. Please just bring me the martini."

"Very well."

Dana departs to bitch about Kellie in the kitchen and spit in her cocktail. Another server brings us the drinks, which arrive quickly. Kellie takes a big sip, okay gulp, and starts talking.

"I've done nothing to that woman and she is always so dismissive." I try to interrupt but Kellie plows through. "You are the *last person* I want disputing that. Look at you. You're like the Prom Queen."

"Oh come on!"

"It's true. You're little Miss Popular."

"Really?" I say.

"Yeah. Desi thinks you're great. Joy *loves* you."

Normally I would chalk up that disdainful tone to the liquor but she just started drinking. The disdain is sincere. I'm guessing that she's wanted to say this for a while now.

"I see what they see in you. I get it. Okay, so you're a little pushy and you wear too much make-up." She pauses to consider the inventory. "And you're too old for that tank top."

"That's nice. Thank you."

"Would you let me finish my point? God! Everyone always cuts me off before I'm done talking, then I get discouraged, clam up and end up looking like an idiot."

I put my hands up and give her the floor. She takes another gulp of her drink.

"You're fun Frances. I didn't expect that at all based on your interview and background check."

"Background check? Excuse m…"

She pauses but only to make air quotes around the title. "You're one of the girls that would never hang out with me in high school. I was busy being the class secretary and you were busy going to all the parties I didn't get invited to."

That wasn't the opening line I was expecting. My response is a cross between a laugh and a stammer. "Kellie…"

"It's true."

"You don't know me."

"Whose fault is that?"

Just as I'm about to answer her, my cellphone rings. I check Caller ID. It's Gladys. That can wait.

I toss the phone into my bag.

"And then there's Matt."

I dropped my guard too soon. Kellie drains her glass and waves the empty in the air. Dana sees her and with a shocked expression goes back to the bar to get her the next Martini. They'll be out of Sapphire before sunset.

"What do you mean Kellie?" I ask trying my best to sound professional. "What about Matt?"

She smiles. "He told me you've been seeing each other." She quickly adds, "It's cool. I'm not going to cause any problems." She grabs my hand. "Really. Don't worry."

"Then what's the problem Kellie?"

She looks over toward the water, not meeting my gaze. I see her wipe away a tear. "I just want to know when it's going to be my turn. When do I get to be the Frances and not the Kellie?"

I've been where she is. I've felt that alone. Never in my life did I expect to relate to her; much less sympathize with her.

That pisses me off.

Eventually Matt joins us. He comes up to the table with pretty tangible dread, like he's approaching a sniper's nest or something.

"So, you ladies have been talking?"

I raise my right eyebrow and nod.

"So you know that I talked to…"

I nod more emphatically. My eyebrow goes up about another quarter inch.

"Yeah. That's what I wanted to talk about."

Kellie finishes the last sip of her martini, and says, "Don't worry, everything is fine."

And it is, until my cell phone rings. It's Gladys again. This time I answer.

"Thank God you picked up."

"Why? What is it?"

"I'm not feeling too well."

CHAPTER
TWENTY

I don't even remember getting to the car.

It's not like Gladys to exaggerate sickness, just the opposite. She'd ignore a broken hip to get to a good party. I made my excuses and headed toward the car. By the time I reached the gate I was running. I didn't even wait for the tram.

She said chest pains.

Okay, okay. That could be anything. Gladys told me she called 911. That's good. What can be done is being done. She is being taken to Sand Lake Hospital, which Matt said is between BVOT and the house. I've already got the directions in my phone.

I hate hospitals; but I love Gladys. Ignore the tightening in your own chest Frances. Concentrate on your friend and drive safely. One person in the hospital is quite enough.

I walk through the door of the Emergency Room and am hit with that sickening smell of hospital cleanliness. It brings back memories I would rather forget.

Where is Admissions?

I see a woman who obviously hates her life. She seems to be looking off into the distance wondering why she didn't pay more attention in school. I look above her. Sure enough, There is the sign identifying Admissions.

Good font. Clear direction. Utilitarian but still with a little energy. Well done.

Why am I thinking about that now?

"Hello."

No response.

"Hello?" Again, there's no response. I'm about to call 911 for this gal. Hopefully she'd get a quick response time, already being in the hospital and all. I wave my hand in front of her face, resisting the urge to slap her. "HELLO?'

She looks annoyed and moves to cover the paper in front of her. It's a grocery list.

"I need to know if Gladys Nelson has arrived yet. She was experiencing chest pains and …"

"She's in cubicle five. You family?"

Common sense prevails. "Yes."

"You her daughter? She said she was expecting her daughter," she checks her computer screen, "Frances." I nod, touched to think that Gladys described me that way. The corners of my eyes get moist. The clerk hands me a tissue. "Okay. You can go in." I start to leave and my manners get the better of me.

"Thank you." She doesn't look up. She is busy writing down Kleenex on her shopping list.

I make my way through a corridor of cubicles. Number One, closest to the door is empty. That's a good sign I think. If Gladys were critical she'd be closer to the entrance, maybe?

Cubicle Two has a drunken woman, who appears to have taken some kind of fall. She's very bruised and yelling slurred words at a husband who looks terminally depressed.

There are three cops in Cubicle Three. They are surrounding a teenager. I slow my pace. A little eavesdropping and it seems as though the kid was shot, not badly, in some kind of altercation off John Young Parkway. Gang activity. Who knew things like this happen here?

I duck under the white curtain surrounding the cubicle. Gladys is lying on a hospital bed shoved into the corner. The bed is a single but it still manages to swallow her. She looks very small. Frail. Normally she's so vital and spry. It's easy to forget she admits to being almost eighty. God only knows how old she really is.

She looks up and immediately her right hand moves to smooth her hair so she'll look her best. "Darling, you're here." Her smile is weak but sincere. She offers her left hand. "Come, sit next to me."

I'm not going to get emotional in front of her. I refuse. That would freak her out. Keep the conversation going. That's the best choice. "What happened Gladys?"

"I had just come in from grocery shopping. That nice Jen Frady down the street took me after she got in from work. I carried in my bags…"

"How many?"

"Three. I was doing just fine. Having a normal day when all of a sudden I got these sharp pains in my chest. I didn't even have the energy to put the groceries away. So I sat down and waited for the spell to pass. When it didn't, I got scared. I thought I might be having a heart attack. So I called 911 and then you. Right after that, I took aspirin, like they say to do on the television."

"Thank God."

"Well, I may have overdone it. Normally I take two but this seemed like an emergency so I took what was left in the bottle."

"How many?"

"I lost count after twelve."

"Has anyone been in to see you?"

"Yes … a charming young resident named Eddie."

"What did he say?"

"That I've had too much aspirin."

"No! What did he say about your chest pain?"

"Oh that! It's heartburn or a minor case of Angina. Nothing I can't live with."

"So are we free to go home?"

"They want to keep me in overnight for observation."

"For the chest pains?"

"The aspirin. It was extra strength."

"Well then, we should make ourselves comfortable."

"Nonsense," Gladys protests. "Go home. I'll be just fine. I have all the care in the world at a touch of this button." She reaches for the nurse's call button but can't find it. It is tangled in the sheets. I smooth them and then hand her the button.

"See? You need me."

Gladys smiles. "Yes. I suppose I do."

That was easier than I expected it to be. She must be scared. Distractions are in order. "I'll run down to the gift shop and get us a few magazines."

"Do they still publish *Cosmo*? There used to be quizzes in *Cosmo*!"

I serpentine my way through the hallways and find the gift shop. Since everybody knows that calories eaten in a hospital are automatically forgiven I get a few Kit Kat bars … milk, dark, and white chocolate. We can do a little taste test. I continue through the maze of corridors. It takes a while but I find the cafeteria.

The day is turning out to be incredibly redundant. Once again, someone who hates her job waits on me. The cashier doesn't even look up. I start to head back to Gladys. I'm rounding the corner when I plow into a woman coming from the other direction.

"Gratciana?"

It takes her a second or two to recognize me. "Yes? Oh, hello. Frances! Hello. What are you doing here?"

"I was just going to ask you the same thing."

"It's so good to see a familiar face." We quickly embrace. "Do you have time for a cup of coffee?"

Two really bad cups of what Grandma Fiore used to call Sanka later, I'm almost up to date. Her little boy, Joey, has been getting sick a lot. I knew that. But it hasn't been getting any better. She's been doing her best to wear a brave face at work.

This morning his fever spiked and he had a seizure. She's been here all day long. We didn't know because of the BVOT Evaluation.

Her husband is at home with the other kids. She's been alone with this for hours. Poor thing. I know what it's like to be alone at a hospital.

"The doctors say it could happen again."

"Could he grow out of it?"

"It's possible. That's what they say. It's possible. What bullshit." She starts crying again. "I'm so scared Frances."

I want so badly to offer her some comfort, but maybe that's not the best choice. Maybe a firm hand is needed here.

"Get back up there."

"He's sleeping."

"He'll wake up and want to see his mother. I'll go with you."

"I just need a short break."

The impulse to yell at her is almost too strong to ignore; but I manage. In my head, however, it's a different story. The words are on the tip of my tongue. "Get your ass up there. Walk past all the women who aren't going to be taking their children home and thank God that you still have hope."

Instead I take her hand and make our way through the labyrinth to the Children's Ward. We hover over her beautiful little boy. Joey is sleeping like an angel. Poor kid. He must be exhausted. He stirs just a little bit and opens his eyes. He sees his Mom, smiles and immediately falls back asleep. I put the milk chocolate Kit Kat next to him so he has a treat when he wakes up.

In my heart I know he is going to be fine. Gratciana seems calmer now. She just needed some company. Even mothers need mothering.

I excuse myself and start following the signs back to the Emergency Room. Snippets of the day come back to me: Matt's long plaid shorts,

Desi's killer legs (that boy in good shape), Joy looking so pretty this morning. The images start to change a little: Kellie's semi-drunken breakdown, Gladys' call, Gratciana and her beautiful little boy.

Friends, the last thing I expected to find when I jumped on a plane to Orlando, Florida.

The mood is broken by a text from Matt.

"Everything ok?"

"Under control. Spendng nite @ the hosp w G."

"U want co?"

You know what? I start to get a little weepy. I do. I really do.

I was right. Sometimes we get exactly what we need.

Matt is waiting for me outside the entrance of the Emergency Room. Jeans and a baseball shirt have replaced his shorts. I give him the Gladys update and tell him about Gratciana as we make our way back to Cubicle Five.

"Hello Mrs. Nelson."

An odd look comes over Gladys' face. "Mr. O'Connell … Frances didn't tell me we were to have company."

"Surprise!" I say trying to make our time at the hospital sound like a little party we've all RSVP'd to.

"Matt, could you give us a moment, please?"

"I'll be on the other side of the curtain," he says as he exits.

"How could you do that?" Gladys hiss whispers.

"Do what?"

"Not give me time to prepare! You best have some make-up with you. I don't know what they teach you up in New York, but NEVER let a man see you without a little spackle."

"Gladys you're in the hospital. No one cares …"

"I don't care if I'm in a pine box on my way to be cremated. I want an even complexion!"

We have a not-so-extreme makeover edition. I smooth a little foundation onto her face, a bit of blush onto her cheeks and comb her hair out a bit. She starts to relax.

"Lipstick please."

I hold up two choices. "Mac Red or Dubonnet?"

"Don't you have something more pink? Those colors are awfully severe Frances." Gladys cranes her neck to peek into my purse. "I can see another one in there."

"Not my Scanty. I just bought it yesterday. I haven't even used it yet."

She looks up at me with big doe eyes and makes a big show of clutching her chest. "Of course dear, I understand."

"No shame at all." I hand her the Scanty. "Get well soon."

Matt comes back in and we settle in for a nice visit. Before I know it, the Kit Kat bars are gone. We all agree I should have given the kid the white chocolate bar instead of the milk.

The magazines come out.

It's time for the *Cosmo* quiz.

"How Seductive Are You?" purrs Gladys as she grabs her glasses from the nightstand. "I look forward to hearing your answers Matt."

"Oh no. I'm not taking that thing."

Once again Gladys starts clutching her chest. Matt tumbles like a house of cards.

"Alright. I'll do it." He shoots me a supposed to be sexy look. "You two are going to learn all my secrets."

"I knew all your secrets the minute I met you," says the saucy landlady as she blows him a kiss with her lips covered in my brand new lipstick.

We fire through the questions and start debating the finer points of seduction.

"Number Eight," says the quiz master. "Your friend brings her guy bud to dinner, and on a scale of one to ten he's an eleven! What's your nab-him plan?"

"Nab-him plan? Come on! Women don't think that way..." says Matt.

The room is silent.

"Do they?"

"Oh grow up!" yells the drunken woman from Cubicle Two.

Gladys starts in on the answers. "Answer A: You hint that a great movie's coming out next weekend. Answer B: Huh? What if he's not single? Answer C: You wait for him to make the first move. Answer D: You slip off his watch and say you're holding it hostage until he calls. Answer E: Be bold! Make the first move yourself!"

Gladys is the first to answer. "I say D. Of course most of the men I meet are so old they would forget about their watch before they call."

Matt says, "Well as a man I'm going to have to answer E. I mean, after all, that's what I did with Frances." He looks at Gladys and motions toward me. "She's more of a C."

Gladys looks at me and winks, "How insightful of you Matt."

We finish up the quiz and flip back to get the results. Gladys gets the highest score. She celebrates by yawning. I look at my watch. It's almost midnight.

"We should let you rest."

"Go home dear," Gladys says while making a shoo-ing motion. "I'll be just fine." A nurse enters and begins checking the monitors in the room.

"No, I'm going to stay here."

Matt looks at me. "I will too."

The nurse smiles, "Looks like you're going to lose this fight Mrs. Nelson." She begins taking Gladys' pulse. "Why don't you just accept that so I can get a good reading?"

"Thank you, nurse."

"Why don't you two take the next Cubicle? It's empty. That way if she needs you you'll be right next door."

I kiss Gladys on the forehead and we make our way next door, climbing into the single bed on the other side of the partition. I start to fall. Matt catches me and puts his arm around me. "For safety's sake," he says. My head falls onto his chest and for the first time I realize what a long day it has been. He kisses me on the forehead.

"Thank you for being here," I say.

"There's no place I'd rather be."

"Should you call Kellie and tell her where you are?"

He tenses. I sit up. So does he. We are eye to eye.

"Oh come on."

"Matt I can't believe you told her. Kellie…"

"... is my friend. You've got to accept that."
I say nothing. "Frances, trust me."

"I do." I really do.

"Then what's the problem?" shouts the drunk lady in Cubicle Two. "Shut up and go to sleep."

"She's right," says Matt.

I smile, kiss him on the lips and put my head back against his chest. Matt's arm returns. For the first time today it's quiet. I get lost in the rhythm of his breathing. I let myself feel not alone, as I close my eyes and fall into a grateful sleep.

CHAPTER
TWENTY-ONE

Progress has been made on Big Project Tiny. That's my nickname for the five point seven million dollar renovation of Tiny Planet. I've finished all the renderings for the individual countries represented in the attraction. France is my favorite. It's based on Mary Binger's sketchpads as a student in Paris. It's very Binger-centric without overwhelming the cultural commitment.

Look at me throwing around corporate talk!

On most projects I have to be very cost conscious. Nonprofit seems to be a theme in my life; personally and professionally. I'm used to working with companies that don't have two dimes to rub together. It's more like a nickel and penny, with the nickel being borrowed at a ridiculously high interest rate. I walk around muttering, "Bigger on Tiny, bigger on Tiny." I've looked at it from above, below, and the side, every possible angle you can get on a CAD.

I've been working at home. Desi keeps the office running. It's been three weeks and four days since Gladys was in the hospital. I might be hovering a little too much. Last week she called me mother; but so be it. I never had a chance to take care of my own parents. I even made soup. Gladys said that might send her back to the hospital, but I didn't let that stop me. Her three kids, Saylie, Valerie and Susan. None of them live here so someone has to keep an eye on her. Landlady is getting my full attention.

Not that it is all altruism. There might be a tiny something in it for me. I can work at home more.

The Vice President in Charge of Corporate Attractions Synergistic Strategies and Implementation is David Cobbler, early 50s, handsome in a disciplined way but *very* short. That's his problem, and by virtue of trickle up, mine. He's like the poster child for the Napoleon complex. During our last meeting, the Little General suggested, "Moving away from Mary Binger and toward a stronger classic Binger presence."

As I mentioned I'm getting much better at the Binger vocabulary. In corporate speak, "Suggested," means *demanded*. No negotiation. Since then I've been struggling with how to do that without destroying the cultural integrity of the piece. Of course the words, "Cultural integrity," aren't necessarily familiar to higher ups under five feet tall.

It's easy enough to come up with the individual cultural visions. Those images already exist so there's clear inspiration and it falls into a context the guests can understand. That's not enough. I want to find a greater unifying idea than, "We waited in line and want to get on the pretty boat and go for a nice ride." The challenge becomes finding something that ties it all together.

Actually, I think that applies to a lot of things. All these big, bold changes in my life have been exciting. Now it's time to integrate. It's time to make it all flow together.

I'm working at Matt's house today. He's having some problems with his cable. He's switching over to Direct TV.

Or maybe he's having problems with his Direct TV and he is switching over to cable; I forget which. It might be his Internet.

Tommy just ran some wires over from Gladys' house and now we get our cable for free. It's a sweet deal and evidently a lot less complicated than going through legal channels for your channels.

Matt was so detail oriented about it all. He had a spreadsheet and everything. It was kind of frightening. Pros and cons, cost effectiveness per channel, he documented it all. Crazy thorough. Almost obsessive.

Ouch.

Damn hand cramps.

Get up.

Okay, that's better.

HAVA NAGILA…

"Teresa? Hi. It's so good to hear from you!"

"Hello?" says the skeptic. "Do I have the right number? Is this Frances Fio…?"

"Yes," I say plopping down on the couch in Matt's den.

"Where are you? I tried you at work and …"

"I'm working at Matt's today. He had a meeting he couldn't get out of and he needed help with the cable guy."

The Next Happiest Place on Earth

"Wow. Have things gotten that serious?"

"I know. It seemed like a big step to me too."

We both pause to ponder the weight of that. For a moment there is silence. I'm the first to break.

"So how are you?"

"Eh."

"Eh?" That's not like Teresa. "Why, eh?"

"Rachel and I went shopping for Bar Mitzvah outfits and everything was so picked over. So last season."

"Where did you go?"

"To the City. 34th Street."

"Not which neighborhood," I say rolling my eyes. "Where did you *shop*?"

"Oh! Macy's and Lord & Taylor for me. Lane Bryant and Forever 21 for Rachel."

"Forever 21?"

"Yeah. I thought it was a shop for big girls that stopped trying to fool themselves. You know forever *size* 21. Turns out it's more of a "I wouldn't let my daughter dress like that" place."

"Yeah," I say. "They might as well have an anorexia counselor on staff. I asked for a size eight once. The only thing I left with was some attitude from the sales clerk. Find anything?"

I hear Teresa grinding coffee beans in the background. "A couple nice things at Macy's, a skirt, on the long side, sky blue. I'll have to wear dark hose with it."

"Your veins?"

"Yeah. Also got a drop-dead gorgeous house robe. Very comfy."

"And Rachel?" I ask as I start crossing into the kitchen.

189

"Not so much. Everything was very old lady. She's a twelve year old girl, not some Nana flying in from Florida for the free shrimp."

"Hey, watch with the Florida …"

I look for anything caffeinated in the refrigerator. There's only Gatorade and a couple of oranges well on their way to becoming dried fruit. I'll pass.

"Sorry."

"What are you going to do?"

"Who's got the time to look? The Internet I guess."

I go back to my laptop and jump onto Google. Teresa and I browse. We navigate through sites like ladiesofsize.com, rubenesque.com, and tonsoffashion.org. Teresa is getting frustrated. I can tell by the clatter of her acrylic nails on the keyboard. She rejects everything. Too mature. Too immature. Too revealing. Not sparkly enough. Too sparkly. Blah. Blah. Blah. The excuses start to blur.

I change my mind about the Gatorade Fierce Wild Berry and head back to the kitchen.

"Teresa, is this really about the dresses?"

She puffs out and sounds a bit haughty. "What do you mean? Are you implying that I'm scared of being alone with my husband after the kids leave the house?"

Where did *that* come from? "Uh - no. Of course not. I'm just saying the kids probably need less attention these days. I know I'd feel…"

"What do you know Frances? You don't have kids."

I stop dead in my tracks.

The silence is heavy.

"Oh my God," she gasps. "I'm so sorry."

I can't respond and start to feel my throat tighten. It takes me an eternity to come up with "Let's just shop, okay?" I turn and head back to the computer.

Eventually, we find a really cute dress. It's a little to the left of prim, enough to bother Teresa, which is a nice bonus. She doesn't care for the sequins or the halter-top. She starts to object but gives in eventually; not because I'm right, which I am, but because she's still feeling bad for what she said. She calls Rachel to the computer to look.

"Auntie Frances, it's perfect!" Her tone changes, "But Mom and Dad said we couldn't spend that much."

"It's my treat honey."

"Really?"

"Yeah."

"Thank you!" she squeals. "Thank you *so much*. It's like you knew just what I'd want."

"Be sure to tell your Mom that."

"Huh?"

"Never mind."

Teresa returns to the phone. "Listen Frances, about earlier? I'm sorry…"

"I know. I know. I'd rather not talk about it, okay? It's fine."

"But…"

"Let's talk about something else."

"Okay." More pause. "How are things with Matt? What's his house like?"

"It's more of a home. It feels so permanent. You can tell just by looking around that Matt's marriage was good."

"Yours was too; for a long time. You forget that because…"

"His marriage was like, thriving."

"Until she died. That's generally signals the end of a thriving marriage."

"Teresa…"

"No. Hear me out. You both have a marriage behind you. So what? Move on. It's time"

"I don't want to fail again Teresa."

"I won't let you talk that way. You've never failed. Things may not have worked out, but…"

I cut her off. "No. My marriage died. The man who was my husband is still alive. He's just not my husband anymore."

"Que sera, sera – what will be, will be."

"That's future tense. I'm talking about the past. What has been has been."

"That too."

"Yeah, well I'm impatient. I want to know more about Matt. I think he doesn't tell me because it involves his old life."

"Frances," says my sister the master spy. "You're all alone, in his house. That's the, excuse the expression, mother lode when you want to get to know a guy."

"Really?"

"Yeah. How do you think I found out about Larry's subscription to *Penthouse?* He ran out to get us bagels one morning when we first started dating. I was all over his apartment like an episode of CSI."

"What did you do?"

"I cancelled his subscription. PS, the improvement in our love life was sudden and drastic. Of course that was before Internet porn, but he doesn't seem to notice I put parental controls on his laptop."

"Well I don't think I could do that. The snooping, I mean."

"Riiiiight," says my sister the private investigator. "Listen, I've got to go. Rachel has choir practice. Oh! Before I forget, there's a concert the night before the Bar Mitzvah. She'd love it if you could come. It's like a Broadway show, what these kids do. One time…"

Pre-emptive strike. "I'll be there. I promise."

"Okay then, go snoop."

"I'm not going to…"

"Riiiiight." She pulls the phone away from her mouth. "Rachel! Get in the van. We're going to be late!" She comes back. "Love you." With an air kiss to the phone, she's gone and I'm left alone with my thoughts.

My nature says don't snoop, but I have become distrustful of my nature. Clearly that means snooping.

I yawn. Rationalization is exhausting work.

I wander around Matt's house with a more deliberate eye and start to realize how much we have in common.

He seems a little trapped in the past too.

The pillows on the couch are ruffled and floral and worn; either he hasn't noticed or he wants to hold onto a memory. I don't know which. The dried flowers on the shelves have a layer of dust on them and have become home to a cobweb or two. I move to clean it but stop myself. Why does doing something nice for him feel presumptuous?

I make my way through the books on the shelf. Thia must have been a reader. It could be Matt, but I'm guessing they belonged to her. Of course he is probably downloading books now. He seems tethered to his iPad sometimes. There are lots of Anne Rice and Stephen King, gothic romances, and a stack of Oprah Book Club titles.

Yeah. These are old.

I hit the jackpot, four yearbooks from Robert M. Lafollette High School in Madison, WI. I grab 1991, good cover, pleasing to the eye, easy to read. I open it. On page 75, between Marty Thering and a pretty girl named Kristina Thomas, an eighteen-year-old incorrectly alphabetized Matt O'Connell stares back at me smiling as though he has been waiting for me for a long time.

I walk to the kitchen, make a quick cup of tea and settle in for a little reading. My fingers run to the index. Page 32, Student Council, Page 35, Matt must wear contacts now because he is wearing glasses on this page. He was a Varsity Mathlete. What the hell is that? Keep reading. I see a woman in horn-rimmed glasses wearing a dress from the Johnson Administration. She must be the advisor.

You equal a good person.
A good person equals you.
Now that's reflexive!
Way to help us win State!
Best Wishes, Mrs. Beverly Lampe

Oh my God. Competitive math! There's no way we would have hung out together in high school.

I probably would have made fun of Matt and his friends during third period lunch.

Page 97, Concert Band, he's the first chair sax from the looks of it. That makes sense. The band kids were usually good at math. The picture is a little blurry but it looks like that's him playing in a concert. The girl next to him, Krissy Kalschuer according to the IDs, has a funny look on her face. Maybe he hit a bad note.

Page 102, Matt O'Connell as Mister Gibbs, fall production of Thornton Wilder's *Our Town*. I never would have guessed that Matt was involved in things like that.

Okay now, this makes sense. Page 114, Varsity Volleyball. He's sitting right next to the team manager, some kid with a perm named Tom Terpening. Matt looks so shy. The coach, let's see, okay, his name is Mr. Halverson has his arm around Matt, turning him toward the camera.

I have to see more. Back to the index.

Nope. That's it. No other listings for Matt.

Wait.

There are two more kids with the last name O'Connell. Siblings? How many people could have that last name?

Page 176, Katie O'Connell. She must be his sister. Pretty girl. Pages 152 and 168, Norman O'Connell. Nice picture. Flip. Flip.

Oh.

Matt's brother was in Special Olympics. He hasn't mentioned having a brother with special needs.

I wonder what that was like.

I look up. On a shelf near the table I'm sitting at is a picture of Matt, his brother and sister. They are older. Katie has gained what I'm guessing is considerable baby weight, which she wears well. Norman is trying to look away from the camera. Matt's arm is around him and they're all laughing. The two blurry people in the foreground must be their folks. They look nice.

I hope it was a good day.

A dried flower falls out of the yearbook. I trace it back to the prom page. If I Could Turn Back Time by Cher was the theme, righteous tune kids. Clearly there was a gay kid on the Prom Committee. I suppose there always is.

There's P.J. Flanigan and Camilla Hammer, the King and Queen of Lafollette High School. There's Matt dancing with, caption please, okay, Bonnie Schulz, who, one second please, according to the Index was Editor in Chief of the yearbook. She must have given him this dried yellow rose with Babies Breath, his boutonniere.

Did she sign an autograph page? Flip. Flip.

Here it is, on the National Honor Society page. Also advised by Mrs. Beverly Lampe. Let's see … what did Matt's prom date have to say?

Matt – I wish we could do it all again. It's been a great year and no MATTer what, I will always love you and treasure the memories. You're the best.

Love, Bon

So there you have it. Matt O'Connell, class of 1991, was and is the kind of guy you can't forget.

The mood is broken by a ringing doorbell.

The cable guy is here.

I leave him to his work. As I round the corner out of the den I notice that a frame on the wall has been taken down. It left one of those dirty outlines. I find it face down on the credenza nearby.

It's a wedding picture of him and Thia. I only look at it for a second and then I carefully put it back where I found it; where Matt intended for it to stay.

I go back to the dried flowers arrangement on the bookcase in the living room and start cleaning. I spend the rest of the afternoon tidying up the house, careful not to disturb the memories. The man from Direct TV leaves. So do I.

Publix is a couple miles away. I buy two good, thick steaks, nice big Idaho potatoes, some rolls, sweet butter, mushrooms, pearl onions, asparagus, a small apple pie, and some vanilla ice cream.

I drive back to his house and time everything perfectly; just the way my Mom taught me to. Matt walks through the door at 5:30. If I had rented twins with an eating disorder this could be *Full House.*

I hand Matt an ice cold Rolling Rock.

"Thank you." His eyes wander up and his smile gets quizzical. "What's that music?"

"A saxophone CD I downloaded today. I thought you might like it."

Our eyes meet again for a moment. Then I feel a little shy, a little self-conscious. I look away, over his shoulder and back toward the shelf of family photos. This time another one catches my eye. It must have been taken in Mexico or somewhere else tropical. His brother Norman and Thia are cheering him on, as Matt dives off a cliff. There is no hesitation on his face. He looks joyful and confident as he jumps into the water with both eyes open.

I'm not sure that I'm totally living in the present. Part of me might be too in touch with my baggage; but maybe that's okay.

Maybe that's just goes with being number two.

"Matt, can I ask you a question?"

He kisses me. "Anything you want."

"Would you come with me to my nephew's Bar Mitzvah?"

True to his nature, he just jumps right in.

CHAPTER
TWENTY-TWO

HAVA NAGILA, HAVA…

Doesn't she know I should be on my way to the airport?

"Hello?"

"Hi! Mother of the Bar Mitzvah boy calling! Things are crazy here." For emphasis she makes it a three syllable word. "Cah-ray-zee! I've got a Frances to-do list that gets longer every second."

"Teresa, I can't talk. Tommy is waiting to take me to the airport."

"Yeah, listen about that…"

"What? Now you're trying to control how I get to the airport?"

"You with the mouth, shut it and listen."

Her wish. My command.

"Tommy left me a voice mail last night," she continues. "He said something about bringing a girl with him to the Bar Mitzvah."

Tommy has always been a little bit of a man-whore; just a little. Not intentionally. It's nothing mean. He just approaches women like he approaches food. You offer him a meal and he's going to take it. Human nature.

"Elena Garastofolis?" I ask. She's his off more often than on girlfriend in Queens. They've been hot and cold since they were in high school. "I heard through my friend Trina who does Elena's nails that she was dating Gus Valases."

"The mortgage broker that works for her father?"

"Yeah," I respond. "Do we know another Gus Valases?"

"Oy. A match made on spread sheets. So it can't be her. Get him to tell you who it is," Teresa orders.

"Please? Get Tommy to talk? I'd have more luck with Katzenberg."

"Listen I need her full name for the computer calligrapher to finish her job. What am I supposed to put on the place card?" asks Mother Frantic.

"The cheap trick banging our brother?"

We laugh, make plans to meet in the City that afternoon and hang up. After several unsuccessful attempts Katz sits on the suitcase and it closes. I start to wheel it out the door. The cat follows me batting at the luggage tags until a small lizard catches his attention.

"You ready or what?" says my brother the keeper of secrets. "Let's get going. We should have left twenty minutes ago." I throw him the keys.

"You drive." He starts to put my bags in the trunk.

Gladys comes out of the house in her robe, quickly checking to see that none of the neighbors can see her. She spies Tommy and smoothes her hair into place before hurrying over to us.

"Darling I just wanted to say goodbye before you left on your trip." We hug. She is the first to break the embrace. "Do not worry about me. I've got Mister Tom here until he leaves to join you in New York City."

"What about while I'm gone?" says Tommy.

"I'm sure Joy would be happy to ccme over," I say.

A funny look passes between Gladys and Tommy.

What have they got against Joy?

"Don't worry precious girl. I talked to my daughter Saylie and she is going to drive over from Sarasota for a few days."

I move to hug her goodbye one more time. As we embrace I put my hand in her pocket and pull out an unopened pack of Capri Menthol Ultra Lights.

"What are these?" I demand.

"How in the world did those get there?" asks the suddenly demure Mrs. Nelson. "I haven't worn this house coat in eons."

"Then you won't mind me taking them," I say.

Tommy snatches them from me. "I'll take them. Neither of you can be trusted with cigarettes." I hug Gladys goodbye again, and this time I find a disposable Bic lighter in the other pocket. I confiscate it, Tommy takes it away from me and soon we are heading east toward the Orlando International Airport in the biggest car on the road.

Tommy is never one for conversation so I start digging through the tapes to find some tunes. The Carpenters start singing "We've Only Just Begun."

How am I going to get Tommy to talk about this girl he's bringing to the Bar Mitzvah? I stare at him for a second. That sweatshirt Joy helped me pick out looks nice on him. He looks happy. Healthy. Nice haircut too. It's usually so unmanageable. The new cut he got really does a good job with the waviness.

"Hey Frances, could we talk for a minute?"

What the hell? I could count the number of times I've heard that from my brother on one finger. Tommy wanting to talk is like hearing Courtney Love ordered milk with her dinner.

"Sure," I say in a nonchalant voice. "What's up?"

"Uh – I've wanted to tell you…"

Silence.

"Yes?"

"That…" pause, "that…" pause, "the car is pulling to the left a little. I'm going to check that out while you're gone."

"Okay. Thank you."

He hits the steering wheel. "And…"

"Yes?"

"I can pay rent this month. Thanks for floating me."

"Is there anything else you wanted to tell me?" Good *Lord*. I should get a dental license. This is like pulling teeth.

He takes a big gulp of air, swallows hard and spills. "Okay, just listen, alright?' I nod. "I've been seeing someone and didn't want to tell you about it because I didn't want to make it seem like a big deal but then it became a big deal and it was like, weird to tell you because we'd been seeing each other for a while. But now she's coming to the Bar Mitzvah with me, so we thought it was time to come clean. I mean, you know, we wanted you to know for a while now. Actually, we've been dropping hints but you never caught on."

"Hints? There have been hints?"

"Yeah. Joy said…"

"What's Joy got to do with this? You talked to Joy about this before you talked to me?"

"I talk to her all the time."

"Why?"

"For God's sake Frances, I'm talking about Joy!"

"I know that but could we please stay focused? What about the girl that you're dating? Doesn't she have a problem with you turning to Joy all time?"

Tommy just stares at me.

Oh.

"You're dating Joy?"

"Finally!" he says, looking toward heaven. "Yeah. I'm dating Joy."

"Why didn't you tell me?'

"Because she's your girlfriend and I don't got the best reputation with women."

"You're right." The realization hits me. "What's different this time? I swear to God, if you hurt her, I'll…"

"Would you shut up and listen?" I oblige. For a second there I sounded like *Teresa*. "I know what an asshole her husband was; cheating on her and all those mind games. No one's going to treat her like that again."

He pauses, searching for the right words. "It's serious Frances. I'm in love."

We pull up to the airport.

I hug my little brother goodbye. There's a rent-a-cop urging him to keep moving as it is a federal violation to blah, blah, blah. There's no time to tell him that I'm happy for him but that's okay. He's never been one who needed words.

As I settle into my Economy Comfort seat I feel pangs of Bar Mitzvah anticipation. I haven't seen my extended family for a while. I hadn't given it much thought. I hope Matt is ready to be thoroughly inspected. I hope no one feels the need to walk him through family history.

Oh God. I hadn't thought of that either.

I distract myself by watching CNN on the in-flight television service, which always freaks me out a little. What if something earth shattering happened while we were in the air? What if there was a news report about our plane? My paranoia entertains me right up until we begin our descent into New York.

We dive into a fluffy blanket of clouds. As they part we follow the Hudson River along the edge of Manhattan. My eye scans the skyline to get my bearings. I see familiar buildings. I start to anticipate feeling the warmth of being home.

It doesn't come.

Instead I feel the accomplishment of having moved on.

I decide to linger. It takes LaGuardia forever to deliver baggage. Why rush?

The two suitcases arrive a little worse for wear; they are, after all, knock-offs of the real thing. I balance them on top of each other and awkwardly snake through the very long queue for cabs.

My mindless zigzag is interrupted abruptly. "Frances! Frances Bettinger!" I look over my shoulder and see Maureen Dudley, a girlfriend from college who married well and stopped calling. I haven't seen her since my wedding. Looking at her is a trip on the road not taken. Her hair is lighter than I remember – probably to soften her face, which despite her smile betrays a touch of sadness and reserve. She at rushes me for an awkward hug. The bars of the taxi line separate us.

I try to smile but that doesn't feel right. Feelings come rushing back; wanting people to know that I'm not beyond repair but being scared they'll think I'm not in enough pain. I embrace her longer and harder than I normally would because I'm dreading the conversation that follows.

"Ladies keep moving," barks the near retirement bowling pin of a dispatcher who clearly could give a damn about reunions in his line.

I should send a thank you note to the guy that barks at us to keep the line moving. Each time the line turns there is another reunion with Maureen.

"You look great."

"I heard about you and Paul."

"I read about your parents. I can't believe what they printed in the papers."

Finally it is my turn for a cab. I hear Maureen yell, "I'm headed to midtown. Want to share a cab?"

"Can't. Headed to Brooklyn and in a crazy hurry. Sorry!" I soften my tone by throwing in a warm, "You look great." I stand there awkwardly for a moment before reminding myself that any action is preferable to none, so I gather my bags and

Greg Triggs

head toward the bright yellow cab. My cab driver has a name that is only consonants. I don't think he speaks English. Thank God.

"West 51st Street, in Manhattan, please. The Washington Jefferson Hotel. It's between eighth and ninth." After an anxious nod from Cabby No Vowels, we take off with a lurch. The cab smells strongly of incense but at least it's clean. I roll down the window and enjoy the rush of fresh air and exhaust fumes.

We make our way toward the City and I lose myself in familiar sights. As we pass Flushing Meadows I spy the Unisphere, still standing guard over the Time Capsules planted after the 1965 World's Fair, still guarding childhood memories.

The cab becomes our very used but my dad can fix anything 1976 bronze with wooden trim Pontiac Grand Safari station wagon. Dionne Warwick is singing a Burt Bacharach tune. My parents sit in the front seat. Tommy is between them lost in his own world quietly playing with a Matchbox Bat-Mobile. My mother is spraying her hair with Aqua Net. The car fills with fluorocarbons that I'm sure will contribute to any respiratory problems I have later in life. My father winces but says nothing. He just smiles and rolls down a window, proud to have such a pretty wife.

Teresa, with a typical sense of entitlement that will carry her far into middle age, has the backseat all to herself. She's wearing a crisp tennis dress with a pleated skirt. A white band is pushing back her long, thick, brown hair. If memory serves she has a perm. Her bangs touch the roof of the car. She's applying another coat of lipstick in anticipation of her lesson

206

from a handsome pro, whose name I can no longer remember. He was Italian or Greek and lived in Astoria. He played in the US Open a couple years later. We all watched it together. My parents had a big party with a bunch of neighbors and the whole family. Cousin Tony, who was maybe twelve at the time, kept trying to get me to bet on the match.

I'm in the car too with our new puppy, a black lab named *Senor Ocho;* so named because he was our eighth pet. The two of us are sitting in the way back, which faces to the rear and keeps me more in touch with where I have been than where I am going.

"Ma, he's so cute," Teresa squeals. "I can barely hold onto my racquet, my hands get too sweaty."

Teresa was using money she earned by babysitting to take lessons at the Tennis Center, not that she was all that interested in the sport. As she put it she wanted to meet, "The right kind of boy."

Always with the strategies that one.

Teresa and I grew up sharing a cotton candy pink bedroom that followed the rooflines of my parent's house in Forest Hills. We had twin beds, side by side with a nightstand in between. A poster of Joey Lawrence hung over my bed. Teresa had one of Gregory Harrison or the replacement hunk from *Trapper John, M.D.* She hoped to marry a doctor and thought it would be good karma.

How I would love to tell that girl that she met Larry Teitelbaum CPA while they were both working at the Rutger's Cafeteria on a work-study grants. Teresa was mixing imitation potato flakes and Larry was looking for rubber gloves so he could clean the grease trap. She'd hate that. She'd be totally inconsolable.

I'd be honest with her. I'd say the lows would be very low but that the highs would be higher than she could ever imagine. It would do no good to tell that to a teenage Teresa. She doesn't listen now. Why would I expect her to listen then?

So why bother thinking about it? Keep moving.

Flash forward to the present. I'm back in the cab, speeding toward Manhattan to make new memories and confront a few old ones.

I check my make-up with the mirror in my compact and fix a little mascara damage. "Frances Fiore," I say to myself aloud, "you're back."

The cab driver politely nods. "Yes ma'am."

And so it goes. Travel all you want. Certain things just don't change.

I'm still a ma'am.

CHAPTER
TWENTY THREE

We pull up to the Washington Jefferson, or WJ as locals call it. It has always seemed like a charming, well-maintained, hotel most importantly the type that doesn't cater to school groups. There will be no marching bands doing tuba drills in the lobby.

I chose it because the price is good and I know the neighborhood. Its only disadvantage is that it's directly across the street from my old apartment; the one I shared with Paul. Still, for $229 a night and free high speed Internet I'll deal.

The neon cross on top of Saint Paul House still blinks, SIN WILL FIND YOU, serving as a beacon to the lost souls of Manhattan. We always meant to have a Christmas picture taken on our front stoop with the lit cross in the background. Oh well.

The bell captain in front of the hotel is busy talking and texting. I schlep my bags up the steps of the hotel myself. I don't want to give into my frustration and ruin my mood. Instead, I visualize the shower and fresh clothes waiting for me. I can already feel the pulsating jets on my skin when the fantasy is snatched away.

Teresa is leaning against the front desk.

"Come on, there must be some sort of discount," she says in her sweetest voice. "Give a girl a break. Do you take Triple A?"

The clerk, probably a struggling actor or model, shakes his perfect head and shrugs his broad shoulders reminding me that life is not fair. He's prettier than I am.

"No Triple A? How about Triple Sec?" She throws back her head and laughs.

"Okay, okay, I'll give your sister the corporate rate," he says in a surprisingly feminine voice. He smiles and scans the room for upper management. "Don't tell anyone I did it, okay?"

Teresa throws the key card down the front of her blouse. The clerk couldn't care less. If he noticed at all it was because he was checking for a label.

I'm checked in and unpacked before I know it. To say the room is small would be unfair. In most cities it would be a glorified closet, but it's clean and gets good sunlight. No complaints from me. I take a quick shower while Teresa watches *The View* on Channel 9. She loves that show. Joy Behar is her role model.

Through fresh eyes and the buzz of Neutrogena Sesame Oil moisturizer, nine bucks at Walgreens, I finally get a good look at my sister.

"What?" she says carefully posing and totally aware of the fact that I'm staring at her.

"You look different." There is a pause.

"What? I lost some weight for the party." She tosses her hair for maximum effect.

"There's more."

"Some highlights…"

"And?"

"Dr. Lowenstein gave me a chemical peel."

"And?"

"Alright already. Some Botox. I had a Botox session," she says defensively; which, of course, doesn't register on her face at all. "You like?"

"Sure. Yeah." Perhaps that took too long? She bristles. I diplomatically add, "You look great," meaning it for the most part. It's just unsettling is all; like seeing your sister in an exhibit at Madame Tussauds Wax Museum, which perhaps not so coincidentally is only nine blocks from here. Maybe she's on a lunch break.

Her breasts look bigger too. No way she'd get a boob job and not tell me, right? She's at least a cup size bigger. Must be all those tasting sessions with the caterer.

I grab my most comfortable pair of jeans but think better of it. Teresa dressed for a day in the City. She's wearing a flattering Gabardine suit that showcases her new look very nicely. Her legs look great. She must be going to the gym. I throw on a white tuxedo shirt and a fitted skirt. Best to remind her that until she gets ribs removed my waist is still smaller than hers.

We head west to 47th and 9th to Room Service for lunch, which is one of those rare, trendy restaurants that actually have decent food. My Pad Thai with mock duck is so good that for a moment I actually forget my older sister looks younger than me. *— wrong but ok. sounds good.*

Teresa hands me a list of errands and things she wants me to do for the Bar Mitzvah. It's overwhelming. Uptown. Downtown. East. West. She has me running all over the City.

"Can Larry's family help with some of this?"

"They are. They're taking care of the errands in Queens and on Long Island. This is the Manhattan to-do list," she says. "I would have put someone else on them, but since you insisted on staying in the City instead of with me…"

My sister, she punishes with errands.

"I'll do my best," I say to the blackmailer. "But, you've got to remember I have meetings while I'm here too."

I was able to avoid using the vacation time I have not yet accrued (my HR vocabulary is expanding) by doing research for Tiny Planet at the Queens Museum. They were endowed with many of Mary Binger's original sketches by her estate.

Even Kellie agreed that it was an untapped resource totally worth exploring. I'm doing it anyway. Hopefully it will give me a new perspective on the project. I sure could use some.

Teresa does her best to put a pathetic expression on her frozen face. "Any help you can give me would be appreciated," my sister says as she wipes a dab of barbeque sauce off the corner of her mouth. "Larry has been so preoccupied; I've ended up doing most of the work myself, which is, of course, my joy. There's just no way I could do everything. I'm only one woman."

"What's up with Larry?"

"Haven't I told you? We made up with Cousin Tony and he is back on the guest list. The little prick agreed to sell the garage."

"Really?"

"Yeah. Larry's putting together the deal. We'll get our money out of it after all."

"Well, that's good news, I guess."

We stare at each other for a second. Both of us are silently saying goodbye to another part of our childhood, saying goodbye to another part of our parents.

"Larry said a franchise came through and tried to low ball them on the price. They're holding out for an independent operator if they can find one."

"A family maybe? That would be nice."

"Yeah. I thought so too." Teresa grabs my hand from across the table. "It's so good to have you here. I miss you every day sweetie, every single day."

I look at Teresa or Newresa as I am starting to think of her, and get a little sad. Her kids are growing up, her husband is distracted by his career and business deals, Tommy and I aren't here. She has to settle for meddling in our lives long distance via phone and text. Even though she looks much younger, she suddenly strikes me as being older than I ever realized.

"Hey listen! I found out about Tommy's girlfriend."

"You mean Joy?" Teresa says as she calls the waiter over for a refill on her coffee.

"You knew?"

"Yeah. For about, what?" She does air math with her right index finger, "six weeks maybe? Tommy asked me to get you to ask him about it. Mission accomplished," she adds, checking off another item on her mental to-do list.

"Why didn't he just tell me?"

"Yeah, that's going to happen."

Okay. She has a point but still, "I don't see why."

"Frances, you've been a little self-absorbed lately."

What the hell? "How can you say that?" I say incredulously. "How long have you felt this way?"

"About four years, but don't worry. It's no big deal. You're coming out of it and it's wonderful to have you back."

I don't know whether to fight the criticism or accept the compliment. I chose the latter. It's less effort.

We move onto the Bar Mitzvah and the headaches she has had planning it. Me, the self-absorbed one, gets her mind onto happier thoughts. She tells me all about her outfit, the centerpieces, and the gifts that have been arriving. She asks about Matt. I describe down to the buttons the gorgeous new suit he let me pick out for the trip.

Teresa and I agree that he deserves a new tie, so we pay the bill and jump a cab to Macy's, which as luck would have it, is holding a Customer Appreciation Day. Fifteen percent off if I use the Macy's AmEx Card that I am holding in my hot little hand.

We get out on the corner of 34th and Broadway and walk through the classic, brass handled, revolving door of the World's Greatest Store. The minute I get inside and breathe the familiar air of retail, I get a tingle. I finally feel like I'm home.

"This is the best," I say to Teresa.

"What? They got Macy's in Orlando."

"Yeah, and they have the Statue of Liberty in Vegas. It's just not the same. This is the real thing."

I look around. The soaring ceilings, the ornate chandeliers, the creamy beige marble, and the inlaid wood take me to another era when clothes were less casual, men wore fedoras, and the pace of living was more gracious. You turn a corner in New York and everything changes. It's magical. Outside everything is dirty and noisy. In here, everything is perfect.

With all of the best intentions we make our way towards the Men's Department. Of course, in order to get there we have no choice but to go through Accessories, Cologne, Jewelry and Make-up. The girl at the Clinique counter, her nametag says Sharona, is really good. She diplomatically gets Teresa to try a softer palette with very smoky eyes and a softer cheek. It looks terrific. Teresa must not be worried about money anymore. She buys more than $200 worth of product after Sharona compliments her on her flawless complexion.

Sharona looks at me and suggests Repairwear Deep Wrinkle Concentrate for Face and Eye as Teresa mouths, "Doctor Lowenstein…"

She's still gloating when we finally arrive at the Men's Department. I get lost in the colors and textures of all the different ties, quietly wondering which one looks most like Matt. Teresa holds up a yellow Ben Sherman that calls attention to itself. Not his style at all. The suit we bought is charcoal gray with little flecks of white running throughout. We also found a crisp white on white pinstripe shirt with

French Cuffs. Tommy lent him a pair of my Dad's cufflinks to wear.

For a minute or two I run my fingers over the ties, hoping the right one will find me and eventually it does. I happen across a Henry Jacobson display and spy a deep red tie made of silk with a geometric design and thin random, gray stripes crossing each other throughout. It's perfect. I hand the tie to the sales clerk, another aspiring model/actor making due with a survival job. He begins wrapping it in tissue paper.

"This Matt, he's good," says Teresa as she walks up to the counter.

"What do you mean?"

"He's sneaking up on you," she says with a sly smile.

Her words immediately strike me as true but I can't give her that and the moment at the Clinique counter. "I don't know what you're talking about."

"You miss him. You've been gone for a few hours and you miss him. It's nice to see."

"Oh, that's so sweet," says the sales clerk. He throws a couple of cologne samples in the bag and sends us on our way. We start walking toward the exit, careful to avoid the allure of the higher floors.

We're almost at the 7th Avenue doors when I hear someone say, "Frances?" I keep walking, certain they can't be calling me; after all, Frances doesn't live here anymore.

"Frances Fiore is that you?"

I turn and look over my shoulder as two familiar faces rush toward us. It's Lorna Pehl and Mary Joseph Landvik. I used to work for them in Brooklyn Heights, but they clearly aren't in Brooklyn anymore. They look fabulous. Both of them scream Manhattan from their shimmering hair to their Sesto Meucci pumps. One carries a Coach briefcase and the other has one of this season's most expensive Kate Spade bags. I instantly feel the typical mix of happiness and jealousy that accompanies reunions with people doing better than you are.

In quick succession I hear of one triumph after another. Their small advertising agency is no longer small. They just sealed a deal with Macy's to do their designer co-op advertising. They did the entire PR campaign for the opening of a Hopper exhibit at the Met. They're taking a meeting with Radio City to do all the promotional work on the Christmas Show.

It finally ends when Mary Joseph says, "On Tuesdays we teach a class to single teen mothers on how to properly accessorize."

"What have you been up to?" Lorna asks.

Teresa jumps in and updates them with a PR spin of her own. She should open an agency, Kvetching Sister, Incorporated. According to Teitelbaum, I'm pretty much in charge of the entire Planet Binger operation and Orlando, Florida is the Paris of the southeast.

"Don't you miss New York?" Mary Joseph asks as she points her implants toward me. "I'd just die if I ever had to leave Manhattan. I'd die!"

"Well," I say, trying to sound pleasant, "I chose to leave. I didn't *have* to." I resist the urge to continue and remind her that I used to work on a card table in her kitchen in Brooklyn.

"Listen," says Lorna, "if you ever decide you're ready to return to the real world, give us a call. I always loved your work." She hands me her business card. "We'd take you back in a New York minute."

"It's great to see you Frances. You fell off the face of the Earth for a while there," Mary Joseph says with sincerity. She moves to hug me. "Glad you're back in the game hon."

I start to beat myself up for being cynical, for listening to my insecurities. We've all changed. I was being too judgmental. After all, they love my work. They want me back. I just got a job offer.

They offered me a job.

Mary Joseph breaks the embrace adding, "E-mail us your address. We still have the Sun Block Council as a client. We'll ship you a case of SPF 45."

She touches my chin and gives it a little squeeze.

"I think you've been getting too much sun."

CHAPTER
TWENTY FOUR

Some sort of rattling sound just ended a great night's sleep. For a moment I wasn't even sure where I was. The sheets weren't mine. The light was unfamiliar. I reached for Katzenberg or Matt, but then remembered neither of them was there. It took me a second or two to realize that a garbage truck or a Blitzkrieg Tank had just gone past the window and woke me up.

I throw on my boots and hit the street. The burst of fresh air and the noise of traffic are almost as effective as caffeine, but not quite. I walk past two Starbucks on the way to my favorite bagel shop on 8th Avenue, a daily habit when I lived in New York. They put their effort into the bagels, not the décor.

Lupe, the owner, is behind the counter.

"Girl, where you been?" she asks.

"In Orlando."

"What the hell were you doing there?"

"Working. I live there now."

"For real? No joke?"

I shake my head.

"That must be why I got more cinnamon raisin bagels at the end of the day."

"That's what I'm here for."

"Toasted brown, with butter and a large black coffee, no sugar, right?"

Coffee, bagel and I head over to Central Park. On the way I pick up a *New York Post* hoping that Page Six and Cindy Adams will offer a nice little distraction.

I make it through the never-ending road construction that has defined the circumference of Columbus Circle for as long as I can remember and enter the Park.

Lorna and Mary Joseph offered me a job. If I want to, I can come back to New York.

If I want to. That's the big dilemma.

What to do?

The only free bench is filthy. I open the Post and sit on Cindy Adam's face.

I sip my coffee and ponder. I eat half my bagel and then remember I need to look good for the Bar Mitzvah. I throw the rest of my breakfast to the pigeons.

My first grade teacher told us during reading class that if you don't know what something means, look around it. That will usually help you figure it out. Later I learned that meant context; study the context to figure out the solution.

So I start looking around. It's still early. The tourists aren't out yet. The sidewalks bordering Central Park West are full of New Yorkers rushing to work so they can pay for their tiny apartments. It makes me kind of sad. They all look so preoccupied, anxious and *pasty*.

In Florida everyone glows.

I reach into the pocket of my jeans and pull out Teresa's list. It's long. I feel like a magician pulling a scarf out of his sleeve.

I run back to the hotel to get my purse. I stop by a deli to get a bottle of water and a few other essentials. I can take the 1 downtown.

As I walk east on West 50th Street my mind wanders to a rainy day a few years ago. I was rushing to a meeting in the Village. I stopped at Duane Reade to buy a pack of cigarettes. It was taking forever but I was desperate. I *had* to have a cigarette. I still had the change in my hand while running with a lit Marlboro Menthol Light trying to get as much nicotine as possible before I caught my train.

"Take your time," said a voice from inside the shadows of the subway entrance. "You just missed the train." A short woman, about the size of David Cobbler, barely five feet tall, was wearing layers and layers of clothing despite the fairly warm and humid spring day. At her side was a well taken care of Golden Retriever. I later learned he was named Gershwin after the theater down the street. His coat was shiny and thick. It looked as though he had just been brushed. The woman's hair was a little matted but her face was clean. The thing I remember best was her smile. It was sincere.

Normally I look away from homeless people. I usually stare at the sidewalk and keep on walking. That day I smiled back. We traded introductions. That's how I found out she was named Sarah, the first homeless person whose name I bothered to learn.

I knew she wanted money. I'm not a fool; but she intrigued me. Whatever her challenges were, she had figured out a way to make a contribution. She told me not to rush so I got to finish my cigarette. That alone was worth the change in my pocket.

Sarah's support of my habit led to a new one. I started to make sure I always had a spare buck or two. Once in a while, I'd stop to buy some dog food for Gershwin before catching the train. Helping them became a ritual for me. Even after the accident, I'd check on Sarah and Gershwin when I was up to it.

One night, an unexpected cold front hit the City. Not that it should have mattered to me. I hadn't been outside for about a week; hadn't showered either. I was the newest member of the Matted Hair Club. Cleaning myself might have interfered with my constant television viewing.

The latest weather model on Channel Seven made me frantic when he announced that evening's record low temperatures.

I threw on my jacket, ran down four flights of stairs and rushed to the subway station. I gave Sarah a hundred bucks from our under the counter cash stash to get a room for the night. I had to know she and Gershwin were safe.

I came home to four hundred and fifty square feet of pure tension from Paul.

"I don't understand," he said clearly hurt. "I can't get you to eat or shower or talk to me, but a homeless person can bring you back to life?"

How could I defend myself? I didn't understand it either. I just did what I thought was right.

Why couldn't Paul trust me? How could my husband not understand?

Knowing that someone needs you gives you purpose, maybe even hope. No matter how bad things get knowing you're needed gives you a reason to go on. I did my best to help Sarah. Sarah took care of Gershwin. I never saw a kid walk past that dog without smiling. It was like that old shampoo commercial, "So on, and so on and so on."

By the time the memories fade I'm at the courtyard of the Paramount Building on 50th and Broadway.

"Frances!" says Sarah once again stepping out of the shadows.

Gershwin runs up to me and starts sniffing. He recognizes my scent and starts whining. His memory is long and I'm associated with food. I throw a can of Alpo to Sarah. Gershwin circles her as she pulls out his bowl and fills it.

"Oh my God, beef, bacon and cheese. You remembered!" she says with a chuckle. He starts licking his chops. "It's your favorite Gersh." I slip her twenty bucks, hoping she'll use it to get herself something to eat.

"How are things in Orlando? It's gorgeous down there, right? I saw it on television once a long time ago."

We chat for a few minutes while Gershwin wolfs down his food. He finishes and jumps up on me just as the train pulls into the tunnel.

I hug him and look up at Sarah. She has a funny look in her eyes. "Frannie, you look better than I seen you in a long, long time." The doors of the train open, I move to enter but think better of it. I go back and hug her, something I've never done before. Sarah looks surprised, but happy. She waves goodbye from the other side of the turn-style as I cross into the train.

Two stops later, I'm at Penn Station making my way toward the shops on 6th Avenue. I pick up feathers, sequins, candles, bunting, Tiffany knock-off gift bags and engraved matchbook covers happily checking off items on the to-do list as I go along.

Somewhere between Starbucks and Starbucks I notice that I have a text message:

IN CAB. C U @ THE HOTEL. M

My heart flutters a bit. I break out in a huge grin and take a few steps toward the nearest subway station. Then I realize I have way too many packages to deal with the train. Instead I treat myself to a cab and rush back to the WJ. I'm having very nasty thoughts by the time I hit the lobby.

He's here.

"What do you mean you can't find my reservation? I have my confirmation number right here." Matt pulls out his phone and starts rattling it off. I didn't know that you were actually supposed to save those, much less use them. Go figure.

"I'm sorry sir," says Teresa's good friend the front desk clerk, "it's not here."

"That's impossible." He starts to repeat the confirmation number, unable to believe that it could let him down.

I tap Matt on the shoulder. "Someone must have canceled it. I guess you'll have to stay with me."

Suitcases, garment bag, and shopping bags all become a blur as we head upstairs. Luckily housekeeping hasn't been to the room yet.

"Welcome to New York."

Waking up for the second time today is much more pleasant. The drowsiness can linger while you ignore the need to untangle yourselves from each other. Slow kisses bring back memories of the more urgent ones that came before. Nothing can ruin the mood.

HAVA NAGILA HAVA…

"Shit!"

I reach for my iPhone. Matt grins looking contented, stretches and ambles toward the bathroom.

HAVA NAGILA HAVA…

"Hello?" I say trying to sound perky and awake. The shower starts to fill the room with a damp humidity.

"Oh my God, am I interrupting? Were you two doing it?" I can hear Larry laughing in the background.

"Shaddup. What do you want?"

"Did you run the errands like I asked?"

"Yeah."

"The napkins from Kate's Paperie?"

"I went to the one on 57th Street. They weren't there."

"No, the one on 13th Street. Oh my God. Oh my God. *Oh my God*." She's hyperventilating.

"Relax. I have them."

"Not nice. Not nice to do to a mother. Larry!" she screams. "Don't worry. She was joking."

"Thank God," he deadpans.

"Anything else?"

225

"Did you get the stuffed animals from Abracadabra?"

"Yes."

She sounds insecure. "Do you like the Safari theme?"

"Yes. It's all the rage this season."

"Really?"

"Sure, I read about it on BarMitzvah.com."

"Again with a joke. Listen, you and boyfriend better get a hurry on. We ordered a car service for you. It's a van. They're picking you up in an hour. Now remember," continues Martha Stewart-Teitelbaum without taking a breath, "dinner at the house tonight. Tomorrow, Rachel's concert."

"Fine."

The toilet flushes in the bathroom.

"Okay then, go pay attention to Mister Man. He gets you for another hour or two, and then you're all mine."

"We can't wait to meet him," screams Larry in the background.

"Rachel! Put down that ice cream. Swear to God, you won't fit in your dress."

"Teresa, I'll talk to you later, okay?' I hang up.

Matt is standing in front of me, fresh from the shower with a towel wrapped around his waist.

Lucky towel.

He sneaks a quick peek into the packages from today's shopping safari.

"What's this?" he asks holding up a stuffed lion.

"Safari theme."

He laughs.

"What?" I ask.

"Her son's name is Christian, right?"

I nod.

"So," he points out, "she's kind of throwing Christian to the lions at his own Bar Mitzvah. That's funny."

He steals a quick kiss.

"No fair distracting me. I have news."

"Okay, no distractions." He removes the towel with a smirk standing there for a moment before he begins drying his hair. "What did you want to tell me?"

I smile and start rubbing my hands together. "Guess who Joy is dating?"

"Your brother."

"What? How..." I say incredulously. "*How* could you know that? I only just found out myself."

"She and I were working late a few weeks ago. He called like eight times."

"Why didn't you say anything to me?"

"I don't gossip."

"Come on!" I protest. "That's not gossip. That is keeping me abreast of current events."

"Speaking of a breast," his hand reaches into my robe. His mouth follows. The robe joins the towel on the floor and soon all thoughts of Joy and my brother are far, far away.

CHAPTER
TWENTY FIVE

The car service arrives in front of the hotel right on time. Shouting through a very thick, clouded plastic barrier that separates us from the driver, I confirm the address in Teaneck. He agrees with a very thick Russian accent; at least I think he does. It's kind of hard to tell.

We're leaving just before rush hour so there's no traffic. Well, of course there is traffic. In New York there's no such thing as no traffic; which is a double negative I suppose. There is no no traffic in New York City.

Whatever. We make our way down 9th Avenue in good time.

"There's used to be Delphinium Home," I say. "It's a great little shop but it moved. I bought my shower curtain there, crazy expensive but totally worth it. Oh! And there's the Westway Diner. They make the best grilled cheese sandwich."

"Yeah?" says a skeptical Matt from Wisconsin, which many consider to be the birthplace of grilling and cheese. "I doubt that."

"The best *ever*," I say. "Stanopolis, he's a waiter there, he told me their secret."

"What is it?"

228

"Can't tell you. I promised."

The wrinkles around his eyes become more pronounced as his cheeks rise and his lips curl. "That's okay. I don't need to know all your secrets."

My cheeks get flush. I bristle but try not to let it show. "What do you mean?"

"Nothing. It's just nice to hear you reminisce. You don't do that very often."

"I'm not sentimental," I lie.

"Okay."

"So you've thought about this? Meeting my family?" I can hear the tension in my voice. I wonder if he can too.

"Are you nervous about me meeting your family?"

"Yeah," I offer. "That must be it."

He puts his arm around me and kisses me on the cheek. I exhale trying to shake the irrational anger or fear that just overtook me and then collapse into the comfort of his strength.

The van gets dark as we enter the tunnel. Flashes of light run across our faces and then the darkness returns for a brief second before the light forces it away again.

I lose myself in the pattern of the tiles that line the tunnel. I try to imagine the men that put them in place. I try to imagine the millions of people that have passed the tile without noticing it. I concentrate on calming my breathing. Matt's profile is reflected in the window as he stares through the windshield, content to be silent for a moment or two.

Sweet Matt, looking toward the future and concentrating on where we're headed rather than where either of us has been.

We make our way through the Lincoln Tunnel. It takes a moment for my eyes to adjust to the sunlight on the other side.

"Matt?"

"What baby?"

Baby?

Why did he have to say baby?

"I want to explain…"

He interrupts me. "No need," he says quickly. Something in his voice betrays him. He's not ready to hear what I have to say. Our eyes lock. He smiles. My eyes remain fixed. He's the first to look away.

He offered me an out.

I take it, delaying the inevitable for a little while longer. We're mostly silent the rest of the way and eventually we are at Teresa and Larry's house, a Tudor in the heart of Teaneck, New Jersey. The Russian driver carries infinite Bar Mitzvah packages into the garage. Meanwhile I time travel and relive my first visit to this particular house.

"A starter home," Teresa said. "We'll be here five years max."

That was fourteen years ago.

She had just found out she was pregnant with Christian. That was such a happy time, lots of good memories. The kinds that carry you through the bad, I suppose. They were in escrow on a new, bigger house in Montclair when we lost Mom and Dad.

"There have been enough big changes. On the other hand a little redecorating, a little renovation, an addition …"

Teresa is one of those people who can put grief into action. I admire that about her.

A mezuzah I made for them during a ceramic workshop I took at Mud, Sweat and Tears on 9th Avenue flanks the right side of the front door. It's chipped and a little worse for wear. I've offered to make her another one but Teresa won't have it.

"So this one is showing its age, so what? Aren't we all?" she said. Of course, that was before she renovated her face with Dr. Lowenstein's help.

"I'm a little nervous," Matt admits.

I smooth out his jacket and run my fingers through his hair. Nothing wrong with a little futzing; I want his big debut to the rest of the family to go perfectly.

Larry and Teresa open the door together. Quick introductions and air kisses follow.

"Where are the kids?" I ask.

"Oh! Christian is on a group date at the multiplex at the Paramus Mall, seeing something get blown up," says his mother. "Rachel is at a rehearsal for the choir concert tomorrow." A deliberate smile cracks her frozen face. "Just the grown-ups tonight."

Conversation flows as freely as the wine. The entrée, "A drop dead gorgeous hunk of prime rib from the people that bought Kleinschmidt's," is complimented with a nice, full Merlot. Teresa isn't drinking. "I want to look fresh for the party."

My sister freely shares the embarrassing stories of my youth. Sneaking out of the house to meet Jason Hunt, my first serious boyfriend, getting caught shoplifting a black lace bra and panty set that my mother wouldn't buy for me just before prom, telling my father that my pot pipe was a tampon applicator.

"Uh, Teresa?"

"Yeah?"

"That was you."

"Oh my God, you're right!"

The laughter around the table is contagious. Larry laughs loudest and with the most appreciation. He doesn't catch me staring at him because he's too busy looking at my sister. When he wipes away a tear I'm not sure if it's from the laughter or affection. Teresa grabs Larry's hand. They smile. It's a loud, quiet, quick moment broken by a shift in priorities.

"Who is ready for dessert?" asks the hostess.

"Count me in Ma," says my nephew who just walked through the door. A quick look between Teresa and Larry confirms that he didn't hear the pot story.

"Aunt Frances, it's good to see you." He's gotten taller since I left, less awkward too.

There's still a little bit of the boy in the man. He's not too big for a hug and a quick kiss on the cheek.

Teresa presents a lemon meringue pie that I immediately recognize as coming from my mother's recipe. "Frances, could you please help me serve the coffee?" says Teresa once again reminding me that subtlety is a total stranger to my family.

"I really like him," she squeals the minute the door to her kitchen swings shut.

"I'm so glad!" I exclaim before going to kiss her on the cheek.

"He hurts you; I take him out with a dull butter knife."

My sister amazes me. She can talk about liking someone and move onto threatening to kill them in the space of two sentences.

The evening settles into a nice comfortable rhythm. Rachel comes home from rehearsal and we all sit around talking late into the evening. Matt fits in, which makes me happy. I can tell they all like him.

And strangely enough, he seems to like them.

I feel surrounded by possibility. There could be a lifetime of evenings like this. I just need to let down my guard and let it happen. Which leads me to wondering if my guard can go down; it has, after all, been up for a long, long time.

Matt. Look at him. He reminds me that it's okay to move on and smile.

I'm not following up on that job offer. I'm going to stay in Orlando. That's it. Decision made.

I could love this guy.

Maybe I already do.

CHAPTER
TWENTY SIX

My cab has only moved half a block and the light has changed three times. Stupid morning rush hour. Damn it. Oh! Vibration. It's my cell phone.

"Hi!" chirps Joy. "Don't be angry. *Please*?"

"I'm not. Not really," I say, surprising myself by how much I actually mean it. "I just don't understand why you couldn't tell me sooner."

"Frances, we both wanted to."

"Riiiiiight."

"But it could have put us all in such an awkward situation." Joy returns with, "What if it hadn't worked out?"

"I could have handled it."

"*Riiiiiight,*" says Joy, using my own sarcastic tone against me. I liked her better before she got all in charge of her life and stuff.

"How long have you two been together?" I ask.

"Remember that day we went to the spa?"

"That was months ago Joy."

"I know," she says with what sounds like just enough guilt. "I took my own advice. You and I had that talk about moving on, remember?"

That was the first night I spent with Matt.

"Yes I do. I remember it well."

"I went into the garage after you left. Tommy checked under my hood and that was that."

"Okay. Okay. Enough already. Spare me the details of my brother checking under your hood."

"Frances!" exclaims Joy. "Oh! Here comes Tommy." She pulls the phone away from her mouth. "I'm talking to Frances," she tells him before coming back. "He's waving."

"Where are you?" I ask.

"Baggage claim at LaGuardia. I wanted to call you right away. We're going to rent a car so Tommy can show me your old neighborhood."

"Have fun," I say, hating myself for letting Joy's enthusiasm sway me so easily. "Make sure he takes you to Nick's Pizza for a slice. It's the best. Oh my God, it's good. The cheese is stringier than Kellie's hair."

I look to the horizon, which is now about three feet closer. We should get through this intersection during the next green light if my New York traffic survival skills are still in working order.

Back to the phone.

"Would you like to join us?" asks Joy.

"Yeah."

"Oh good!" she says.

"But I can't," I admit.

"Why not?"

"I have to work today, remember? I'm on my way to the Queens Museum."

"Oh, that's right! You have to do the Mary Binger research for Tiny Planet," says my friend in charge of exposition.

"Have fun."

"Okay. Goodbye!"

I'm just about to throw my phone into my purse when it goes off again. Caller ID. It's Matt.

"Hello is this lover?" I ask using my sexiest voice.

"Uh Frances, you're on speakerphone," replies lover.

Oh no. No! He's calling from his Tiny Planet budget meeting at Binger Headquarters on Park Avenue. All the suits must have heard me. Crud. Think quickly Frances.

"I was just joking," is the best I can come up with.

"Me too," says lover. "You're not on speakerphone."

"You ass!" I scream into the phone, which startles the driver.

It takes a while for Matt to quit laughing and get his breath back. He punctuates his own joke with, "Oh God that was funny."

"You got me," I admit.

"Really?" he says. I can hear what sounds like a very nasty smile.

"It's starting to look that way."

"I just wanted to let you know my meeting went well. They approved the budget and moved up the deadline. Six month turnaround."

"You're kidding." I immediately start to panic.

"Don't worry. We've got plenty to keep us busy until the last drawings are ready. We're going into production as soon as possible."

"Oh Matt, congratulations!"

"Thanks," he beams. "You too. They said we make a hell of a team. I told them they don't know the half of it."

We say goodbye just as my new deadline and I pull up in front of the Queens Museum of Art.

When we were making arrangements for this meeting, Desi said, "I love this country. Where else would the Queens get their own museum?"

I used to come here for Art Camp when I was a kid. Artists from Manhattan would come to Queens and teach in the summer for survival money that got them through the fall. How I admired their passion. I was always too practical for that life, practical or insecure.

Either way, I love coming back here as an Art Director. When they heard that someone from the company was coming to review the Mary Binger Archives they fell over themselves making sure everything went smoothly. I'm glad she didn't leave her papers to MoMA or the Met. They're both too arrogant to give that kind of service.

"Ms. Fiore we have all the pertinent Binger portfolios pulled for you," says the Queens Museum Archivist dressed in a very professional dark blue suit. I almost bought the same one at Bergdorf's for an interview with the Republicans for a freelance gig during the 2012 National Convention. It's *very* conservative; especially with a white blouse and red flats.

We leave the public area and start down the hallway toward the viewing rooms reserved for VIPs. Today that would be me. She's on her best behavior. Non-profit trying to impress profit I guess.

Truth told it is I who envies her. She doesn't have to wear a nametag.

"Here's the viewing room. Let me know if you need anything," she says with all her teeth before departing.

I turn into the room filled with stacks of Mary Binger's work and various documentations. I had no idea there would be this much to go through. I slowly make my way through the piles of sketchbooks, magazine articles, lithographs protected in acid free sleeves, animation cells and slide carousels.

Oh my God, slide carousels.

I haven't seen any of those in a while.

I feel like my mother. She used to go to yard sales every weekend unless there was a funeral or a wedding. Even then sometimes she'd hit a sale on the way to the Funeral Mass. My father thought it was a waste of time.

"What are you looking for?" he'd ask.

"I won't know until I see it," was her standard reply.

I've gone through about most of the collection and I don't really feel as though I know Mary Binger any better. I wanted to get to know Mary Binger the woman and artist, not the corporate icon.

"Ms. Fiore?"

It's the woman in the Barbara Bush blue power suit. "Yes?"

"I brought you some coffee."

"Lovely."

I put out my hand. She doesn't give it to me.

"If you could just step away from the collection…"

"Oh! Of course! How stupid of me." We sit down on two chairs at the edge of the room and finally

I am given coffee. "Thank you," I pause. I don't know her name.

"Margo."

"Thank you Margo."

"You're welcome." There is an awkward silence. "How is everything going?"

I stick out my jaw, raise my eyebrows and suck air through my side teeth.

"Not great, huh?"

"No. I'm so disappointed. It's all just the typical Binger stuff that I was hoping to escape. I really wanted to learn more about who she was away from the cute little barnyard menagerie."

"Oh," she says haltingly.

I smell hope.

"I thought you might be looking for something more personal, but my boss said she knew you would just want the animation stuff." She looks off to the side. "I knew it. I just *knew* you were looking for something else. But my boss can be such a…" She catches herself. "Never mind."

"Believe me, every company has one."

"I wish it was just one," she says with eyes rolling toward the ceiling. "Excuse me just a second."

She returns with boxes less professionally archived, and by less I mean not at all. She puts them down on a table in my pristine workroom. Her suit is covered with dust. "I hope these help," she says with a smile. "Be sure to tell my boss where you got 'em, okay?"

As I roll up my sleeves I realize there must be more to this Mary. What was her maiden name? Thompson. There has to be more to this Mary Thompson Binger than I realized. I start digging.

There are tintypes of her as a young girl, growing up in San Francisco. The images are so alive you can almost hear an upright piano in the background. In one, she looks to be about seventeen, maybe a little older. She's wearing a wide brim hat, a starched white blouse, a long, full, pleated skirt and button up shoes. Written over it, in her own hand I imagine, is, "Off to France, August, 1919."

In the subsequent pictures she begins to look more serious. Her hair is down and her brown eyes become worldly. There are smudges on the corners, graphite and charcoal I think. She must have been looking at them after taking her art classes in Paris.

The last one says, "Left Bank with school chums, 1922." The group looks to be in a café, raising wine glasses and saluting the camera or whoever is behind it. If I'm not mistaken the man with his hand on her knee is a very young Art Binger.

Another box. This one is for hats from Hattie Carnegie's Salon on East 49th Street in Manhattan. It's very frail. I put on the gloves provided by Margo, lift the cover, and look inside. Layers of ancient pink and lavender tissue paper guard the contents. I gently push them aside.

There is a journal, very frail. The ink is faded but there could be something here. I'll ask Margo if they can get an archivist working on it.

As I go to put the journal back some snapshots fall out of the journal. There are several pictures of a pretty little girl. I turn them over to see if there are any notes, but no one bothered to label them.

After wrapping up I head back to the hotel to meet Matt. I'm rewarded for my hard work by the car the service sent. It's a luxurious black Lexus with soft buttery leather. I melt the minute I sit down. I roll down the window to enjoy the faint chill in the brisk air that floods the car as we speed closer to the lights of Manhattan. It's the kind of moment you wish you were sharing with someone.

Vibration. Cell phone. Caller ID says number unknown.

"Hello?"

"Frances, is that you?" Suddenly a perfect moment becomes even better.

"Gladys! How are you?"

Silence.

"Gladys?"

"Yes darling, I'm here."

"We must have a bad connection. I asked how you are."

"Everything is lovely. And you dearest?"

"The trip is going very well."

"Yes. I can hear it in your voice."

I catch her up on all the details. I tell her about Joy and Tommy. Of course, she already knew. I was the last to find out. Even Katzenberg must have known about it before me.

"How are you and your daughter Saylie getting along?" I ask.

"She's here with me now. She's waving."

"Hello back," I say.

"We're having a wonderful reunion. In fact, we're having so much fun that my other two children are coming to join us."

"That's wonderful! You'll all be together."

"Yes, for the first time in a long, long while. Perhaps they'll still be here when you get back and you can meet them."

"I hope so."

"I suspect that will be the case," she reassures me. "You know, you and your brother being in New York reminds me of one of our family vacations when the children were very young; barely out of diapers."

"When were you in New York?"

"We took them to see Mister Ed Sullivan's television show. It was being performed at a studio right on Broadway just up from Times Square. It was wonderful. Afterwards we went to the Serendipity Ice Cream Parlor."

"Right. On the East side," I say as though I'm Google Maps or something.

"We also saw Miss Ethel Merman in, *Call Me Madam*," at the Imperial Theater."

"It's not there anymore," I mention.

"No, I suspect it's not," she says sounding more than a little wistful. "That was a long time ago when I was still young."

I correct her saying, "You're still young."

"Well if I am, it's due in no small part to the good fortune of you driving past my house." There is a pause. "I love you very much," she says.

"I love you too Gladys."

"There's no need to tell me. You show me every day." Her tone changes, "Would you listen to me?

I'm getting all sentimental and I'm going to see you in just a few days."

"That's right. I'll be home soon."

"Home. That's right. This is your home."

"A gift from you."

"It is you that has been the gift," says my landlady. "By the way, check in the side pocket of your suitcase." She giggles. "I hid a surprise in there. A trinket."

"What is it?"

"Oh good Lord Frances, a surprise isn't much of a surprise if someone tells you what it is."

"You're right."

"I always am. Don't you ever forget that," she says with total certainty. "Now you hurry up and get back home."

The time at the hotel is a blur. I'm just there long enough to take off work clothes, put on a hot Aunt outfit I've been saving for this evening, collect the boyfriend, leave, return to spray a little cologne, and leave again.

"Wait," says boyfriend.

"What?" I say awkwardly doing so mid-step.

"This," he says, handing me a little nosegay of violets before he starts walking away. How sweet, of course now I have to carry my purse and the bouquet, but still, it was a very sweet gesture.

"Wait," I say.

"What?" says boyfriend.

"This," I say, giving him a slow and hopefully romantic kiss. When we break I head down the hall and he heads back toward our room. I laugh. He whimpers.

"There will be time for that later," I promise. "Come on. We have to meet Tommy and Joy for a drink before the big concert."

We make our way to Teaneck and arrive right on time at the Jerusalem Pizza Sushi Bar on Cedar Lane. We're still waiting twenty minutes later. My mood has started to wilt along with the violets. In the spirit of being even more multi-cultural the management has hired a polka band. Matt is looking at me over our plate of nachos with a "we-could-be-back-at-the-hotel-having-sex" look when my iPhone starts to vibrate. Thank God I didn't change the setting. It would be impossible to hear over the oompah-pah of the band.

"Don't hate us," says Joy. "Here's Tommy."

Silence.

"Hello," I say.

"We aren't going to make it tonight."

"WHAT?" I say loud enough for the accordion player to shoot me a look.

"Don't worry," he says.

"I'm not worried. I'm angry," I start to say before Tommy cuts me off.

"I'll explain tomorrow. Listen, I gotta go."

"Don't you dare hang up Tom."

Click.

A slight case of indigestion follows us all the way to Thomas Jefferson Middle School. We are led to the auditorium by yellow construction paper signs. Teresa and Larry wave us over. Christian is slouched over in his seat, too cool for school. We start to sit down.

"Thank God you're here," says my sister. She looks over her shoulder at one angry mother in particular, "the vultures were circling around these seats." Thank God for dimming lights. It keeps the conversation to a minimum.

"Better than Broadway," my sister mouths to me before it gets too dark. I start to laugh but catch myself when I realize that she was being sincere.

A faculty member dressed as what I'm assuming is supposed to be Thomas Jefferson comes out and stands center stage. "Greetings Town Folk," he reads from a parchment scroll. "Tis time to make merry!"

Two boys from the sixth grade drama club, or rather the two members of the sixth grade drama club, perform, *Zoo Story,*" by Edward Albee. One boy has a very pronounced lisp but it works for the character.

Next up, the dance troupes. If I were a parent, I would run up on stage, cover my daughter, and sue the school system. Middle School is what, sixth thru eighth grade? These girls are gyrating with belly busters and tight spandex pants. The elastic waistbands from their thongs are clearly sticking out above their waistlines.

Of course it gets my nephew's attention, but still.

Three and a half days later the 8th grade show choir finally takes the stage. I crane my head to see my niece. Why is Rachael stuck in the back?

"That pisses me off," I say to Matt.

"Frances, someone has to be in the back," he replies.

"Not my niece."

The eighth grade orchestra starts playing "I Won't Dance." They're not bad. It actually sounds like, "I Won't Dance." Teenage boys start to sing and dance. They look like they'd rather be in Iraq. Well, that's unfair. Several of the boys look thrilled to be dressed in their tuxedos; although those boys might prefer to be dancing with each other.

I look at Rachael. Her curly brown hair, just like mine, is up. One strand, however, has fallen away and frames her face, keeping time with the dance steps.

I just wish she wasn't stuck in standing in the back.

Perhaps God is here in the auditorium of Thomas Jefferson Middle School in Teaneck, NJ because right on cue the choir parts and Rachael steps center stage to sing a solo as they break into "Dancin' in the Streets." When she's done, she's hit with a spotlight and begins dancing.

My niece is not a small girl. For one second long buried school fears come bubbling to the surface. I worry that the students in the audience are going to make fun of the fat kid trying to dance. No one does. She has them enraptured, and I'm not just saying that because I am her aunt. She's large and in charge like a young, white, Jewish Aretha Franklin wearing tap shoes.

She finishes and the audience cheers. Teresa and Christian stand up and start screaming. Larry is too preoccupied with shooting video on his iPad Mini to do anything but protect his shot. A shrill whistle comes from my left. It is Matt who is standing up with the rest of the audience.

"Some kids have to be in the back, eh?" I tease.

Matt squeezes my hand and returns with, "We all have to pick the moments we move up front."

CHAPTER
TWENTY SEVEN

I wish we were sitting next to Tommy and Joy at the synagogue, but they got here late. I know this not because I've been sitting on this hard wooden seat with a numb ass for the last ninety minutes; no I'm not that smart. Joy is the smart one. She knew to arrive late and then apologized for it by pointing to her wrist, rolling her eyes and mouthing, "We got here late. Oops!"

Eventually my nephew gets up to read from the Torah. He clears his throat, smiles nervously, looks to his mother and father, and begins. His voice cracks occasionally. His sister is the performer, not him; but Christian does his best. His confidence grows. His posture straightens and again, time starts playing games with me.

Standing at the front of the synagogue is a boy and a man in the same body. I can see Christian the teenager but I also see the child on his fourth birthday. He asked to spend the night with Paul and me in the City. We promised to have him home in time for his party that night.

Christian adored his Uncle Paul. Larry was so jealous. Teresa told me so, all the time. Both of them kept urging us to have a kid of our own.

Christian was sitting on Paul's lap when he blew out the candles on the small birthday cake I picked up from Magnolia Bakery.

"What did you wish for Christian?"

"Elmo!" said the boy that somehow became the man standing in front of all of us today. One wish fulfilled. Paul had gone out the night before to about twenty stores to find that season's hot toy. He finally found one from some sidewalk vendor in Times Square.

My heart was so warm that night. It was impossible to imagine that flame would ever extinguish. I remember looking at Paul with such love through the wafting smoke of those four little candles.

"Did you make a wish Uncle Paul?"

"I sure did Buddy." He looked at me as he kissed the top of Christian's head. I read his mind and knew that someday we'd make that one come true too.

For a split second I can imagine that I'm still married to Paul. The accident never happened. The drunk driver never hit us. My parents are still alive. Sam, our perfect little boy, is sitting next to me – right where he always is.

The knot in my stomach returns extra tight, to remind me that it never really goes away. It just hides.

The knot underestimates me.

I'm stronger than I used to be. I look up at my handsome nephew. Today is his day. The what-might-have-been game can wait for another time.

Sweet Christian. Suddenly he is a man. I can imagine his wedding day. I can see him watching his own son's Bar Mitzvah. My parents aren't here but Christian is. I can see the continuity to that. I'm sure somewhere in the Talmud it says that this is how things are to be.

He looks so relieved when he finishes. The congregation applauds and he looks mortified. Shy. The little boy is back.

The Rabbi walks towards what I want to call the altar. It could be called a podium, the dais, I don't know. He goes to the place where the Rabbi talks to the congregation, or the worshippers. I wish I knew what the hell it's called.

I'm the worst aunt ever. Not only do I know very little about my nephew's religion, I just used the word hell in a synagogue.

I don't think Jews believe in hell, so maybe it's no big deal.

The Rabbi, for whom my cat is named, has white hair and sparkling eyes. There is something about him that instantly comforts me, although I am not aware of being upset. It's like being in the company of a nondenominational Santa Claus.

"Look at this Jewish boy, this proud Jewish *man*, named Christian. I wish his middle name was Buddha." Rabbi knows his audience and pauses for the laugh. "Take a good look ladies and gentlemen. What you're looking at is a bridge. This is a boy who brings people together."

A little tear trickles down my cheek. Matt squeezes my hand and looks at me with eyes similar to Paul's from that day so long ago.

The service ends and the obligatory bagels are served. "Oh my God, these are good," says boyfriend who happens to be from Wisconsin. He's right. You can't get bagels like this anywhere else in the world. You could send the same ingredients to Orlando and we'd still win. People say it's the water but I'm not so sure. Bagels just suit the Northeast better.

I look around the room and see very few of our relatives. Not even Cousin Tony made an appearance. It's mostly Larry's family since they're Jewish and live in Jersey. Teresa wanted to make sure that the Fiore's came, so the reception this evening is in Floral Park.

Matt and I make our way toward Tommy and Joy. Tommy is wiping his mouth with leopard striped napkin that has been engraved with Christian's name and the date of his Bar Mitzvah. When he is done Joy's acrylic fingernails go after a little cream cheese hanging onto his upper lip. As we arrive they are rising to leave.

"Where are you two going?" I ask.

Joy starts to explain and Tommy cuts her off. "Business to take care of. See you tonight."

"Tom," says Joy, his official spokesperson. "Can't we just have a cup of coffee together?"

"Okay," says my brother, grabbing what is left from his Styrofoam cup and downing it. "There you go. Now let's hit the bricks," he says sounding more Queens than I have heard him sound in years.

Joy shrugs her shoulders. "See you tonight," and then they are gone. Larry follows them out as Teresa approaches us. "What the hell?" she says, gesturing toward them.

"I know," says Matt. He then adds, "it's *meshugina*," in perhaps the most heavily Midwestern accented voice that has ever attempted Yiddish.

Teresa nearly chokes on her kugel before her throaty laugh fills the room. She kisses him on the cheek before leaving to work the room. She continues laughing and repeating, "*Meshugina*," to herself as she makes her way toward the Widow Kleinschmidt from whom she bought my car.

The reception winds down. I notice Larry's parents Carol and Lee walk out. Teresa is clearly simmering about something. Matt and I walk over as the conversation goes from simmer to boil.

"What the hell did she mean by saying, much nicer than she expected? Was that another one of her *Goyim* jibes?"

"What the hell am I, my mother's interpreter?"

"No, of course not," says Teresa as she brushes off the lapel of Larry's suit. "I just figured she'd hear me through those apron strings she has tied around your balls," Big Sister retorts. She moves up to his tie and begins vigorously tightening the knot. "How dare she say something like that to me *today*? That bitch..."

"Isn't here," I say moving her arms down to her side. "Don't let her ruin your day."

"Yeah," says Matt. "That'd be *farkatke*."

Again she laughs and sanity is restored.

"Oy, this one with the Yiddish," says Teresa, doubling over. "Thank you. Thank you." She turns to her husband. "Darling, I overreacted. I'm sorry. Instead of complaining we should both be thankful."

"Right," says Larry.

"After all, you could have married a woman as demanding and controlling as your mother." She spits between her fingers. "And I could have been that kind of mother."

The silence that follows is really awkward.

I pull the Joy maneuver and look at my wristwatch. "Listen let's gather up Rachel and head to the beauty shop for our session with the stylist."

"Honey," Teresa says, "would you mind wrapping things up here?"

"What's left? Pay the caterers?"

"No, I did that. Start wrapping," she says, "literally. I'm not throwing out these leftovers. We can eat for a week. I bought Saran Wrap in bulk at the Costco. It's in the trunk."

"I'll stay and help," Matt offers.

"A *Mensch*, that's what this one is," says Larry.

"What's that?" says Matt as the men walk away.

We gather up Rachel, commandeer the waiting limo, and head to Teaneck New Jersey's most glamorous salon, Bruce Lieberman's House of Style. The driver is a cute college boy from Hofstra. Rachel pointed that out several times.

We enter a rather austere shop in the business section that looks more like a barber joint than a ladies salon. An elderly man in a zebra print smock walks up to us. "What? You pretty ladies are here to tamper with perfection?"

Three women and three reactions; Teresa giggles, Rachel blushes, and my mouth is agape. I take Teresa aside, "You can't be serious. Let's get out of here."

"You with the book and the cover, judging this sweet old man," says Teresa with a self-righteousness that can only be described as extreme.

"But his hands are shaking. That's not good when it involves scissors, right?"

"So?" says my sister managing to sound more incredulous than ever before in her life. And that's a saying a lot. She must be compensating for the lack of expression on her Botoxed face. "Lotte Abromowitz said he was a magician."

"Yeah – in vaudeville!"

"Sit down already. Today is stressful enough without you causing more headaches." She starts crying before getting nauseous and running into the ladies room with her smock trailing behind her like Batman's cape.

Rachel goes to check on her as I am led to the shampoo station. Bruce of Teaneck makes some very disconcerting noises as he runs his soapy fingers through my hair. I think I know why he has chosen to become a hairstylist. He has a follicle fetish. Rachel returns. Teresa is right behind her popping an Altoid and holding a damp towel on her forehead.

"Sweetness, run to the corner and get Mommy a Diet Coke. Wait!" she says urgently as though the fate of the free world hinges on changing her order. "Make that an orange juice."

Rachel begins to leave as I ask, "Are you all right?" Teresa's watches clearly waiting for her daughter to get out of earshot.

"I'm fine." She pauses before smiling. "So is the baby."

What?

"Frances, I'm pregnant. PS, the kids don't know. We didn't want to steal anyone's thunder."

I search my sister's face for a moment trying to figure out if this is a good thing or not. No luck. She might as well be wearing a mask. Her face has lost its ability to register emotion.

"Congratulations?"

"Damn right, congratulations!"

We both scream in unison and begin hugging. My soggy hair whips around and hits Teresa in the face. She sputters but doesn't stop yelping with glee. "IwantedtotelyouaboutthisbutLarrymademepromise…"

"Slow down Teresa. Breathe if only for the baby's sake."

"You're right. You're right," she says with her hand to her chest. "I know you've noticed how irrational I've been lately."

"What? You? That's crazy talk."

She ain't buying what I'm selling. "Annnnnyway, Larry and I have been trying for a while now. I've been on hormones and some minor fertility drugs. My emotions have been all over the place. He's been stressed out about trying to sell the garage. Not a fun time."

"Why didn't you say anything?" I ask.

Another look.

"Okay, I know why. Go on."

"Well we chose the date of the Bar Mitzvah so I wouldn't have my period, right?"

"Okay…"

"Anyway I was in the thick of the planning and getting ready when all of a sudden I realized I was more than a week late. I waited to take the test until this morning. I thought Christian's big day would be good luck."

"And it was positive?"

"I don't know. I haven't looked at the results yet."

"What?"

She smacks me on the head. "Of course it was positive you *yutz*. I said I was pregnant right? Of course for all I know I'm having a litter, I was on so many damn drugs."

I smile and our eyes connect. "Everything's going to be fine."

She bites the corner of her lower lip. "Are you okay?"

Not being happy for Teresa won't bring anything I lost back so I smile and nod. It's so close to being sincere that for a moment I feel hopeful it will be soon.

Rachel returns with some Tropicana, Extra Pulp and soon Hairdini the Magician has us in various stages of his process.

Two hours later I have to admit Teresa is right. The man is a magician; unfortunately his act is circa 1965. We all have shellacked hair strategically woven into skyscrapers hovering above our heads. These hairdos could be rented out as cell phone towers.

My face must betray me. He steps outside the cloud of Final Net that seems to follow him and says, "What? You don't like?"

I try to answer but no words come.

"Listen my dear," says Mister Bruce, "I know from hair. The party is not until this evening. I used a little extra hold. Come cocktail hour it will be perfect," which he emphasizes with a little grunt as though he was visualizing it and enjoying the image a little too much.

"I love it," says Teresa the hormonal mess as she begins to cry. "You look beautiful."

"Trust me," continues Mr. Dippity Don't. "I know from structure. I was a maintenance engineer on the George Washington Bridge for thirty five years."

"That would explain why my hair has two levels," I retort through a strained smile.

"You noticed," he says with pride. Ugh. His hands are back on my head. "Later tonight if you pull out these three bobby pins your hair will fall in perfect curls around your shoulders. The effect will be," his pelvis twitches, "remarkably sexy."

I check in with Matt from the limo on our way to get our make-up done. He's gone back to the hotel to work. He sent all the Mary Binger documentation back to Florida. Now he's working on budgets. Matt is an over-achiever. He never takes a break. I'm sure if he has time he'll work on his Yiddish for tonight's party.

"Any chance you'll be able to come back here before we have to be at the reception?" he asks.

"You just want to have sex," I say under my breath hoping that Rachel is too busy flirting with the driver from Hofstra to notice.

"Guilty. I'm a bad boy. What's my punishment?"

"Delayed gratification."

"You're evil."

"Some things are worth waiting for Matt."

"I know it Frances. I know."

Larry's sister Stephanie, "Meet my husband Doctor Kober the cardiologist," joins us to get our make-up done. She and Teresa dish the relatives from this morning. I get to spend a little time with my niece.

"Are you having a nice day Rachel?"

"Mostly," she says trying to put her best foot forward.

"Mostly? What does that mean?"

She smiles in spite of the tears welling up in the corners of her eyes. "I wish Grandma and Grandpa Fiore were here," she says before starting to cry a little.

Part of me is touched, part of me is sad and part of me is devastated that such a young girl has such a heavy heart. "I wish they were here too Sweetie. Every day."

"I shouldn't be talking to you about this," she says with a touch of remorse.

A memory comes back to guide me.

My mother was very generous in her own quiet way. Generous might not be the best word. My mother was thoughtful. When she'd visit someone who had just brought home a new baby she was always careful to have something for the older children. She wanted people to know they mattered. My mother always made sure that her family and friends knew that.

I'd like to be that kind of woman.

"Rachel you can talk to me about anything."

She reaches out to hug me. I feel her fighting the impulse to cry some more. I pull back to look at her. "Honey if you're going to cry, do it soon before you ruin your make-up. What will Hofstra the driver think about that?"

Rachel begins to laugh and sob at the same time. I open my purse and hand her a tissue. Then I find the perfect tonic wrapped up inside a handkerchief.

"I want you to have these," I say as I hand her my mother's earrings; the ones I have always worn on special occasions and first days.

Rachel's eyes get wide. "Oh no Aunt Frances, I couldn't possibly take these. I know how much they mean to you."

"You mean more," I say pressing them into her hand. "Besides you're my favorite niece."

Now the wide eyes are rolling. "I'm your only niece."

"So far," I say protecting the secret I share with Teresa. "So far." Then I add, "Please take them Rachel. It would make me and your grandma so proud." I take them out of her hand and clip them on her ears. "Wear them tonight."

I lead her toward the mirror. Looking back at us is the past, a present, and the future.

"Perfection."

CHAPTER
TWENTY EIGHT

Larry's sister Stephanie is still here. Evidently her husband the cardiologist is a cardiologist; a fact she brings up with amazing regularity. She's also an eavesdropper prone to dropping her opinion into conversations in which she really wasn't included.

"Joy," she says while applying a lipstick that is too dark for her outfit, "aren't you worried about the future? I mean he's just a mechanic. Now my husband Ron is a cardiologist. It gives me such peace of mind to know that our future is secure."

"Just a mechanic?" challenges Teresa.

Joy stops her.

"I don't look at it that way," Joy says in a calm voice. "Tom is healthy and even tempered. That's much more important to me." Teresa crosses to Joy and puts her arm around her.

Joy outlines her lips. "I mean if I had a stressed out husband that needed to lose thirty pounds and smoked like a chimney I'd be worried."

Winner, Joy.

I give myself a final once over. God bless him, Mister Bruce was right. My hair has relaxed

Greg Triggs

and looks perfect. The dress is not perfect, but
pretty good. Glam App says you can't show leg
and cleavage at the same time, so I played the
middle and ended up with a bit of leg and a bit
of cleavage.

"You don't look happy Frances," says Joy.

"This dress just isn't working."

"Ladies we have a fashion emergency!" announces
can-do Joy. Soon the room is full of scissors
and hemming tape and thread and needles. Before
I know it the dress is perfect, falling just a
little above the knee and a little below the
collarbone. Okay, a lot below the collarbone.
I'll have to lend this dress to Teresa when she's
breastfeeding.

"It's great," I enthuse.

"Are you kidding?" asks Rachel. "That dress
could cause heart attacks."

"Well if that should happen, everyone please
remember Stephanie's husband *is* a cardiologist,"
says Joy as she opens the door.

The ladies of the family gather at the top of
the staircase to make an entrance. Matt, Tommy,
Larry, Christian, and the Cardiologist are all
waiting for us in the foyer.

"Are we the luckiest guys in town, or what?"
Larry beams as the men raise a glass to us.
We make our way down the stairs and are each
handed a glass of Champagne by Tommy. Rachel and
Christian each get Sparkling Cider, which I see
Teresa discreetly trade out for her Champagne.

"Before we leave I have something to tell
you all," Tommy says with more authority and
confidence than I usually hear coming from him.
"Joy would you please join me?"

She makes her way past Stephanie and Doctor Ron as Tommy grabs her hand and pulls her toward him. She glows as she settles in beside him.

Tommy stammers, uncomfortable to have all eyes on him. Joy loudly whispers, "Go ahead. Tell them the news."

"Would you please do it?"

She grabs his chin and looks him in the eye. "You can do it Tom."

He takes a deep breath and starts to tear up a little, which is evidently contagious. Never in my life have I see so many people cry in one day. His confidence returns after a deep breath.

"We rented an apartment in Astoria this morning. I'm moving back home and Joy is coming with me because we bought the garage from Tony."

Joy pulls a ring out of her evening bag. Tommy puts it on her finger, which she holds up as she squeals, "We're engaged!"

A cheer fills the room and toasts are proposed.

"To your success!"

"To your happiness!"

"To my ex-husband!" toasts Joy.

The room falls silent.

"Why the hell would we drink to him?" says my hormonal sister.

"The 401K he had to give me half of provided our down payment!"

Laughter and hugs and good wishes flow freely from everyone but me. I stand on the outskirts watching, wishing I could be unselfish enough only to be happy for them and not aware of my own sadness. I already miss them and they haven't even left yet.

Joy makes her way through the crowd and makes her way toward me. "So…"

"So," I return. "Congratulations."

"Thank you. Thank you for everything Frances."

"It's good, right?"

"Better than I ever could have imagined," says Joy, who is finally living up to her name.

Tommy walks over. "You okay?" he asks.

"Better than that, I'm really happy for you." Evidently it is my turn to cry. I hug him and whisper in his ear, "I'm proud of you." I pause. "Tom."

Matt slips beside me. "Should I consider this your two week notice, Joy?" She laughs. More hugs and champagne follow until the limo driver arrives to carry us to the party.

Teresa and Larry let Christian choose the car, which is never a good choice when you're dealing with a thirteen year old. It's one of those white stretch SUV monstrosities with speakers you can hear half a mile away. It makes the Bingermobile that they sent to pick me up when I first moved to Orlando look understated. Matt must be able to read my mind.

"How about we follow behind you guys in case you need an extra car?"

We are handed the keys to Larry's C Series Mercedes, which he calls, "A starter luxury car." My first thought is of the new baby. Goodbye two door Mercedes! You're going to be traded in on something more practical in a few months.

It's nice to be quiet for a minute or two and let the day unwind. There are so many things to be thankful for as New Jersey slowly morphs into New York. Before I know it, we are in Floral Park.

An occasional memory pops up as we drive past familiar spots like the Pizza Hut where I used to work, but I reject them in favor of relaxing while resting my head on Matt's shoulder. His concentration is steady in spite of being on unfamiliar roads. He's content to get us where we're going and leave me with my thoughts. We pull up to Floral Terrace, the old Vaudeville Theater renovated to become the finest party facility in all of Queens.

The valet parking staff is very subtly dressed in Pith Helmets and safari gear from the Eddie Bauer Store at the Paramus Mall, which is managed by Larry's college roommate from Rutgers. He gave them a twenty-five percent discount on the clothes as his Bar Mitzvah present to Christian.

We get into place in the line of other C Series Mercedes as it slowly inches forward. Evidently it is the car of choice amongst forty-something accountants.

"You look beautiful."

"Thank you," I say as a blush brightens my cheek. To cover my embarrassment, I take a second to look at Matt. He's so handsome tonight, so distinguished. The white flecks in his suit bring out the wisps of white in his hair and make his smile even brighter. The tie Teresa and I bought at Macy's is tied in an elegant Windsor knot against his crisp white shirt.

We steal a quick kiss.

"I love you Matt," just slips out. No hesitation and, after taking a quick inventory, no regret. Only one thing could make the moment better.

"I love you too."

And that's it. Quiet and strong. Confident and natural. It has been said. One more kiss, this one longer and more meaningful and we slip next in line to have our car taken. Matt doesn't wait for the attendant. He opens his own door. He's on his way to my side but the valet, Tonique LaGrange according to his nametag, beats him to the punch.

Matt tosses him the keys and says, "Watch out for stampeding rhinos." Tonique looks at him like he has two heads. Matt being from the Midwest feels the need to explain. "The safari? Rhinos. Get it?"

Tonique is smart enough to pretend that a hip-hop black teenager from Queens finds this hilarious. One has to be savvy out on the Savannah if one wants one's tip. "Good one Sir. Rhinos. Very funny." He is given five dollars for his efforts.

Floral Terrace is a turn of the century building that got a bad renovation and became a party facility in the late 80s. It reminds me of a marriage between an old man and a much younger woman. It's incongruent and tacky but decorum demands you pretend not to notice.

There is sandstone, beautiful masonry, and gorgeous marble floors that must be a hundred years old, with lots of glass walls, floating modern staircases and gold accents.

As is her nature, Teresa ignored all that and did exactly as she pleased. Amongst the geometric fountains with color wheel lights are bar stations with middle-aged bartenders dressed in dashikis. Servers make their way through the growing crowd carrying mini corn dogs for the kids and pate for the adults - both hugely popular when trekking through Camercon.

I scan the room and see many familiar faces. I reach for Matt's hand. "Promise to protect me from my family?"

"If you promise to protect me from the strangers."

"You got it," I say before stealing another kiss for strength.

We head over to the shortest line and order a drink. "White wine for the lady. Scotch and soda with a twist for me," says Matt as he throws another five bucks in the tip jar.

Before the bartender can even finishing pouring the drinks we are drowning in a sea of relatives. By the end of the cocktail hour Matt has met my Mom's sister Dorothy and her husband Ray who own an aluminum siding company in Rockaway, their blind daughter Sharon and her date Tim, Cousin Andy and his "roommate" Chuck who have lived together since 1971, and Cousin Rhonda who used to be an exotic dancer until she and her insanely large implants discovered Jesus.

"This is my first Bar Mitzvah, but Pastor Graf told me there is no harm in all of us being here," she assures us before crossing herself. "Different strokes for different folks."

The timing of that comment was very unfortunate for Cousin Rhonda. Precisely at the moment she said it Aunt Abby from Flushing who recently survived a stroke rolled up in her wheelchair. For a second I mistook Rhonda's stammering for speaking in tongues. The backpedaling was quick and divine.

As we walk away from Cousin Rhonda's repetitious mea culpas I run smack into Cousin Tony, the only man I've seen so far that isn't wearing a suit. His acetate shirt and Caravacchi pants fit the décor nicely but that doesn't make it appropriate.

"Hey Frannie!" he says, knowing that I hate being called that. I've told him a million times.

"Hello Anthony."

Introductions are quickly made.

"You hear the news?"

"Yes," I choose to be diplomatic if only for his parent's sake. Uncle Nick and Aunt Josie were the best. "Congratulations."

He salutes me with a can of Diet Coke. "Nah, no congratulations for me. I fucked up and got thrown a life preserver."

"Lucky you."

"Yeah, well, this time is different. I've learned my lesson."

"I hope so Tony."

He smiles with weary eyes. "After rehab I just went back to my old crowd and partied too hard. I got to get the hell out of here, for a while at least. I'm moving to Miami."

"Good luck," I say meaning it despite my concerns that Miami isn't exactly known as a place to escape partying.

"Hey, my folks would be so happy to see you doing good," he says. Then he turns to Matt, "You take care of her, okay? Miami ain't so far from Orlando that I can't drive down there and kick your ass."

For a second I consider correcting him and letting him know that Orlando is up from Miami, but I decide against it. That little piece of information would only make it easier to find me.

The main hall opens and we find our way to one of the head tables. We're seated right by Tommy and Joy.

"So how did you pop the question?" Matt asks.

He looks at Joy, deferring to her with a nod.

She lights up like a Christmas tree - which might be an inappropriate thing to say at a Bar Mitzvah but, screw it. That's what she lit up like.

"It happened yesterday around lunch time. I remember because I was hungry. Anyway, we had just finished finalizing the deal with Tony. Business was kind of slow."

"Does he still have that old soda pop machine?" I ask.

"Yes, we were right next to it. The floor was filthy and I almost slipped, so Tommy lifted me up onto the hood of one of the cars being worked on and pulled a rag out of his back pocket."

Always the mechanic.

"I thought he was going to wipe up the floor but instead he got down on one knee and said…"

Tommy puts his hand on Joy's and takes over. "Will you marry me Joy?"

"I screamed yes and the garage is so big it kind of echoed," Joy says before rubbing her cheek on Tommy's hand.

"Are you going to change much at the garage?" Matt the businessman asks.

"The name. Right now it's called Tony's and he isn't leaving with the best reputation," Joy answers. "I want to call it," she pauses for effect and her eyes get bigger, "Tom and Joy's Garage."

"And I want to call it Joy and Tom's," says my little brother with a shy smile.

What is it about a Bar Mitzvah? Suddenly all the boys in my family are becoming men.

A drum roll quickly changes the mood. A loudly dressed man runs into a spot light that has popped into the center of the dance floor. "Hello Ladies and Goyim, my name is MC Purnick. I'm a Jewish rapper. Oy to the vey!"

Is it just me or do all DJs at weddings and Bar Mitzvahs suck? I've never seen a good one but I don't want to give up hope that somewhere, someone is enjoying this DJ.

"Welcome the Teitelbaum Bar Mitzvah Safari!" he says as he hits a button that cues up, "Baby Elephant Walk." Four dancing girls dressed in gold lame jumpsuits wearing tails and cat ears enter and do a quick dance with four boys dressed as Safari Guides.

The festivities have officially begun.

Larry's father cuts the large loaf of bread. He looks very proud as he begins to slice. Members of the family are called up to light one of thirteen candles, one for each year of the person going through the Bar or Bat Mitzvah I suppose. Tommy and I are called up third, right after Rachel and Larry's parents. As each of us light our candle a lovely glow begins to take hold. It reminds me of Christian, still growing, getting stronger, going out into the world and spreading light.

Funny thing about wonderful moments; they are by definition temporary and can only last so long before they are replaced by something far less than wonderful.

Standing on the edge of the crowd, barely caught by the glow of the candlelight, is the one familiar face I did not expect to see this evening.

Paul is here.

CHAPTER
TWENTY NINE

"Are you all right?"

I hate to lie; especially to Matt, but somehow I'm guessing that this is not a time for the truth. "My stomach is just a little upset. I'm going to go to the ladies room." Inspired cover story, yes? "It must have been that third corn dog I ate."

Details always help craft a convincing lie. I learned that from the ex-husband that just crashed my nephew's Bar Mitzvah.

Joy stands up. "I'll go with you."

"NO!" I say way too loudly. "They're starting to serve the salads. Sit down. Eat. *Enjoy*," I grab my purse and start to exit with a saucy over the shoulder, "I'll be right back."

Matt stands up and kisses me on the cheek, which makes me feel even worse but I can't take time to indulge the guilt. A girl has to have her priorities and right now I have to find out if that really was Paul.

As I weave through the crowd ignoring the occasional, "Hi Frances!"

"Frances hello!" says someone with a little more moxie, someone who refuses to be ignored politely. A hand on my shoulder spins me around. It belongs to my Great Uncle Philip, a conspiracy theory addict who believes that multi-vitamins cause cancer because he got a small melanoma after taking Centrum for a week.

"How are you?" he asks with the very inconvenient and arrogant expectation of an answer.

"Fine," I say looking past him and into the crowd. "Fine. If you'll excu…"

"I'm so glad to hear that. It's quite a shindig, eh?"

"Wonderful."

"These caterers though. They're using balsamic vinegar on the salads. No good. It causes ulcers my darling. I was reading on that the Internet. Your Aunt Nancy and I recently bought a Dell computer from the Home Shopping Network, which is no coincidence because her mother's name was Adelle…"

After hearing my eighty-year old Uncle pontificate on everything from nutrition to why Diane Sawyer is obviously a lackey in the hip pocket of the teeth whitening industry I realize I'm starting to relax a little bit. We're in a high traffic area with great visibility. If Paul were here I would have seen him by now.

"And that's why you shouldn't eat potassium. Bananas are a silent killer, but the Chiquita people suppress the studies. They suppress it. The studies are suppressed."

What the hell? Is he conjugating the verb suppress? I suppress the temptation to say, "The only thing bananas around here is you." Instead

I say, "Thanks Uncle Philip. I'll keep that in mind. I promise."

"Just taking care of my family. That's all. Nothing is more important than family."

"You're right…"

"I mean, who else would hide you from the right wing power base when their plan to punish the blue states goes to the next level?"

"Riiiiiiiiight."

Oh great. Now I really do have to go to the bathroom. "If you'll excuse me, I was on my way to the ladies room."

"Of course you do! Corn dogs have an additive supplied by the toilet paper industry. One leads to the other," he says, kissing me on the cheek. "Save a chicken dance for your favorite uncle."

I turn toward the bathroom and run right into Paul.

It's disorienting for just a second, as though I'm back in my old life. I'm Frances Bettinger and there's a mini-van with personalized plates in the parking lot. It's here to take us down the road not taken.

That good old reliable knot in the pit of my stomach quickly brings me back to reality. So does the tension between us. It's almost like Paul and I are opposing magnets. Even if we wanted to be together we couldn't; yet all one of us would have to do is flip over, literally turn the other cheek, and we'd be on top of each other.

An eternity passes in all of two seconds.

"Paul."

"Hello Frances," his jaw clenches but his eyes brighten.

"Uh – I was just on my way to the ladies room."

"Oh! Oh. Don't let me stop you."

"Will you…"

"Wait?" he still finishes my sentences.

"Yes," I say with a smile. "I won't be long."

"Really," he says. "You've changed."

Was that supposed to be some sort of dig? Probably not. Relax and put your best foot forward Frances. I start down the hallway on less than steady heels. I bought a few minutes to collect myself. That's something, right?

Luckily the one available stall is relatively clean. Just as I finish doing my business my handbag begins vibrating. Someone's trying to call me. I catch it just before it starts to ring.

"Oh my God," barks Teresa. "Did you see him? DID YOU?" She's talking so loud that it hurts my ears.

"By him, to whom do you refer?" I ask knowing there's only one possible answer.

"He who has no name, that's who. I'm talking about your ex!" As if I had forty-five ex-husbands, she feels compelled to continue. "Paul is here!"

"I know. I just saw him."

"What are you going to do?" Teresa asks which is surprising. I expected her to tell me what to do. Being asked is a nice surprise.

"So far my master plan has consisted of running into the ladies room. He's waiting for me to come out."

"What?"

"The ladies room. I'm in the ladies room."

"No way. So am I."

We disconnect. The sound of two toilets flushing echoes through the tiled room; we both exit our stalls and meet in the middle of the ladies john.

Teresa grabs my hands and gives them a, "I'm here for you," squeeze. "Are you all right?'

"I suppose."

So deep is my sister's empathy for me that her Botoxed and chemically peeled face actually registers a little emotion. Her hips shift, and she hits me on the shoulder. "He looks good, right?"

As much as I'd like to say he has fallen apart without my supervision, Paul is holding up very well.

The sports coat I recognized. He bought it when we were together. The pants and shoes, they're new. Very trendy, as are the blonde highlights mixed in with his naturally dark brown hair. The overall effect screams of dating someone inappropriately younger, which isn't exactly a big surprise. After all, he was doing that when we were still married.

"He wants you back," she says without a moment's hesitation. "Why else would he be here?"

Paul is waiting right where I left him. He's looking at his watch with a smile. "Right back, huh? You haven't changed."

"I have."

"Really?" he says with that arrogant smirk that used to piss me off, and evidently still does. He thinks I haven't changed? It's been three years and he thinks I haven't changed? I'll show him.

"I'm more direct now," I say moving toward the inevitable. "Why are you here Paul?"

He looks around. "Uh - Christian's Bar Mitzvah?" he says. "I wanted to drop off a card."

What kind of ex-wife would I be if I weren't to let that slide? "You could have mailed it."

"You're right - but then I wouldn't have run into you," he loses a little of his confidence, "accidentally."

"Accidentally?"

"Come on Frances. You moved to Florida without even saying goodbye."

I smile in spite of myself and feel my eyes soften. "How are you Paul?"

We trade updates. I was right. He's seeing someone; which hurts a little to hear out loud, but it's nothing I can't handle. He says it's not serious yet. I don't want to get competitive so I don't mention Matt.

He goes on to tell me about his career and catches me up on old friends. Some of the details escape me. I try to concentrate but my mind wanders.

I look into Paul's eyes and remember tears. I look at his perfectly styled hair, and remember waking up to see it pointing in a million different directions. I look at his hands and remember them holding mine when I woke up in the hospital. I hear him saying, "You were the only one who made it."

I look at his mouth and think of his kisses for me, and then others. I remember more tears when he finally admitted it. "Yes Frances, I had sex with her." The memory of his voice becomes the white noise of a subway. I look at him and remember the final moment we were us.

We were on our way to a fancy party at London Terrace being held by his friend Patrick. I didn't want to go. I was wearing a pair of passive aggressive jeans. Paul was dressed up. He may even have been wearing the same sports coat. I don't recall. We walked to the C train on 50th Street. It was right after our last session with Carl, our third and final therapist.

As the train pulled into the station, Paul said something optimistic. It was the last thing I wanted or needed and I resented that I felt obliged to return the effort but I tried. I really did. I just couldn't do it. Some part of me still loved him, but I was done.

It was over.

The platform was crowded. Paul stepped onto the train, assuming I was behind him. He turned around to look for me just as the doors were closing; just as the thin metal and glass door made our separation a literal fact. I was on one side. He was on the other. He stared at me but there was no confusion. As the train pulled away I could swear he looked relieved.

"And my Mom is doing well too."

"I didn't ask," I say, throwing in a little chuckle at the end in the hopes that he'll know it was just a joke.

Mostly.

"It's nice to hear you laugh Frances. I missed your laugh," he says with bittersweet eyes.

So comes the pivotal moment, the opening.

I reach to embrace him to see how it feels to be back in his arms. We move towards each other but then a four year old boy runs between us. He might be five. He could be three and tall for his age. But to me he is four. And he'll remain four until next year when all the little boys become five. Their names will always be Sam.

Any foolish notion that was entertained is gone; evaporated and vanished. Paul feels it too. I can tell. There's no need to talk. This is not a time for discussion.

"It was good to see you," he says.

I nod and we finally embrace. Safely, like getting to touch a memory and say goodbye to someone you once thought was the air you breathed.

"So long." He walks away. Fifteen steps, one for each year and I call out to him. "Paul?" He doesn't turn around. One more try, "Paul?"

He hears me and turns around. I remember now. You always have to say it twice to get his attention.

"I just wanted to say it was good to see you."

"You too," he says before starting away again.

Quickly, before I lose my resolve, "And, that I forgive you. I forgive you and hope you can forgive me too." Then I add, "And that you're happy. With all my heart, I hope you're happy."

He comes back and kisses me for what I'm guessing will be the final time. "What I would have missed not knowing you. What I would have missed."

He walks away and keeps going until I can't see him anymore, as though he was that subway car so long ago. I travel in the opposite direction.

Matt, ever the gentleman stands when he sees me arrive. "Are you okay?" he says.

I nod.

Joy says, "You missed the salad."

"Oh well. It's just the starter. Bring on the second course. I'm ready."

The rest of the night is perfect: good food, family, friends, and dancing. The best part is seeing all of it in the moment through Matt's fresh eyes. It's wonderful but before I know it the safari is over. We're headed back to the civilization of Manhattan. We're back at the hotel getting ready for bed.

Instinctively I reach for my earrings only to remember that they belong to Rachel now. I search through my suitcase for make-up remover and feel something through the thin nylon pocket at the side of my suitcase. I push aside the zipper.

There it is; the bracelet Gladys' father gave to her mother. I slip it on my wrist and watch light dancing off the small diamonds.

"I can't believe she gave this to me," I say to Matt. "She's too generous. I'm returning it the minute I get home."

Probably.

I stretch and yawn. What a day. Christian's Bar Mitzvah. Joy and Tommy announcing they are getting married on the same day I finally said goodbye to Paul; the same day Matt and I said, "I love you," for the first time.

And Teresa is pregnant.

I gave Rachel Mom's earrings. And now Gladys has given me this wonderful bracelet. Perhaps the Buddhists have it right. Sometimes you have to give up something to make room for something new. It's the natural order of things.

A quiet reflective moment ends too quickly. And it turns out it is to be the last happy moment I'll have for quite a while.

The hotel phone rings. Matt is in the bathroom slipping into a thick white cotton robe after a quick shower. The steam lingers above our heads like thunderclouds.

"I'll get it!" I say extra loudly so he can hear me.

"Hello?"

"It's Desi."

"Hey! What's up? Wait 'til you hear everything that's been going on. Have I got news for you."

"Frances, can I speak to Matt?"

"Matt?"

Wait a minute. Desi is my friend, not Matt's.

"Why do you want to talk to Matt?"

"Just let me speak to Matt. Please."

By now he's in the room. I hand him the phone silently, unable to concentrate on anything other than my growing sense of dread.

The conversation is brief.

"Thanks for calling." Matt hangs up the phone slowly as he sits on the edge of the bed, motioning for me to join him.

"What is it?" I say slowly and evenly. I don't think I want to know.

"It's Gladys," he says staring at the floor. "Sweetheart, she had a heart attack."

"Okay," I say, getting up and walking the same five steps back and forth. "Okay. Let's call the airline. Find out how soon we can get back. She'll need us."

He doesn't move.

"Matt, call the airline," I demand. "Call now."

But he just sits there so I grab the phone.

"Fine. I'll do it myself," but I don't start dialing. I already know that there's no need.

Matt stands up and puts his arms around me.

He opens with "I'm so sorry."

And then he says it.

"She didn't make it sweetheart. Gladys is dead."

CHAPTER
THIRTY

I know Matt was trying to be sweet upgrading us to first class but what was he thinking; that wider leather seats and real silverware would make me forget that Gladys is laying in a box somewhere waiting to be buried?

Part of me wants to give into the gray creamy softness of my seat, lean into the strength of Matt's shoulders and close my eyes but that's not going to happen.

The silence gets heavier with each mile, for me at least. Matt is wearing his Bose Quiet Comfort 2 Noise Blocking "Consumer Reports says they're best" Headphones.

"OH!" he says too loudly but unaware thanks to the headphones, "I called Kellie and told her about Gladys. She's extending your time off."

"Why?"

"What do you mean?" as he takes off the headphones.

"Why would you tell Kellie about Gladys? It's none of her business."

He looks confused, "I was just filling her in on staffing; besides she already knew. Desi told her."

"Don't bring him into this. Why would you tell your little lap dog Kellie anything about me?"

"Lap dog? Come on…"

"Don't change the subject."

"Keep your voice down," Matt demands. "People are starting to stare."

"Someone dies and you turn to Kellie." His eyes are wide. My eyes are narrow. "That's what you did when Thia died, right?"

"Don't compare this to Thia. It's not the same."

"Gladys was old. Her death matters less. Is that what you're saying?"

"I didn't say that."

"Really? That's what it sounded like."

He looks away, but then turns back. "I'm not going to defend myself over something I don't think and didn't say."

"Really?"

"No."

"What do I know about grief, right? You're the only one that's ever suffered a loss."

"I didn't say that," says the sweet man sitting in seat 2B on Delta flight 238.

"Ladies and gentlemen, this is your captain speaking. We are experiencing a bit of turbulence."

No kidding Captain.

"Please keep your seatbelts on."

Matt looks up at the little seat buckle insignia and then back to me. His eyes go from angry to soft in a matter of seconds.

"I know what happened Frances."

Instinctively I get up but my seatbelt pulls me back down. My head jerks toward him but the same instinct makes me instantly look away toward the window. I push away from him but the window and wall allow me to only get so far away.

"It's okay," he says as he reaches for my hand.

"It's *okay*? No it's not. It's certainly not. How long have you known?"

"It was part of your background check before we hired you."

"Part of my background check? So you've known since before we met?"

"Yes."

"You knew before we became involved, before we slept together, and you waited until now to tell me?"

"It wasn't like that…"

"What? You figured let's hook up with the other one in the office who's been knocked around? Maybe grief and a little sangria …"

"Frances, don't say that," he says. I can tell by the set of his jaw that he's uncomfortable, but I don't care. All in.

"What should I say? I know. Let me fill in the blanks and tell you the rest of the story. The parts a background check might not tell you."

Images come flying back at me. I choose one and begin. "The dining room of our apartment was going to be the nursery, until we bought a bigger place. There was a mural spelling out his name in stars, like a constellation. Sam. I painted it myself."

"Frances, you don't have to put yourself through this."

"Paul was out of town for work. He almost didn't go because it was close to our due date. I stayed with my parents in Forest Hills in case anything happened. Paul was due back, so I wanted to go home. My parents didn't think the subway was safe for a woman in my condition. That's how they put it. They drove me home."

"We were on the BQE, the Brooklyn Queens Expressway, driving toward Manhattan. A car crossed the median. My Dad twisted the wheel to protect Mom and I, and Sam I suppose. We flipped over."

Again, he nods. As though he knows. Then I remember. He does know. He knows all of it.

"I was in a coma for 4 days. No, wait. I don't want to exaggerate. It was just under 96 hours; so less than 4 days. When I woke up, I wasn't pregnant anymore and my parents were dead. Paul was there, waiting and told me everything."

Another image flashes – I see Paul unshaven, bags under his eyes, slouched, weary and sadder than I'd ever seen anyone before or since.

"Did you know that Jews believe bodies should be buried within 24 hours of death?" I don't wait for an answer. "Of course you didn't. You're from Wisconsin. Why would you know that? Teresa talked Paul into following tradition. Everyone was buried as soon as possible – Sam was buried in my mother's arms, or so I'm told. I wasn't there. I was in the hospital, in a coma."

Matt reaches out and rubs my arm.

"I was the only that survived. The drunk speeding to get her kids from school, the one who was having an affair that she was rushing home from? Dead – so there was no one to punish. There was no one to direct my anger toward, is what a therapist told me. I feel bad for her kids; but at least they got to meet their mom."

"I'm so sorry Frances."

"The story isn't over yet. It turns out there was probably a slight tear in the placenta that I didn't know about. The impact tore the rest away and that's what killed the baby. I read all about (it) in *The New York Post*. My medical information, Sam's medical information, right out there for everyone in New York to read. *The Daily News* reported, not directly about me of course but in an article about the accident, that mothers using cocaine are more prone to Placenta Abruption." A nasty thought flashes. "Is that why I had to take a drug test when you hired me?"

"No. No."

"I've never used cocaine in my life; but there are probably people who think I have. Those are the people that think I caused my baby's death."

"You'd have to be crazy not to be depressed after something like that. I think some days I was both – crazy and depressed. The doctors prescribed meds. So now in addition to hormones and sadness and God only knows what else, I now have chemicals in my body. They couldn't get the dosage correct, so I got worse. I would stare at Paul and get so angry. He held the baby. He got to see him, got to touch him and then he signed the papers that allowed Teresa to do whatever she wanted to. I barely talked to her for a year. Turns out you can't divorce sisters. Just husbands."

"He tried to ride it out, but I was so nasty, so angry, that eventually he turned to someone else … okay, lots of others, which is not who he really is. He's a good guy. So I even feel guilty for that. I took all my disappointment out on him until he became another disappointment."

Again I see the subway doors closing. There's Paul looking at me on the other side of the door between us.

"After the divorce I went through the motions. I'd force myself to wash my hair. Force myself to meet deadlines. Force myself to go outside. Everywhere I went people seemed to know my story. So I decided to go where people didn't know me or what had happened."

"Orlando," Matt says.

"Right, the happiest place on Earth." I smile. "I can't tell you how nice it was not to be the woman who got in a car and lost everything she thought she'd have for the rest of her life … but I guess it wasn't real. Nothing is real in Orlando, right? It's all make-believe."

"No it's not. It's not all make-believe. A lot of it is real. You and me, we're real."

"You were letting me believe what I wanted to believe. You knew. Maybe others. Maybe Kellie."

His silence tells me I'm right.

I take another sip of my drink and think of my father. He always said there's a reason why arms aren't amputated with emery boards. "Some things need to be done quickly." That's what my father used to tell me.

Part of me wants to fight the urge to run, to create distance; but it's too familiar not to give into and I keep talking.

"So no baby, no husband, no parents, no Gladys … and no boyfriend."

"What? No boyfriend?"

Matt starts to say something else, but the flight attendant interrupts.

"Another Bloody Mary?"

"No. No thank you. I've had enough"

The seatbelt sign has been turned off while I was talking. I unlatch, stand up and find an empty seat back in economy where I belong. No one tries to stop me.

CHAPTER
THIRTY-ONE

"Hello?"

"Hi Lorna, it's Frances Fiore."

"Oh thank God. Things are frantic around here. *Please,* tell me you're calling to follow up on our little offer."

"Well, that all depends on how little the offer is."

"How soon can you be back in New York?"

"Just as soon as I finish up a project I'm on here in Florida."

Goodbye Planet Binger. Hello New York.

"Frances?" Joy walks into the room as I hang up the phone. "Tom packed the last of his things. It's time for us to go."

"Are you sure?"

"Never surer."

I push myself away from the desk and out of the office Joy set up when I moved in here. We start to walk toward the front door.

"Listen, if you need to talk I'm just a phone call away," says my only girlfriend in Orlando who happens to be leaving Orlando in a matter of minutes.

"In case I need to talk? You're the one marrying a mute."

"That just leaves more time for him to show me how he feels," says Joy as she licks her lips and moves her eyebrows up and down.

"Okay, ick. That's my brother you're talking about there. Talk to your other girlfriends about the sexy stuff."

"But you're my best girlfriend," says my future sister-in-law as I push the lacy pink bra strap up over her shoulder.

Joy and I are still hugging as Tommy walks up. My arms move from her to my little brother, suddenly all grown up.

"Bye," is all I can manage without choking up.

"Frances, I just wanted to say," a text alert comes from his phone. He mouths the words as he reads.

"Oh geez! It's from Teresa. She says we got to leave now if we want to beat rush hour traffic in Atlanta."

"Okay," says Joy climbing into the passenger side of Tommy's truck.

He starts to follow her, but pauses and turns back to me. "Thanks for everything. You know, being here changed my life. I mean, look at her," he says, motioning toward Joy. "She's," he searches for the right words, "everything."

"Okay, you've got everything. Now go find more."

Tommy says, "Eh, take your own advice," and shoots me a meaningful look before starting the engine and pulling away.

I'm still staring at the taillights when a woman runs over toward me, which isn't easy. She's a big girl.

I start to walk away.

"Miss Fiore? Miss Fiore!"

I turn and give her the most sincere smile I can muster. "Yes? May I help you?"

"You're a very hard woman to get a hold of."

"I'm sorry … have we met?"

"My name is Saylie, Saylie Nelson-Barrett, Gladys' daughter?"

"Oh yes!"

"We wanted to thank you for being so good to our mother. She spoke very highly of you."

I can feel the tears behind my eyes, but I will not let them escape. My grief does not compare to this woman's. Deep breath and recover.

"Your mother was incredible."

"We missed you at the funeral. We got the flowers though. They were lovely."

"I thought it might just be family."

"Well, I think my mother thought of you as family Miss Fiore." I look into her eyes and see little pieces of Gladys shining through. It's her eyes really. She has her mother's eyes. I start to relax a little bit.

"Frances. Please. Call me Frances."

"She left you this property Frances, both houses."

"What? No. There must be some mistake."

"No mistake. The probate will last for at least a year, given the size of the estate, afterward you'll be free to sell or stay. She amended her will right after her last stay at the hospital. She told me about it at the time.

She said she wanted to make sure you always had a sense of home."

"But you and your sisters, surely you expected …"

"Don't worry about us. I'll admit we were surprised, but Mother's trust left us all very well off."

"Trust? What do you mean? I don't…"

"Know? You didn't know? My mother's maiden name was Binger. Her parents were Art and Mary Binger."

"What?"

"Mother never liked people to know who her parents were. I don't think she much cared for sharing them with the world, so she talked about *who* they were, not what they did."

"Your mom was an original - full of surprises."

Saylie laughs. "Wasn't she? That's how I'm going to remember her. I didn't know who all those people were talking about at the funeral."

I think I like this Saylie woman. "Would you like to have some tea?" I ask.

"No."

"Oh, of course not."

"If were going to spend time reminiscing about my mother I think we ought to make something a little stronger."

My new friend and I spend the afternoon toasting Gladys Nelson with Harvey Wallbangers garnished with maraschino cherries.

CHAPTER
THIRTY-TWO

"Thanks for the latte Frances," says Desi of the frothy milk moustache. "You got the skinny, sugar free, right?"

"Just like you said. Why? You're not dieting are you?"

"Yeah."

"Why?"

A smile that could be an ad for whitening strips breaks out across his face.

"Because of this!" Desi turns around his computer screen. There is a montage of pictures of what is easily the most beautiful man I have ever seen. "His name is Jorge."

My jaw drops. My mouth hangs open. There are no words to describe the beauty of this man.

"Right? Gorgeous no? He's from my village in Cuba. Turns out he's been in Miami for years. He finally came to Orlando."

"And?"

"We've been seeing each other for three months."

"Three months? Why didn't you say anything?"

"Well you haven't been in the office much. And, you know, after you and Matt broke it off…"

"I broke it off, you mean. I broke it off."

"Whatever."

"Say it…"

"Okay, you broke it off."

He shoves his glasses down onto the bridge of his Nose and looks over the rims. Can I finish now?"

"You may…"

Desi gives me a shy smile. "I just didn't seem like the best time to talk about love or anything…"

"Love?" My smile grows. "Do you LOVE him?"

Desi's blush confirms everything.

I start to sing a little song, "You love him. You love him."

"Stop it!"

"Details! I want details! How did you meet?"

"Okay, well, I ran into him during Gay Days at Planet Binger."

Allow me to explain.

Gay Days at Planet Binger, evidently they've been happening, well forever. I mean when isn't it gay day at Planet Binger? It's been official for about 20 years. Gay boys from all over the world descend on the parks during the first weekend in June. Hundreds of thousands of them book all the hotel rooms in Orlando. They wear pink t-shirts or tanks, the tighter the better, rabbit ears and little tails, which kind of make them look like Playboy Bunnies; which is funny because that's all about being straight right? Some of them even wear fishnets and pumps. Well, according to the pictures I've seen Desi wore fishnets and pumps.

We will actually give you free clothing if you didn't know and show up to the parks wearing pink that weekend. It's like all the parents are worried that their six-year-old daughter is going to be labeled a baby lesbian or something.

"Good for you Desi."

"Yeah. He's almost done with medical school, and…"

"Wait-a-minute! He's gorgeous and he's a doctor?"

"Yeah! Crazy, right?"

"Sometimes life just isn't fair."

"There's more," he says biting his upper lip.

"What? He's won the lottery too?"

"I might go with him for his residency, which would be in Los Angeles …"

"Oh, well that's great Desi. That's great. Good for you. Good for *him*."

What is the word for feeling sad and happy at the same time? I'm happy for Desi but sad too. There should be a word for those two feelings when they combine. Sappy? Had? Bittersweet, that's it.

I don't know why this is bothering me so much. I mean I'm moving back to New York.

But I'm doing it alone.

Aha.

It seems like everyone else is heading to the ark two by two. Tommy and Joy and Desi and Jorge. And Frances and her cat are waving from the pier.

I start to feel a little tense and look around the room. "Well listen, I should get going."

"He's not here Frances."

"I'm sorry. What? I don't know what…"

"Matt. Matt is not here. He is in meetings at corporate all day long. Remember, you had me check his Outlook?"

"Well that's really none of my business."

"Okay. It's none of mine either, but I've got to say I think you're making a mistake."

"Mine to make, right?" I gently put my hand on his arm before gathering my things. "Mine to make."

I stop to say goodbye to Gratciana and push open the door. I walk outside. Kellie and Matt are directly between my car and me.

Shit.

I drop the papers in my hands. Loose-leaf paper and poster tubes spill out everywhere. It's like a little tornado of office supplies.

"Hello Frances," says Kellie, who bends down trying to help me. Dammit. Don't be helpful. I hate you.

Wait a minute. Something is different.

"Kellie … your hair …"

She stands up and frames her hair with the palm of her hand as she bevels like a beauty contestant.

"Do you like it?"

"The color…"

"It's my natural color. Just between us," she looks around for effect, "I wasn't a natural redhead."

"No kidding?"

Matt takes advantage of being behind her and taller to shoot me a look, the subtext being, play nice.

I hear myself say, "Kellie, it looks really good," which is the truth. It's shorter and modern.

It gives her a whole new style. Okay, it finally gives her a style. So do her clothes. "I like it."

"Thank you." She looks up at Matt. "Lots of things have changed. Maybe we can catch up sometime and talk? There are things I'd like to tell you."

"Maybe. You know I'm working from home these days."

"Yes. We hardly ever see you," says Matt.

"Speaking of which, I should get going." I rustle some papers to make it look official and start to walk away.

"Kellie, could you give me a minute alone with Frances?"

Dammit.

We both watch Kellie walk away. Is it the new clothes or has she lost weight? Something is going on there.

"How are you?" asks Matt. From the set of his mouth I can tell he's no more comfortable than I.

"Good. Fine."

Pause.

"How about you?"

"Getting there."

Matt was removed from the Tiny Planet project after we broke up. Neither of us raised the issue. It was corporate policy. I felt bad when it happened but looking at him now, I can't help but think maybe it was for the best. As a consolation prize he was placed on the task force for a new park in Australia, which is considered a promotion; besides, working together everyday would've been awful.

God knows this is hard enough.

Now it's his turn to walk away.

He turns around at the last moment. "You know, it didn't have to be this way."

"Please don't."

"Life isn't meant to be a punishment. It's not about suffering. Bad things happen."

"No kidding."

"Life is about the grace you show when bad things happen. It's about keeping an open heart. Thia, Sam, your parents, Gladys, it's about living by their examples, not closing everyone out so you don't get hurt again."

He moves closer.

"Be happy Frances, with or without me. Just give yourself permission to be happy. That's what I'm trying to do," and then he finally walks away. I follow him with my eyes, until I see him rejoining Kellie at the door. She gives him a little hug and they walk inside together.

The rest of the day is a mess. Nothing works out because all I could think about was seeing Matt and what he said. He makes it all seem so logical and easy; but it's not. Not for me.

So here I am hours later sitting in a lounge chair, with one of the cigarettes I found in Gladys' stash. Without warning a thought bursts into my head, just like the fireworks that are exploding overhead in the evening sky.

Matt is giving himself permission to be happy.

Life is about keeping an open heart.

Kellie wants to talk.

She waited for Matt at the door.

Dammit.

Another two just got on the ark.

CHAPTER
THIRTY-THREE

Crossing in through the front door of the house I can't help but expect Gladys to walk in with a pitcher of Whiskey Old Fashioned cocktails in Mad Men era frosted glasses.

Thinking of Gladys makes me happy. I walk into the kitchen done with sentiment and ready to work. "I'm going to start in the attic, okay?"

Gladys' daughters look up from the pile of Tupperware in which they're drowning. "Okay. If you need us, we'll be here trying to figure out which pieces have a cover."

"Why did she have so much Tupperware? She didn't cook."

"She and Daddy were friends with Earl Tupper," says Saylie.

"He was the inventor of Tupperware," adds Valerie, the one who looks the most like Gladys.

Susan, the one who I'm pretty sure has had some work done, brings it home. "Let me tell you the story."

Forty minutes later I'm heading toward the attic weak with laughter. Those are three apples that did not fall far from the tree. The sisters Nelson know how to tell a story. How Gladys hosted a Tupperware party that ended with her getting drunk with Steve Lawrence and Eydie Gorme on their tour bus is beyond me.

Katz runs past me toward the attic. I pause to re-tie the bandana covering my head. The girls are right, this is a lot of work, but maybe it'll be a nice break. Tiny Planet has fallen into a big black hole. If I don't get an idea for the big ending I'm going to be stuck in Orlando forever.

My hands stumble along the wall. It's dark up here.

iPhone out. Flashlight app.

Okay, here's the light switch.

The attic fills with light and I immediately miss the dark. I've haven't seen this many boxes since the ending of the first *Raiders of the Lost Ark*. Is it possible Gladys was a well-organized hoarder?

Thank God I hear the girls heading up the stairs. Together we'll get through this a lot quicker.

"We're heading to Yellow Dog to pick up lunch, says Saylie. "What do you want?"

Ten minutes later I've gotten through one box and started piles for each sister. I open another box, which appears to be stuffed with Happy Meal Binger Bunnies when I hear my cell phone.

HAVA NAGILA...

I pick it up before the second HAVA, thankful for the distraction. Any distraction. There's enough dust up here to take out a convention of asthmatics.

"Hello Teresa!"

"Hello? You sound awfully happy to hear from me..."

"Always."

"Well not today you're not." Teresa definitely has an edge to her voice this morning.

"Why?"

"I've got news." She pauses for effect and sucks on her teeth. "Big news."

"Okay," I answer, getting a little nervous.

"I just got back from the doctor."

"Well the news can't be all bad. I can hear the kids laughing in the background."

"Oh yeah. They're laughing now," she says loudly. "They're laughing now," she says louder. I break in before she can go for loudest.

"What did the doctor say?"

Christian and Rachel chime in at the same time. "She's having triplets!"

"Damn fertility drugs!"

"You're kidding, right?"

"Why would we kid about such a thing?" Teresa's pregnancy hormones kick in. "WHY WOULD I KID?"

"Okay. Okay. Well," I struggle for the way to turn around such news, "Let's look on the bright side of things."

"BRIGHT SIDE???"

"Yes." What is the word Christian used at his Bar Mitzvah? "It's a *brokhe*, a blessing."

"HOW IS THIS A BROKHE YOU CRAZY GOYIM?"

"Well, you wanted babies, right?"

"Yes, of course I wanted a baby. A baby. One. Not babies," she says lingering on the plural for a long, long time.

"Well, you've been blessed with an abundance."

"I'm listening…"

"It's like a baby sukkit."

"A baby, what? Did you say suck it?"

"No, *no*. The harvest holiday. Sukkit."

"You mean *Sukkot*?" says Teresa. "Oh my God, you thought we had a holiday called suck it? That is hilarious."

"Teresa, let's not …"

"Suck it! HA! Larry, listen to what Frances said…"

The story is repeated. I hear everyone laughing in the background. This story is sure to be told at the triplets Bar or Bat Mitzvahs.

"So, what else did the doctor say?"

"To say hello to my beautiful sister. Dr. Mendelsteen was very excited to hear you're coming back to New York. He just divorced his third wife. He had a pre-nup this time so he's still sitting pretty."

"No Teresa, about the babies. Your *triplets*, remember? What did he say about the babies?"

"Oh! One boy. Two girls, thank God. Three boys? I don't know what I'd do."

Biting my lower lip I ask, "Are they all healthy?"

"Oh my goodness. What do I know about telling a story? Yes! Yes! One is a little small. That one will be my favorite during the birth, but otherwise everything is fine. Fine."

Teresa pauses before asking, "But how about you? How does this make you feel?"

"Fine. I'm happy, happy for you."

I can hear her starting to sniffle and choke up. The pregnancy hormones are kicking in again. "Oh wow. Wow."

"What?"

"I'm having three healthy little babies, at my age. You're right. It *is* a blessing."

Of course we have to start talking baby details. What kind of aunt would I be if we didn't?

The nursery is going to be classic Binger. Of course the news comes with strict instructions to use my 40% discount, which I would have offered if she hadn't asked.

Sometimes I wish my sister would wait to ask until I've had a chance to offer. Ah, wishes. What do they get you really?

"Have you decided on names?"

"I have, but don't tell Larry. I've got to find a way to make him think these names were his idea." She continues of course, "I was thinking of Florence for Momma and Frances, because it's pretty and you don't hear it much these days."

I hesitate before asking, but have to know.

"What about the boy?"

"Well, every family should have a Sam."

My sister. She does things right.

Later, I hear the door open from downstairs. "Hello?"

I can't quite place the voice. Is it Susan or Valerie? "Still up here!" I yell, anticipating the taste of my sandwich. I hear the sound of stairs being climbed. "That was quick."

Wrong again.

"Hi Frances."

Really God? Really?

"Kellie, this isn't really a good time."

"You're going to keep saying that," says the newly assertive Kellie, "until I give up, which isn't going to happen." She crosses her arms and sticks out her hip. "We might as well talk right now."

"Okay. Let's talk."

"Really?" she says as her face lights up. "Great!"

Pause followed by awkward pause.

"Oh! Okay. I'll start. I mean that makes total sense. I'm the one that wanted to talk after all."

I put extra effort into sounding as patronizing as I possibly can, "Right."

"So how are you?" Pause. "No? Okay, well then let's cut to the chase. I'm here, partially, in an official capacity to talk about the resignation letter you turned in on Friday."

"What about it? It's rather self-explanatory. I quit."

"Why?"

"I explained that in the letter."

She pulls a copy of the letter out of her black leather purse. Next come her glasses.

"Let's see where is it? Oh yes, here!" She slides the glasses further down her nose and clears her throat. "I am leaving to take a position with another company in New York." She looks up and shrugs her shoulders.

"What more do you want to know?"

"Why are you really leaving?"

Okay, here goes.

"I'm sick of being hurt and disappointed."

"By what?"

"For starters you and Matt. For months you knew about everything that happened to me and never said anything. You just let me go on thinking I had a fresh start."

"What else were we supposed to do? Come up to you in the middle of a workday and say, "I'm sorry your life was destroyed by a drunk driver?" Is that what you expected us to do?"

How am I supposed to respond to that?

"Because I am Frances, I am so sorry that happened to you. I cannot even imagine what that felt like. You had everything anyone could want and then to wake up and find out it's all gone. I can't imagine the strength it took to get up the next day after something like that happens."

I go back to the box I was unpacking. Kellie puts her hands on my shoulders and turns me back toward her.

"Your strength, your talents – I wish I was more like you. I truly think you're a miracle Frances."

Then for some reason she starts walking toward me.

My God, she's going to try and hug me. She's going to try and *hug* me.

"No, no. No hugs. No girlfriend moment. Kellie I appreciate everything you just said. Thank you. I wish I was gracious enough to accept it all and become your friend, but now that you're with Matt…"

"Huh?"

She backs away, looking confused."I'm sorry. What?"

"You. And Matt. You and Matt. I've known all along that you had feelings for him and now you have him, so the two of you just float away on your little pixie dust cloud…."

"Pixie dust is Disney," corrects Kellie.

"Okay, whatever. *Whatever*. The two of you just go be together forever and ever. Have a baby. Name it Binger for all I care. Just leave me be."

Kellie starts laughing.

"Are you laughing at me?"

"No. No! Well, yes. Yes I am."

"I don't think this is anything to laugh about."

"It's not. It's not!" shrieks Kellie as she crosses her legs to keep from peeing. "I'm not with Matt. That's the last thing in the world I would do."

"Well that's harsh. Matt's a good guy."

"Yes. Yes he is. He's like my brother."

"What?"

"Oh Frances, I'd be lucky to have a guy like Matt; not Matt, but a guy like him."

"You're not with Matt?"

"No," she hesitates. "Listen, can I tell you something? Just between you and I?"

"If you must."

A tense silence is broken with a strong exhale. "I was involved with David Cobbler for the last eight years."

"Who?"

"Mr. Cobbler."

"That uptight VP? The synergy guy?"

"Yes, the *married* synergy guy," she says looking hopeless and staring up at the ceiling.

"The bald one? Cobbler, as in elf? Short?" I stick out my hand so it lands at my ribs. "Like 5 feet tall?"

"Oh now, be fair. He's 5' 2"."

We both laugh.

"Oh Frances, don't you see, that's what I wanted to tell you. Knowing you, and what you've gone through, it finally made me see that I wasted," her face goes deadpan, "*eight years* of my life with something that wasn't going anywhere."

"Wow."

"Exacty. He liked submissive women, so I became submissive. He wanted me to wear my hair curly so I got *eight years* worth of perms. Who gets perms anymore? Just me! He liked redheads, so I became a redhead! He liked leather so I went out and bought…"

"Kellie, I get it."

"My point is Frances I got stuck." She grabs my hand. "Don't let that happen to you. You want to go to New York, go. If that's what you want. But if even a tiny part of you thinks you might have a future here, with or without Matt, why don't you stick around and figure it out?"

There's only one thing left to say.

"Mr. Cobbler? Really?"

We laugh all the way to her car.

"Think about what I said, okay?"

"Do I have to?"

"Yes … and remember your nametag."

"God I am going to hate not hating you anymore."

She smiles as she waves goodbye on her way home to walk her three-legged dog.

Later after a very satisfying Johnny Rocket Sandwich from Yellow Dog Eats I make my way back up to the attic, which was not entirely voluntary.

"You're an honorary Nelson now. Get up there and empty that attic!" says Saylie. The other two sisters make the sound of a whip cracking.

It's a good thing I like these Nelson sisters so much or I'd resent their bossy, pushy ways, which they clearly get from their mom.

I halfheartedly return to the box I was working on and dig through the first layer of toys.

There, waiting underneath is the prize in the box I never could have expected. It's the same picture of the little girl I found at the museum in Queens.

It's Gladys.

CHAPTER
THIRTY-FOUR

A Planet Binger map seldom provides the most efficient path between attractions. Guests of the Rabbit are taken down twisting routes that actually take them further from their destination. Consequently people sometimes get stuck somewhere they never intended to be.

Today I forgo the detours. I wake up prepared for the day. I shower, put on my clothing, spend a few minutes petting my contented cat as he stretches under a sunbeam, notice the time, grab the bag that's beside the door of my house, get in my new car, and head to my office.

The day is uneventful, but rewarding. I leave knowing I have something to look forward to. I walk past the iconic castle - a symbol of make believe to some, for others real life. When I reach the construction fence in Binger's Kingdom of Enchantment I flash my credentials and head exactly where I am meant to be.

"Hello everyone," says an executive I've never met. "Thank you for joining us this evening. You are amongst the first to be welcomed to the new Tiny Planet."

308

Fiberglass boats pull up on cue. The gates silently open and we are invited inside the attraction to take a ride.

I quickly scan the crowd.

Former Planet Binger Ambassador Shelaylee Ward is at the front of the line. She's here with her husband the magician who has a kind, impish face. "Hello Frances. Nice to meet you," he says with a flourish before pulling a coin out from behind my ear.

Kellie and Donny, the short man she met working at an animal rescue called A Better Life run up and quickly say hello. She casually and openly grabs his hand. With a perpetual giggle she says, "Let's get a seat in the front!" before running off to get in her boat.

Gratciana is here with her children all of whom are happy, healthy and thriving.

Representing the Binger Family are Saylie, Valerie, and Susan, their children and all eleven of Gladys' great-grandchildren.

Standing just a little ways off, on the border of it all is Matt O'Connell looking as handsome as ever. It doesn't escape my attention that he's wearing the tie I bought him in New York. The butterflies in my stomach fly away as I motion for him to sit next to me. Once again, for now at least, we're in the same boat and it's nice.

Just before we leave Binger Bunny appears underscored by a quick fanfare. People applaud as he sits down next to Matt and me. The boat rocks for a bit before finding equilibrium.

Soon, the hot Florida sun is replaced by darkness. We hit a wall of mist and are on our way. The water, "Deep enough to create the illusion of depth," says the executive, parts with a gurgle as we round another corner.

The simplicity of riding through Tiny Planet is deceptive. There's no evidence of the countless hours of planning, meetings, budgets, building, revisions and rebuilding that it took to make all this happen. It doesn't begin to tell the stories of all the women and men behind the magic, the people who have created these attractions that become precious memories of childhood. The world will never know them but their hard work made dreams real for generations and generations of families.

I'm proud to be one of them.

In the front boat I can see Sherman Stamper. He wrote "Tiny Planet," with his late brother Craig for the 1965 World's Fair.

Their song begins to play.

We all see the sunrise
We see the sunset
We all love someone
we haven't met yet
Though mountains divide
It can't be denied
It's a tiny planet after all

Smiles are bright
Tears can be shiny
As our hearts get bigger
The planet gets tiny
Oceans keep us apart
But we know in our heart

It's a tiny planet after all

Little children represented by one-dimensional figures and dolls, pop up to say hello in their native languages. They used to be very stereotypical in a cute way I suppose. These new ones were actually created by school children from around the world. I hear Gratciana's little boy Joey in a boat behind ours.

"There's mine!"

American kids from all 50 states are represented. So are children from France, Chile, Brazil, Qatar, Afghanistan, Australia, and Japan. We even have a drawing from a child growing up in Antarctica – every country that wanted to participate was included, making the planet very tiny indeed.

Desi's friend Maya, the dancer in Cuba sent a charming drawing done by one of her children. It's shows a boy and girl dancing together on top of a giant pineapple.

There are kayaking koalas, limbo-ing giraffes, ice-skating squirrels, ballerinas dancing on music boxes come to life, anything a child could imagine. It's the ultimate playground, a place where any child might love to live.

Now we are in a tunnel passing by video images of Binger Bunny. It does not go unnoticed by the rabbit sitting next to me. He blows a loud kiss to himself as we pass.

We start to travel backwards through time. Binger de-evolves from his current computer generated incarnation to hand drawn animation to a simple line drawing on a pad of paper in Mary Binger's farmhouse kitchen.

The segment ends with a photo of a pretty little girl named Gladys sitting on her mother's lap as she draws. Just the two of them. No studio. No theme parks. It's just a mother and child, close together – before their world became a planet.

Saylie turns back and mouths, "Thank you," before turning to kiss the head of the grandchild that sits on her own lap.

As the ride ends we enter a large dome. The boats leave their linear track, because when is life ever linear? We orbit the circumference of the room. Mixed in with pictures of the Binger family are pictures of guests enjoying the park that day and pictures of families and people from all over the world via Facebook and Instagram, the co-sponsors of Planet Binger's latest attraction. #Binger

Matt looks at me with surprise. "Is that a picture of Thia?" he asks.

"Do you mind?"

He just shakes his head and smiles.

The montage of pictures ends with a sonogram, normally hidden behind my parent's wedding picture in a silver frame on a high shelf in my home. It is meant to represent the future. Only the strongest of eyes could make out, "Baby Bettinger," in the upper left hand corner, but I know it's there and that he was too.

Sam Bettinger was here.

Quietly under his breath I hear Binger Bunny say, "Wow," as the boat moves on.

The nameless executive offers his hand to pull me out of the boat. "Wonderful work Miss Fiore."

"Thank you."

"I'm sorry to hear you'll be leaving the company."

"Oh, but I'm not. I've decided to stay."

"Good news, right?" I hear his smile in Matt's voice. I turn around and he takes me in his arms.

Our kiss is tentative but hopeful. That's enough for today. I open my eyes in time to see the castle silhouetted against a burst of red, followed by blue, golden yellow and then a shimmering silver shower of starbursts. The show has begun.

Fireworks will light my way home.

ACKNOWLEDGEMENTS

The irony that you can find real life in a land of make-believe delights me.

I moved to Walt Disney World without an expectation of anything other than a steady paycheck, a dishwasher and good weather. What was supposed to be one year became twelve. I lost and found love, got hit by a truck, learned to walk again with the help of friends & had a home filled with people I will treasure for the rest of my life.

In Orlando I learned that you have to stop and enjoy the fireworks because they are inevitable - and also because roads are closed to prevent potential litigation.

The world thinks Central Florida is about theme parks, chain restaurants and t-shirt shops. It's not. Orlando is about the amazing people that make all of that and so much more happen.

As an improviser I'm not used to having a permanent record of my work. Years from now I'll reread this book and see only what I wish I'd done differently - but that's all in an imagined future. For today I am simply proud and grateful. I hope the response to this novel will provide enough encouragement to write another.

Greg Triggs

If you enjoyed the book please recommend it and post reviews. If you didn't, feel free to keep that to yourself.

First and foremost I want to thank Lorna Landvik for the gift of being one of the first people to read *Patty Jane's House of Curl*. In that moment she taught me that real people – not icons, write books.

To Iris Rainer Dart, Nancy Schlick and Mary Pulver aka Monica Ferris, thank you for taking time to mentor someone well past the age we are thought to need mentors.

To editor Susan Dalsimer – thank you for pushing past my old habits and helping me craft a stronger story. Abby Maretsky, you're a generous friend - thank you for finding the time to proof read and provide feedback.

To my wonderful teachers Dr. Gloria Link, Susan Saunders, Elizabeth Dean, Keith Larsen, Jeanette Butler, Henry Barney & Barb Jung thanks for taking time to notice a kid ~~that~~ who might've otherwise fallen through the cracks.

To my improv teachers - Mark Bergren, Chris Wright, Stevie Ray, Christine Decker, Jim Detmar & Chris Oyen thank you for providing the foundation of how to tell a story and countless nights full of laughter.

Pete Aguero, Lori Alling, Jen Bascom, Michele Greenwood Bettinger, Michelle Goeke Bloodwell, Leslie Dallas, Rachel Dart, Taylor Jack, Cecile Kohrs Lindell, Kate Pappas, Mary Joseph Pehl, Steve Purnick, Andy Redeker, Jeff Scherer,

Rebecca Vigil & Nancy Witter – thanks for being amongst the first to read NHPOE and provide feedback.

Tommy Terpening, to me you're a brother. Patrick O'Connell our friendship has changed my life in infinite ways. Laurie Fuller in a different reality I'm sure I asked you to marry me, and you had the good sense to say no. Donny Jacobson, you're dear to me, then, now & forever.

The spark for this book came from a column called "What Would Greg Do?" which I wrote for *Watermark Newspaper* in Orlando, FL. Founding Publisher and dear friend Tom Dyer, thank you for everything.

To The Robert M. MacNamara Foundation, thank you for the opportunity to finish the first draft of this book in a beautiful place with inspiring company. Maureen Barrett, from the first moment we met your generosity has been precious. I hope in some small way I've been able to return the gesture.

To the casts of TSZ Mpls, Dudley Riggs' Brave New Workshop, Streetmo, the Adventurer's Club, the Comedy Warehouse, CSZ NYC, CCL, the beloved Bruised Fruits and of course, Broadway's Next Hit Musical (www.BroadwaysNextHitMusical.com), thank you for allowing me to share a stage with you. Waiting to hear what will be said next has been thrilling.

Ralph Buckley, Deb Rabbai and Rob Schiffmann, thank you for being exceptional partners.

To the casts and production staffs of *Hold Me, Suitehearts, Say Goodnight Gracie, I am a*

Camera, Dino-Land Grad Students, Pleasure Island, Super Soap Weekend, *the 2000 Super Bowl Half Time Show, Murder is a Drag, Fairy Tales, The Lion in Winter, Miss Firecracker Contest, Who's Afraid of Virginia Woolf,* the Philadelphia Zoo, *Cinderella's Princess Court, the Pirates of the Caribbean Invade NYC, HSM,* the Tribeca Film Festival, The Doha Tribeca Film Festival, the World Science Festival, *the Rockin' Ski Party, Believe, Viva, Cannery Row, Waggin' Tails, Sea Lion High,* the Walt Disney World Children's Activity Centers, the Disney Magic, the Disney Wonder, the Disney Dream, the Disney Fantasy and Aulani: a Disney Resort & Spa, it has been an honor to work with almost all of you.

Annie Schiffmann & Katie Hammond, thank you for being such an important part of how this book gets into people's hands. Robert Z. Grant, your work surpassed my imagination of what I thought the cover would be.

Daniel Holmes, a huge thank-you for ten years of friendship, laughter and hard work. You only just left and you're already missed so much.

Thank you to Budge Threlkeld who always told me that the story would tell me where it wanted to go. Louie Gravance, thank you for teaching me to see past clichés. Carl Sword thanks for listening.

Mr. Ronnie Rodriguez, you're a Disney legend. Thanks for the first chance.

David Duffy, Maureen Landry-Mancini, Peter Downing, Reed Jones, Ken Harris, Ray Coble, Vickie Lynn Fielitz, Tommy Costanzo, Sharon Davis Aguillen, Michael Fletcher, Thomas Tryon, David

Patrick, Susan Waldrip and countless others, thank-you for not allowing geography to prevent me from doing the world I love so much.

To Delta Airlines, thanks for my medallion status.

The animal rescue that Kellie Holden works with actually exists. Jodi Chase and Rita D'Angelo Tikador are making a huge difference in the lives of animals and the people who give them homes. Please support their wonderful work by visiting www.betterlifepets.com.

To the Nolen family – thanks for making me feel like an in law long before the real law allowed it.

To the Triggs Radke Fiore Fisher Ryerson Rubedew family – I wouldn't trade you for anything in the world. Emily, thank you for taking me to see *Cabaret* and Lily Tomlin and so much more. You were a lifesaver - the perfect big sister for a kid like me. Susan, your sense of adventure helped me to find my own. Valerie, the way you face each day reminds me that I have no excuses not to do the same. Butch who now insists on being called Raymond, how lucky was I to grow up beside one of the best people I know. Art, I miss you every day. You were more father than brother. I'd give almost anything to see you one more time.

Dad – I'm sure you were thrilled to have a son who chose rehearsals over deer hunting. Thanks for never trying to change who or what I was going to be.

Mom – thanks for storing your old paperbacks in my bedroom. When I couldn't sleep I'd pick up a dusty Jacqueline Susann novel and dream of a glamorous life in New York City. While I'm not a Broadway star sucking down dolls like they were Good & Plenty, in some small ways those dreams have come true. I wish you were here to share in it. The thing I'm most proud of is being your son.

Matt Nolen, thank you for showing me things I cannot see on my own. From the moment we met I knew my life was changed for the better. That has proven to be the case almost every day since. I can't wait to see what happens to us next.

And finally, thanks to everyone who took the time to read this far. It means the world to me that you chose to visit *The Next Happiest Place on Earth*.

ABOUT THE AUTHOR

Greg Triggs spent 12 years cleverly posing as a Disney Cast Member to learn everything he could about the theme park industry. Currently he lives in Harlem and Narrowsburg, NY with his husband Matt Nolen, a ceramic sculptor and college professor at Pratt Institute. Triggs tours with and co-produces the improvisational revue Broadway's Next Hit Musical. In between shows he works as a freelance writer/director for clients including the Tribeca Film Festival, the World Science Festival, Disney, Disney Vacation Club and Disney Cruise Line. His writing has regularly appeared in *Watermark Newspaper* and *MetroSource Magazine*. *The Next Happiest Place on Earth* is his first novel.

Printed in the United States
By Bookmasters